Walk away, walk away, walk away.

The words echoed in Emma's mind as she left the festival. Josh's gaze—filled with shock—bore into her back. She wouldn't be surprised if she found a bruise between her shoulder blades later. Her blood sizzled and all she wanted to do was run to her car, but he'd know how his warm body made her skin tingle and her pulse hum in her ears, and there was no way she'd admit to that shame.

He was supposed to date her best friend.

Best friends didn't poach boyfriends. Or potential boyfriends. Or matches, no matter how improbable the match might seem.

Best friends didn't inhale the scent of the man as they hugged him. Heck, best friends didn't hug the man, period.

Especially when, the more time they spent together, the more interesting they seemed.

Dear Reader,

This first book in my Matchmaker, Matchmaker... series might just be my most favorite book I've ever written. It's got a loving grandmother determined to see her grandson through a huge life change; an independent and feisty heroine who has overcome a tough home life and managed to thrive; a matchmaker who thinks she's made the perfect match—of course, but whose mistake adds conflict to the story; and a hero who is absolutely irresistible, even if he fights change every step of the way.

One of the things I love about writing Jewish romance is the chance to infuse the value of *tikkun olam*—repairing the world—into the story arc. The town of Browerville has always been a small town with a big heart, and I've loved populating it with people who are willing to step up and help out when needed. New bookstore needs help? Of course the town is willing to pitch in! Winter doldrums got you down? Come to the winter festival, check out the ice sculptures, and indulge in some powdered donuts and hot cocoa.

But it's more than that. By making my hero a rabbi, I've had the chance to give you a peek into why Judaism is a religion filled with joy, even when times are tough. That joy can be found in the glow of Shabbat candles, the warmth of a celebratory holiday meal, or in the satisfaction that comes from helping out people with food insecurity.

So join me as we get to know Josh and Emma. Get excited as Emma achieves her dream of opening up a bookstore and heals the rift with her family. Feel the touching love between Josh and his grandma as she ages and moves onto the next phase in her life, all while helping Josh to see that change, although inevitable, doesn't have to be scary. And fall in love with our hero and heroine as they learn that they can do anything they put their minds to, as long as they are together.

Jennifer Wilck

FALLING FOR THE RABBI

JENNIFER WILCK

SPECIAL EDITION

If you purchased this book without a cover you should be aware that this book is stolen property. It was reported as "unsold and destroyed" to the publisher, and neither the author nor the publisher has received any payment for this "stripped book."

ISBN-13: 978-1-335-18030-8

Falling for the Rabbi

Copyright © 2026 by Jennifer Wilck

All rights reserved. No part of this book may be used or reproduced in any manner whatsoever without written permission.

Without limiting the exclusive rights of any author, contributor or the publisher of this publication, any unauthorized use of this publication to train generative artificial intelligence (AI) technologies is expressly prohibited. Harlequin also exercises their rights under Article 4(3) of the Digital Single Market Directive 2019/790 and expressly reserves this publication from the text and data mining exception.

This is a work of fiction. Names, characters, places and incidents are either the product of the author's imagination or are used fictitiously. Any resemblance to actual persons, living or dead, businesses, companies, events or locales is entirely coincidental.

For questions and comments about the quality of this book, please contact us at CustomerService@Harlequin.com.

TM and ® are trademarks of Harlequin Enterprises ULC.

Harlequin Enterprises ULC
22 Adelaide St. West, 41st Floor
Toronto, Ontario M5H 4E3, Canada
www.Harlequin.com

HarperCollins Publishers
Macken House, 39/40 Mayor Street Upper,
Dublin 1, D01 C9W8, Ireland
www.HarperCollins.com

Printed in Lithuania

Jennifer Wilck is an award-winning contemporary romance author for readers who are passionate about love, laughter and happily-ever-after. Known for writing both Jewish and non-Jewish romances, she features damaged heroes, sassy and independent heroines, witty banter, yummy food and hot chemistry in her books. She believes humor is the only way to get through the day and does not believe in sharing her chocolate. You can find her at jenniferwilck.com.

Books by Jennifer Wilck

Harlequin Special Edition

Matchmaker, Matchmaker...

Falling for the Rabbi

Holidays, Heart and Chutzpah

Home for the Challah Days
Matzah Ball Blues
Deadlines, Donuts & Dreidels

The Fortunes of Texas: Fortune's Hidden Treasures

Fortune's Unexpected Gift

The Fortunes of Texas: Secrets of Fortune's Gold Ranch

A Fortune with Benefits

The Fortunes of Texas: Fortune's Secret Children

Fortune's Holiday Surprise

Visit the Author Profile page
at Harlequin.com for more titles.

To Julia Bendis of Match by Julia, for teaching me all about matchmakers. Your help was invaluable, your stories were hilarious and I appreciate everything you've done to help me with this book. Thank you!

To Courtney Riseborough of Belvidere Books in Belvidere, NJ. Thanks for helping me with the behind-the-scenes info about owning and running an independent bookstore. I can't wait to stop in and visit yours.

And to my parents, whose matchmaking "mistake" through IBM's Project Match has led to fifty-eight years of love. The rest of us should only be so lucky. Love you!

Prologue

Muriel Axelrod bustled into the office of Ms. Match, Browerville's first and only matchmaker, rang the bell on the desk and tapped the toe of her orthopedic shoe on the gray laminate wood floor. The reception room was empty, other than an electric menorah left over from Hanukkah sitting on top of the reception desk, all nine candles aglow. She glanced at her wrist with the gold-and-diamond watch her husband had given her when they married sixty years ago.

A cloud of citrus perfume made her turn in time to see a woman enter. She was in her thirties with bright red hair. "May I help you?" she asked.

"I have an appointment to talk about engaging your services for my grandson, Josh."

The woman's gray eyes brightened, and she looked behind Muriel. "I'm Anya Rubenstein, also known as Ms. Match. And he is…?"

Muriel scoffed. "Oh, he's not here, God no. I need to present this to him as a done-deal. Otherwise, he'll never agree."

Ms. Match frowned. "Why don't you come into my office and we'll talk."

Muriel followed the matchmaker through a door into a light and airy office with bright windows that looked out over the Browerville Green. Ms. Match's office was decorated in soothing lavenders and grays. Plants sat on a table by the window, and a small stone fountain burbled in the background. Photos of loving couples gazing at each other adorned the walls.

Muriel wondered how many of them were real and hoped her plan would succeed. She sat in a lavender-and-gray-upholstered chair and folded her hands in her lap.

Ms. Match looked at her across her desk. "I've been matchmaking for what seems like forever."

Muriel laughed. "You don't look old enough for that, honey."

With a shrug, Anya continued. "Maybe not, but it sure seems that way. I've never set someone up who didn't want to be. I'm not sure how kosher this is."

Muriel brightened. "My grandson, Josh, lives and works in Manhattan, but he's going to be home for a month helping me move into Marble House. He's upset I've sold our house, but it's for the best. And I thought while he's home, he could use the distraction of meeting some nice women."

"So he's not dating anyone in Manhattan?"

Muriel scoffed. "He's using those dating apps." She leaned forward. "I don't know how anyone expects to find the love of their life with a swipe."

Ms. Match's eyes twinkled. "You know, one of the services I offer is to set up online dating profiles for people who prefer the apps to my full services. I think it depends on personal preference."

"Really?" Muriel leaned back against her seat, dumbfounded. "I never thought of that. It's different from how my Howard and I met. We used a traditional matchmaker, a shadchan, who set us up after meeting with our parents. And we were married for fifty years, until he passed ten years ago." Her eyes filled, and she blinked. She didn't want this young lady across the desk to dismiss her as a fragile old woman.

Ms. Match leaned forward. "I think it's lovely. And I'd love to try to help you, as long as ultimately, your grandson buys into the process. I've set up lots of clients both locally and in Manhattan. So many people work in one place and live somewhere else, it won't be a problem to find him someone regardless of where he's located. So how about we get started, and when he comes home, you send him to me, and we'll complete the process? Okay?"

Muriel nodded, relief washing through her. Josh was going to have a tough time with all the changes as she moved onto her next chapter. He'd need a distraction, and hopefully, a wonderful woman by his side to help him. With Ms. Match's help, Muriel had every intention of setting that up for him.

Determined to help her grandson, she gave Ms. Match all the information she requested and rustled through her handbag until she pulled out a few photos of Josh. "Isn't he handsome?"

Ms. Match smiled. "He is." She shuffled through them. "I'm going to scan these two to use in his profile." She placed them on her desk and used her phone to scan them, before returning the originals to Muriel.

"Obviously I'll double-check everything with him," Ms. Match said, "but why don't you tell me his hobbies?"

"Hobbies, ugh. That's the problem. With his job as a rabbi, he doesn't have a lot of time for hobbies." Muriel paused, thinking for a few moments about what Josh liked to do. "Well, when he comes home, he's always helping me fix things around the house."

Ms. Match nodded. "So he's handy?"

"Very! And he loves to go out to new restaurants. He makes me keep a list of the ones that open nearby so we can try them."

"He's an adventurous foodie?"

"Yes."

Ms. Match tapped her glittery nails on the desk. "What are his career goals?"

Muriel frowned. "You might have to save that question for him. He's only been a rabbi for a few years."

"So he likes to help people."

"Absolutely."

"What about the type of woman he's interested in?"

Muriel wasn't one hundred percent sure, but she did know the kind of woman she wanted Josh to be with. "She should be Jewish, confident and independent and smart."

"Age range?"

"Well, Josh is twenty-eight, so somewhere around his age would be good."

"Okay, let me put all of this together and see what I have as far as potential matches. I'll send you some options." Ms. Match leaned forward, folding her arms on the table. "I will definitely need to talk with Josh, though, when he's here, to firm up his options. Other matchmakers have different rules, but I don't set anyone up anonymously or against their will."

Muriel shook her head. "Oh, I'd never trick my grandson into doing anything." She winked. "A little nudge here or there, though, isn't out of the question."

Ms. Match nodded. "I can't argue with you. As for my fee, usually I charge for a certain period of time, like six months, let's say. But with you, since you're setting it up for your grandson…"

Muriel waited.

Ms. Match tapped her ruby lips, a pensive look on her face. "How about this. You pay me five hundred today to work up a bare-bones profile and get started pulling a few match options. Once I meet with Josh, I'll send you the bill for the rest, which will be fifteen hundred dollars. And I'll talk to Josh about length of time. Ideally, I like to work for six months, but I can be flexible."

"And I can grease the wheels a bit for you so he's…more amenable to the process when he meets with you."

Ms. Match's nostrils flared, and Muriel thought she might be restraining a smile. "I would appreciate that."

Pulling her checkbook out of her purse, Muriel wrote out the check and signed it with a flourish, confident Ms. Match was going to find Josh the woman of his dreams.

Just like the shadchan had done for her sixty years ago.

It was going to be perfect. And if not, she wouldn't hesitate to find him someone herself.

Chapter One

Emma Geffner's pulse raced with excitement as she drove to her lawyer's office on a cold, gray January day. She looked across the center console at her best friend, Samantha.

"Thank you so much for coming with me," she said as she navigated the icy Browerville streets. Midmorning on a weekday, the streets were filled with cars, and she gripped the steering wheel. The last thing she wanted to do was skid into anyone.

"As your best friend, and a lawyer, I'd never let you sign anything without me," Samantha said. "Your timing is perfect, because I worked on a huge case at the firm, we won, and my boss gave me the week off with a nice bonus as a thank-you. You're the best reason to come home from New York City."

Emma smiled her gratitude. She was finally signing the contract to purchase the building to house her brand-new bookstore, The Book Nook. Browerville was a center of activity and filled with lots of great shops and restaurants. But the one thing it was missing was a bookstore. When a grad school class assignment to create a business plan for a retail business caught her imagination, and after lamenting the lack of a bookstore in her hometown, a lightbulb went off in her mind. Now, having achieved her MBA—and aced that project, by the way—she'd taken her business plan and found the perfect location.

Pulling up to Prime Law Offices, she grabbed her canvas messenger bag and walked inside with Samantha, ready to take the next step toward her dream.

The teenager behind the welcome desk looked up, blinked her neon eyeshadowed lids, tucked a lock of hot pink hair behind her pierced ear and tapped silver-beringed fingers on an iPad. "Hi, welcome to Prime. Can I help you?"

Emma could barely contain her excitement and resisted bouncing on the balls of her feet, although her entire body was jittery. "I have an appointment with Arlene. Emma Geffner."

The young woman nodded before motioning her to take a seat. "She'll be with you in a sec."

There was no way Emma could sit. Instead, she paced back and forth in front of the desk as she waited.

"Emma, relax," Samantha said. "It's all going to be fine."

A few moments later, Arlene appeared. The older woman stepped forward, hand outstretched. "Are you ready?" Her smile matched Emma's before her gaze fell on Samantha. "Oh, you brought a friend?"

"This is Samantha Drucker. She's a lawyer, too, and my best friend," she said as they walked with Arlene to the conference room.

Arlene stiffened but didn't object. "You're a little early, but it's fine. Meanwhile, can I get either of you any coffee or tea?"

Emma demurred. "I don't think caffeine is a good idea for me right now, but water would be great."

She sat at the large conference table, and Arlene handed her a glass. "You can both start looking through the documents if you'd like."

Ugh, this was the boring part of the process. Luckily, Samantha was with her, and, if the speed with which she picked up the documents was any indication, she was eager to check everything over.

Emma planned to read everything as well. She wasn't an idiot, and understanding all the fine print was essential. But someone should have figured out a more interesting way to phrase all the legalese. Swallowing her frustration, she began reading the first of many documents stacked in front of her. She'd gotten through about a third of them, when Samantha nodded and rose.

"Everything looks good to me," she said. "I'm going to run next door for a bagel. Text me when you're done." She leaned over and gave Emma a hug. "Congratulations," she said. "You're going to be amazing."

More confident now with her best friend's stamp of approval, Emma continued reading.

The squeak of the door handle made her raise her gaze, and she stretched her back as Arlene opened the door.

"Mrs. Axelrod," Arlene said. "Hello. Come on in."

Emma turned. Arlene led in an older woman with short white hair and a stooped back. Despite the wrinkles of age, her blue eyes were bright and her step quick.

The previous owner of the house, she'd been a picture-perfect seller, allowing Emma to return to her house multiple times before making her decision, answering all of her questions and offering suggestions about how Emma could turn the three-story house into a combination bookstore and living space. During the weeks-long buying process, Emma had grown fond of the woman.

"Emma, dear, nice to see you again," the woman said.

Smiling, Emma rose and leaned toward the woman, extending her hand. "Hi, Mrs. Axelrod. It's nice to see you, too."

"Are you excited to take ownership?"

Emma nodded. "I am. And I can't wait to show you my plans. You gave such great suggestions, I think you'll love them."

"Wonderful. Oh, here he is. You haven't yet met my grandson, have you?"

Emma followed Mrs. Axelrod's gaze to the tall man, about her age, wearing a small Yankees skullcap.

Emma blinked in surprise. His brown hair was short and wavy, and his eyes were the same color as his grandmother's—a deep Yankees blue. "Hi, I'm Emma." She held out her hand. *His Yankees kippah matches his eyes.*

He clenched his jaw, brows drawn, and waited half a beat before shaking her hand. "Josh."

Emma swallowed. Apparently, his only similarity to his grandmother were those beautiful eyes, because he certainly hadn't inherited her charm.

He stuffed his hands in his pockets, his gaze darting between her, his grandmother and the stack of papers on the table. He reminded Emma of a beady-eyed squirrel judging whether or not he could cross the street before a car raced by and squashed him.

Emma straightened her spine. "Is there a problem?"

He strode to the table and sat next to his grandmother. "Only if you consider giving up your home a problem."

She grimaced. Mrs. Axelrod wasn't giving up anything. Emma was paying her a significant sum that easily reflected the value of the house and location.

Before Emma could respond, though, his grandmother placed a veiny hand on his arm. "Joshy. Hush."

Joshy? Really?

A laugh gurgled its way from Emma's belly to her throat, but she drowned it with a big gulp of water. She hadn't forced Mrs. Axelrod to sell. She'd simply expressed interest when she saw the For Sale sign hanging outside. In fact, Mrs. Axelrod started out more eager for the sale than Emma was in the beginning.

"Grandma, are you positive this is what you want?" He turned to her, a look of desperation crossing his face.

A slice of sympathy wormed its way into Emma's heart, even as anxiety raced through her. The time to get out of the sale was long gone.

"We can hire people to help you," he said, "and I can come home from Manhattan more frequently to pitch in."

His grandma shook her head. "We've been through this. The new place is best for me. I'll have lots of friends. Our house is way too big." She looked over at Emma and winked. "And I love what Emma's going to do with the place. It's perfect. You'll see."

Emma breathed a small sigh of relief and glanced at Josh, whose expression looked like he didn't see at all. Emma's sympathy gave way to annoyance. *Where the heck was he during the weeks of negotiations?* If he thought he was going to come in here at the last minute and torpedo her dreams, well, he had another think coming, along with a kick of her brand-new, pointy-toed leather booties. She swung her foot beneath the table, trying to remain calm.

If only Samantha had stayed. She'd defend Emma, the sale and anything else necessary. But she'd left.

Josh glowered, and Emma was tempted to glower right back. But she didn't want any more negative energy getting in the way of her dream. Instead, she gave him a blank stare before glancing over toward the door as Arlene reentered the suddenly icy room.

Arlene sat at the head of the table and looked between them, reminding Emma of a tennis spectator. She cleared her throat. "All right. If everyone is ready, we can start going through the forms. The first document is…"

Emma followed along, one ear listening to Arlene's instructions while the rest of her brain focused on the annoying man seated across from her.

The blue button-down he wore hugged his wide shoulders nicely. She'd never been one to fall for the preppy-looking guys, and even his deep voice—one of the things that always attracted her—couldn't make up for his bad attitude and poor timing. She was not going to allow him to sink the deal.

The longer they stayed in the room, the higher her blood pressure rose. Her temples throbbed as he continued to frown at her, his hand in a fist on the table.

Finally, the last document—the one that allowed Mrs. Axelrod to stay in the house for another month after closing—was signed. A huge check, whose size made Emma's nerves tap-dance with anxiety, changed hands, and with the capping of her pen, the house was hers.

Now she could exhale and hopefully lower her blood pressure. The annoying grandson hadn't pulled out some last-minute surprise. Her mouth creased in a smile as she expelled a big breath, and she shook first Arlene's hand, followed by Mrs. Axelrod's.

Should she shake Josh's hand? Turning to him, she watched him stuff his hands in the pockets of his khakis.

Okay then.

"Thank you so much," Emma said, turning once again to Mrs. Axelrod and ignoring her grandson.

"You're welcome, my dear. And you should feel free to come over any time you want. I know you need to get started with renovations." She turned to Josh. "We should leave out snacks for the workmen and Emma. All that work will make them hungry."

Emma withheld a laugh. "You don't need to do that, Mrs. Axelrod, but thank you."

Josh's entire body bristled at the exchange. He turned to

her as they were getting ready to leave. "Make sure you call first before you come over."

She swallowed her retort, as her humor was replaced with a sour taste in her mouth. As if she'd ever show up unannounced.

Josh seethed as he ushered his grandmother into his Mustang, helped her find and snap her seat belt and shut the door before jogging around to the driver's side. He slammed the door shut and jammed his finger pressing the ignition button. Ignoring the pain in his knuckle, he reversed out of the parking space and swung out onto the road to the sound of honking horns and screeching tires.

"You know, if I wanted two wheels, I'd have ridden here on my bicycle," his grandmother said.

He glanced over at her, noting her white-knuckled grip on the door handle. He blew out a breath and eased off the gas pedal. He shouldn't be speeding on icy roads regardless of how upset he was. "Sorry, Grandma."

She nodded, remaining quiet until they passed the town square. "Pull over here, please," she said, her voice low but firm.

"Here?" he asked, but quickly turned on his signal to change lanes. "I thought you wanted to get home."

She turned to him as he pulled into a parking space and arched a white brow. "I haven't expressed any of my wants since we left the lawyer's office."

Swallowing, he turned off the engine. That chiding look and tone had put him in his place when he first came to live with her at age twelve, and it continued its magical hold to this day.

"Sorry, Grandma." With the motor off, the car was silent, and his apology echoed.

He stared out the windshield at the bare branches of the

trees outside, the Revolutionary War statues and the large stone fountain, now turned off for the winter. Decorations left over from Christmas and Hanukkah decorated the park. Bundled up moms with blanket-covered strollers walked the stone pathways, passing lampposts festooned with fir boughs and blue, silver or red ribbons. Employees from nearby offices carried steaming coffee cups in gloved hands on their way to work.

"Want to tell me what's bothering you?" his grandmother asked.

He sighed, unsure exactly how to explain his mood. "I hate that you're leaving our home."

The three-story Victorian was where his grandfather had brought his grandmother to live after their wedding. It was where his mom had grown up until she moved away after college and married his dad. And it was where he'd come to live when his parents died in a car wreck when he was twelve.

"We've been over this. It's an expensive house to keep for one person."

"But I can contribute funds." Maybe he could return here when his lease was up. "And I'm there, too, on weekends and holidays," he continued. "I can take it over in a few years." His tone sounded desperate even to his own ears.

"And it's a lot of stairs for my knees, Joshy."

"We could move you to the first floor. Or install an elevator."

His grandmother snorted. "Where I'd be alone." She placed a hand on his leg. "I want to move to Marble House. Half of my mah-jongg friends already live there. There are activities to keep me busy, staff to help me if and when I need it, and it's what's best for me."

He covered her hand with his, giving a gentle squeeze and noting how fragile it was. "Why do I feel like I'm abandoning you? Why won't you let me quit my job and move in with you?"

His grandmother shook her head, her white curls bouncing. For some reason, they reminded him of Emma. He blinked, and the image subsided.

"Absolutely not. You're a young rabbi. You need the freedom to lead your own life and do what you want to do. You should not have to curtail your professional or personal activities to take care of me in this large house. I would hate that." She pinned him with her blue-eyed gaze, making him squirm.

"But you took care of me when I needed it. It should be my turn."

"Nope. Not in that way. You don't owe me anything. We don't do things because I owe you or you owe me. We do things for love. I know you love me. Just as you know that I love you."

His allergies must be kicking in because his eyes prickled. He sniffed, and she patted his leg again.

"You want to show me how much you love me? Visit me. Oh, and let Ms. Match set you up with some women while you're home." She winked, and the sob that started to form in his throat turned into a laugh.

How she always managed to do that to him, he had no idea. One minute she was tugging at his heartstrings, the next she embodied the stereotypical Jewish grandmother, trying to find him a girlfriend.

"Grandma, come on. A matchmaker? I can find plenty of dates on my own."

She patted his hand. "Of course you can. But a date and a girlfriend are completely different. Come on, what do you have to lose?"

He could fight her on this. Or he could let her win. With an exhale, he nodded. "Fine. I'll do it."

"Excellent! She's expecting your call."

He glanced sideways at her. "Pretty confident, weren't you?"

She gave him one of her looks, like he remembered from his teenaged years. "Where do you think you get it from?"

"I'll call her when we get home," he said.

Home. That word now possessed two separate meanings. One brought back memories of his childhood. He'd been furious at the loss of his parents. He'd hated having to move towns, change schools, find new friends. But his grandma had supported him throughout all of it, supporting him, admonishing him and loving him. She'd created new memories for him—holidays spent with just the two of them, yet never feeling lonely; her presence at every school event, even when he begged her to skip them.

The second meaning looked to the future. As much as he tried to come to grips with his grandmother moving to Marble House, the idea of her in an assisted living facility, even if it wasn't a nursing home, made him shudder. What if she was wrong? What if it wasn't the best thing for her?

As they returned home, he straightened his shoulders. He'd give it six months. If he wasn't satisfied with how she was doing, he'd figure out an alternative plan, even if it meant he needed to alter his life. He wasn't going to abandon her.

Forty-five minutes after her meeting with the lawyer and two thirds of the way through Samantha's everything bagel with egg, provolone and avocado, Emma sat across the table from her in Isaacson's Deli and swatted her brown curls out of her face.

"Samantha, I swear I'll go to the ends of the earth for you. And I'm tremendously grateful for all your help with the legal end of buying the bookstore. But a matchmaker? You are out of your freakin' mind. How can you possibly think a matchmaker is going to know you better than I do?" She rose from her seat, jammed her hands on her hips and glared at the woman across the table from her. "I'm your best friend!" Emma cried. "I know you best."

The sudden silence in the crowded deli punctuated her rant, and she looked around the dining area, which moments before was filled with a cacophony of voices. Her cheeks heated, and she skewered her friend with a glare before plopping onto the seat again.

Samantha brought her coffee cup to her lips, blue eyes lined with gray liner sparkling with humor as she sipped her hot drink.

The background noise resumed, and with it, Emma's doubts.

"Aren't I your best friend?" Emma growled. If she could have shot lasers from her eyes, she'd have done so.

Finally, after entirely too long—seriously, how much did one need to drink before stopping for a breath, especially when the liquid was hot?—her best friend put her cup on the gray marble tabletop.

"You know you are, Em. There's no need to make a scene." She brought her napkin up to her lips and dabbed at the corners of her deep red lips.

Emma wanted to shake some sense into her—or at least get her to admit to the depth of their friendship. Sam's nonchalance was killing her.

"Why would you consider asking a matchmaker for help meeting men?" Emma asked. "You want to date some guy who's filled out a form and is waiting for some plastic, two-dimensional piece of perfection to float into his inbox?" Her friend was much more than that. She deserved someone who saw the depth of her character behind that perfect mask.

Samantha flared her nostrils and smoothed her flat-ironed,

dyed blond hair. "Of course not. That's not what they do, and that's not what I want. You'd be surprised how popular they're becoming, Em. A lot of single women in my office use them. The matchmaker weeds out all the people who don't share the same interests and values, so I only match with people I have something in common with. After all the random dating I've done, and the horrible dating apps filled with guys who are only looking for sex, I want a relationship with someone I can relate to."

For a brief moment, Emma understood. She'd love a relationship, too…someday. "You make it sound like you've been dating for fifty years. Or worse, like you've entered some sort of alternate *Fiddler on the Roof* universe. Tell me she doesn't wear a shawl around her head!"

Sam scoffed. "Of course she doesn't, Em. She's probably in her mid-thirties. I met with her yesterday."

"And you're only telling me about this now?" Emma sighed. "I can't imagine someone else deciding who I should or shouldn't date. I love my freedom too much." It was bad enough her parents needed to intrude into her education choices. Using a matchmaker felt like too much of the same vibe.

"Em, I don't have the time or energy to wade through a ton of Mr. Ughs before I find someone I like enough for a second date," Sam said. "This woman weeds through everyone I'd turn down anyway."

"We're only twenty-seven, Sam. We've got plenty of time to find men. Besides, do you think one meeting is enough?"

Samantha nodded and tapped her manicured fingers on the table. "She interviewed me in-depth, found out exactly what I want and don't want, and she'll only send me men who fit my profile, location preferences, et cetera."

Emma ran her hand through her messy curls, trying and

failing to keep them from falling in her face. "Honestly, if you're looking for help finding a boyfriend, why don't you let me do it?"

She and Samantha had been best friends since kindergarten. Samantha, with her ruffly pink dress, huge pink bow in her hair and perfectly polished shoes, took one look at Emma's purple overalls, red unicorn T-shirt and green sneakers, looked her up and down and decided they were destined to be besties. Through elementary, middle and high school, they'd been inseparable. Emma pushed Sam to get more creative and daring, and Sam reined in Emma when she was liable to jump off one-too-many bridges. Despite their opposing personalities, their friendship remained tight.

The look of horror that crossed Samantha's face would have been comical. Except something in her best friend's gaze pierced the edge of Emma's heart. She'd made the mistake of dating a guy Samantha had liked in the past. It wasn't intentional, and Samantha said at the time it was no big deal, but every once in a while, when they talked about men, something in Samantha's gaze showed she hadn't forgotten.

"Don't you trust me?" Emma asked.

Sam reached for her hand. "Of course I trust you."

Emma squeezed her friend's fingers, reassured. "I know plenty of guys who would love to date you. Ones I think you'd like. I'd be happy to set you up."

Samantha leaned forward and grasped Emma's arm. "You lean toward artsy. The only art I want is on my wall. I like buttoned-up finance guys who make their first million by thirty. Ones whose Judaism is important to them, and who aren't interested in having kids." She gave a dry laugh. "You'd be surprised how hard they are to find."

Growing up, neither Emma nor Samantha were particularly religious, celebrating Jewish culture more than the religious observances. But in college, Samantha was active in her university's Hillel and had grown a little more observant. It wasn't something Emma understood, but she respected her friend's choices.

Emma scrunched her face up. "While I can't remember how observant the Jewish students in my MBA program were, I think there are probably a few candidates you'd like."

Samantha sipped her coffee. "I still don't understand why you let your parents talk you into that degree."

Emma swallowed the bitter taste in her mouth. "Because there's only so many times I can be compared to my perfect sister—and found lacking—before I cave. And although I would never tell them this, they made some good points. Plus, they paid for my education. Now I get to use what I learned to my advantage. And to yours, if you let me set you up." None of the guys in her classes had appealed to her. They'd been good study partners, but that was as far as any relationship went. Which meant many of them might be perfect for Samantha.

"I could set you up with Joe," Emma said, snapping her fingers as she grasped for his last name. "He works for an investment bank. Tall, blue eyes, blond hair…"

Shaking her head, Samantha turned her coffee cup around, as if stalling for time. "Emma, I want to try this. She's already sent me someone she thinks will be a fit." She pressed her fingers to her forehead. "Justin… Jonah… I don't remember. J-something. And he's a rabbi! Think how perfect he could be."

"I don't know, Sam, a rabbi? I know religion is important to you, but are you sure you want to go in that direction?"

"Emma, I'm excited about this. The guy sounds great, and if he isn't, the fact that she immediately found him for me means she can find others if he doesn't work out. But can't you see me as a rabbi's wife?"

Emma stared at her friend. "Not really," she said. Of course, she'd always celebrated Judaism's food and culture more than the religion itself, so maybe she was wrong. Still, she couldn't imagine a matchmaker knowing more about her best friend than she did.

"It's not that I don't trust you, but who knows what this matchmaker is going to choose? At least take me with you on the first date"

Sam wrinkled her usually perfect facial features. "Like that wouldn't be weird at all."

Emma pleaded with her. "It's for a good cause. I'll help you evaluate whether or not there should be a second one. You know I'm good at spotting red flags."

Sam's gaze danced with merriment. "Yeah, you were the only one who realized Bradley had a side hustle," she said.

"And don't forget the fetish guy you brought home from college. What was his name?"

Samantha covered her face with her hands. "Marty. Don't remind me."

Emma bit her lip, but remained quiet for an extra beat. "Seriously, please?"

Expelling a huge breath, Samantha nodded. "Fine. But first date only. And we need to make it a double date so it's not weird. Deal?"

Emma held out her hand, racking her brain for a suitable guy to bring along. "Deal."

Chapter Two

Two days later, Josh walked into Mamma Mia's, one of Browerville's most popular Italian restaurants, phone in hand, and scanned the entryway, decorated with snowflakes. According to Ms. Match, the matchmaker his grandmother "gifted him," the woman he was meeting was due to arrive in five minutes.

He didn't expect her to be early—in his dating experience he was always the one who arrived first—but still, he glanced at the patrons waiting for tables on the off chance she'd beaten him here.

A guy sat on the bench in the waiting area, a family of four stood next to the hostess station, and another guy shifted from one foot to the other, before his face brightened and he kissed a woman on the cheek.

Nope, he was early.

He sighed in relief, glad he'd get to take the first look at his date before she knew he was waiting for her. If he had to go through with this matchmaking attempt, he wanted a semblance of the upper hand, if only not to appear too desperate.

Because wasn't that what people who used matchmakers were?

His grandmother had retreated in horror when he'd suggested that. "Joshy, don't you know a matchmaker set me up with your grandfather?"

He'd swallowed in embarrassment. "No, I didn't. Or if I did, I forgot."

When his parents were alive, he'd been too young to pay much attention to family stories. After they died and he'd gone to live with his grandmother, most of the family stories she'd told him had been about his parents, to keep their memories alive. He couldn't recall ever hearing about her with a matchmaker.

"I want you to give her a chance," his grandmother had said. "Ms. Match is supposed to be excellent, certainly better than the dating apps you've tried."

"But, Grandma, I don't live in Browerville."

"That's okay, she can set you up with people anywhere."

And now, standing in the restaurant, he reluctantly decided that his grandmother might have a point. He hadn't had much luck finding anyone using dating apps. Maybe the matchmaker would be more successful. And going on a few dates while he was home wasn't such a bad idea. For all he knew, this woman tonight was amazing. He should at least give her a chance.

A tap on his shoulder made him spin around.

"Josh?"

The woman in front of him was almost his height with glossy blond hair and a pleasant voice. "Samantha?"

She gave a small wave, before gesturing behind her. "And this is my best friend, Emma, and her date, Rob. I hope you don't mind if they join us. I thought a double date might be less awkward."

He glanced at the two people with her and froze as he zoomed in on the woman. "What are *you* doing here?" The question—and his accusatory tone—escaped before he could stop it. His breath hitched. He was usually much better at controlling his emotions. As a rabbi, it was a requirement.

"What am I doing here?" Emma responded. She turned to Samantha. "*This* is the guy your matchmaker set you up with?"

"Do you two know each other?" Samantha asked.

"Yes," Emma said.

"No," Josh said at the same time. Sitting across a conference table didn't count.

"Emma, what's going on?" Samantha asked.

Good question, Josh thought. He frowned at Samantha. She'd brought another couple on a first date. He was all for women's safety, but the least she could have done was warn him. Too late now.

"His grandmother owns the house I bought. I didn't know he was a rabbi," Emma added.

Samantha's turned toward Josh. "A rabbi. That must be interesting. I didn't know you lived in Browerville. Ms. Match said you're from Manhattan."

And suddenly, Josh was under the microscope, having to answer questions in the entry of a restaurant in front of an audience. He took a breath. "I lived here with my grandmother when I was a kid. Now I live and work in Manhattan, and I come home to visit her frequently."

"Maybe we should sit?" The guy—Josh thought his name was Rob—made a good point.

Josh nodded, his gaze bouncing off the two women.

Shifting his gaze to Emma was like looking at a reverse image of his date. Where Samantha was tall, Emma was short, only reaching his shoulder, max. Samantha's hair was straight and light, not a strand out of place, while Emma's was a mass of dark curls in every direction. Even their expressions were opposites. Samantha's was interested and friendly. Emma's was wary, bordering on suspicious.

Did she think he was a serial killer?

It was stupid to get hung up on Emma when his date was with Samantha. He shifted his focus to the other guy and held out his hand. "Good idea," Josh said. "Nice to meet you."

Rob nodded and grasped his hand in a tight squeeze. "You, too."

Josh readjusted his assumptions and massaged his hand. The guy looked like a computer geek—tall, gangly, with glasses. But that grip? Wow.

Okay, clearly, nothing about this date was going to go as planned.

Swallowing, he announced their arrival to the hostess, explained they needed a larger table, and after a moment or two, led the group to a corner near the fireplace—and their not-so-romantic table for four.

He pulled out Samantha's chair. Was he supposed to sit next to her or across from her? He'd been raised with manners, but no one taught him the etiquette for when an uninvited second couple crashed your first date.

Before Josh could do anything more than wonder, Rob pulled out the chair next to Samantha and sat across from Emma.

Problem solved.

Now if only he could convince the other couple to move to a different table. Across the room. He was normally a friendly guy who liked meeting new people. But this was supposed to be a date. With Samantha only.

Instead, from diagonally across the table, Emma pinned him with her brown-eyed stare, surprising the heck out of him. He'd always thought of brown eyes as doe-like, liquid, soft. But hers? There was nothing soft about them. They held him in place like fossilized amber. He hadn't noticed them at the closing.

The thought of his grandmother actually moving on to the

next phase of her life crushed him, only for mind-numbing anger to replace it when he realized there was nothing he could do to prevent it. But now, he couldn't help stealing glances at Emma as he stared at the menu. Why did he feel like the large leather menu was a shield? And even more, why was he thankful for it?

"They make an amazing chicken piccata, if you like that," Samantha said. "Also their branzino is delicious."

He changed his focus to Samantha, where it was supposed to be. "Thanks for the suggestion. I've been here a few times before, actually. My grandmother and I celebrated her eightieth birthday here last year. Their veal is amazing, too."

Did Emma scoff? He looked over at her, but her face was buried in the menu.

"The way those baby cows are raised," Rob said, making eye contact with Emma. "It's cruel."

Emma nodded, a small look of horror on her face. "I stopped eating it as soon as I heard."

He hadn't thought of that. But now, he remembered the articles he'd read, and his stomach flipped. Josh wanted to sink beneath the table. Except there were too many feet.

After placing their orders, he tried to get to know Samantha better. "Samantha," he began, "or do you prefer Sam? Where do you live?"

She smiled at him. "Either is fine. I split my time between here—my parents live on the other side of town—and the Upper West Side of Manhattan, where they have an extra apartment. Since I work in the city and my hours can be crazy, I stay at my parents' apartment as often as necessary. At some point, I'd like to get my own place, but with their place usually available and being way nicer than I can afford…" She shrugged.

I'll bet that apartment's nice. "The matchmaker said you're a corporate lawyer," he continued. "What do you like about your job?"

"I like the rush of a job well done. We just won a big case, and I'm proud of the work I did on it. You know," she said, leaning forward, "everyone is always concerned about the little guy, and I get it, but big corporations aren't always in the wrong. There are plenty who are big but also do a lot of great things for the community. And I think that gets overlooked."

Her face lit up as she talked about her work. She was pretty, and her enthusiasm was contagious. He could imagine having fascinating conversations with her. Even if he didn't agree with her.

"Sometimes big corporations are actually good at doing good," he agreed. "My personal experience, though, isn't that favorable." He clenched his jaw as he thought about all the large developers who'd salivated over his grandmother's home, wanting to buy it up and turn the lot into a high-priced condo. The thought of the house he'd grown up in since he was twelve disappearing, along with all of his memories, twisted his stomach into knots.

At least Emma wasn't planning on tearing the place down. He hoped. He looked at her again, wanting to ask, but now wasn't the time.

At Samantha's quizzical look, he elaborated. "I'm helping my grandmother pack up her house. Well, our house. Unfortunately, due to her age and a desire not to burden me with taking care of her—despite the number of times I've begged her to let me—she's decided to move into an assisted living facility. The number of developers who've tried to purchase her house is astounding. They sort of remind me of grave robbers."

He gave her a smile to gentle the metaphor. What he didn't say was that he'd hated every smarmy one of them. Thank

God the move was of her own making, giving both of them control over who they sold to. Which, apparently she'd taken to mean Emma.

Again, he looked at her, wondering what his grandmother saw in her. It must be something, based on how sweet his grandmother was to her at the lawyer's office.

Sympathy crossed Samantha's face. "I'm sure that was tough, but think about the money she'd have for the rest of her life. They don't swoop in without compensation, you know."

Except life was more than money. His grandmother taught him that. It was why they'd said no to all of them.

Every time he thought about his grandma getting older, he wanted to rage against time. If someone else was going to move into their house that was filled with memories and love, it needed to be the right person.

What about Emma made her "right"?

Emma put her menu on the table and stared at him. Did he have something on his face? Was she trying to gauge his suitability for her best friend? Or did she want to burn him with her laser-like eyes? Any of those things were possible, and he tried not to squirm.

Women had never made him feel this way before.

"How about you?" Samantha continued. "You're a rabbi. That's incredible. Do you love it? How observant are you? Your hours must be crazier than mine."

Emma's eyes widened before she quickly looked away. Lots of people reacted in odd ways when they found out he was a rabbi, but why did she care? For that matter, why was he noticing *her* reaction?

He returned his gaze to Samantha and tried to focus solely on her. "Since I'm only a few years out of rabbinic school, and I work for a huge synagogue in Manhattan with several senior rabbis above me, it's not as crazy as it could be. But you're right, a rabbi is kind of on call all the time. The senior rabbis do all the big stuff, but I'm the substitute if their schedule is busy." He sighed. "It's a balancing act, like everything else."

"So you're expected to put your plans on hold when they need you?" Emma asked.

He bristled. What right did she have to judge him? She was a small business owner. Did she expect her bookstore to run itself?

Jumping on the words of the best friend of the woman he was trying to impress was probably not the best way to go. He took a breath before he responded, "It's hard, especially when it keeps me away from my family, but being a rabbi is a calling," Josh said. "It's something I've wanted to be for as long as I can remember. I like helping people. And as for how observant I am, well, it depends. Clearly, I don't keep kosher." He smiled.

Samantha's gaze softened at his words, and he warmed. As he continued chatting with her, he couldn't help notice Emma's look of boredom. *Excellent, maybe she and her date will leave.*

"You're close to your family," Emma interjected again when there was another lull in their conversation. "You mentioned helping your grandma."

He jerked. He'd expected her to be the silent observer. Now she was entering the conversation, too? Glancing at Samantha to see if she minded, he was confused when she sat there, waiting for him to answer.

"I'd do anything for her," he said, turning to Samantha. "She raised me from the time I was twelve, after my parents died, and now it's my turn to repay her for everything she sacrificed. She missed out on traveling and retirement, and I feel obligated—no, I need—to make her life now as easy as possible. How about you? Are you close with your family?"

A mask seemed to slip over Emma's face, before she turned toward Rob and whispered something. Since he'd directed the question to Samantha, Josh tried to ignore Emma's reaction, even if a part of his brain couldn't let it go.

Samantha raised her chin slightly. "I'm not, despite my flagrant use of their apartment. But I admire your dedication to your grandmother. She sounds like a wonderful woman."

"She is," Emma said.

Josh switched his attention toward Emma, feeling a little like a spectator at a tennis match. Wait until the matchmaker learned about this double date.

The server arrived with their meals, and thankfully, Emma focused her attention on her date and their food, sharing each other's meals, exclaiming over the taste. Finally, she was staying out of the conversation.

"Do you see yourself staying in this career long-term? Or is there something else you hope to do in the future?" Josh asked Samantha.

She nodded. "I'm exactly where I want to be, and where I see myself in the future." She forked a piece of chicken Parmesan and swallowed before continuing, "I love being a corporate lawyer. As a kid, I loved playacting courtroom scenes. You remember that, right, Emma?"

Emma groaned. "Don't remind me. I was on the other end of your interrogations one too many times. I still get PTSD every time you ask me a question."

Samantha turned and addressed Josh. "How about you? Do you want to be a pulpit rabbi?"

He nodded, his pulse racing as it always did whenever he talked about his dreams for the future. "I love working at such a big synagogue because I get to experience a lot, but ultimately, I'd like to be the senior rabbi at my own congregation. I love teaching the kids about Judaism and providing comfort and guidance to people." He shrugged. "I guess I like helping people. Especially the kids."

Samantha paused, her posture tense. "Oh?"

That's odd. "I love working with the youth groups during the year and at sleepaway camp in the summer. How about you? Were you a Jewish camp kid?"

"My parents couldn't wait for drop-off day," Samantha said. She laughed, the sound throaty and warm, and for the first time, a little of her personality shone through.

The rest of their dinner flew by. Emma and Rob had the grace to mostly keep to themselves, which gave Josh a chance to focus on his date.

Before long, the server arrived with their bill. Josh scooped it up before Samantha, or anyone else, could take a look at it, pulling out his card and laying it on the table.

"Here, let me split it with you," Rob said, handing over his card as well.

"Thank you for dinner," Samantha said ten minutes later as they rose to leave. "I enjoyed getting to know you, and I'll be sure to let Ms. Match know I enjoyed our time together."

He nodded. "I did, too," he said. Although he definitely would have preferred something more intimate, less distracting.

They headed toward the door. Outside, Emma and Rob continued walking down the block, giving him and Samantha a little much-needed privacy.

For the first time all evening, Josh relaxed. "Maybe we can do this again? Just the two of us?"

Samantha nodded, before waving goodbye and walking in the opposite direction from his car.

As Josh climbed in and started the engine, he vowed to make sure that next time the date would not include Emma.

***

"Joshy, you want coffee?" His grandmother's cheery voice grated early the next morning.

He shook his head. No matter how old he was, he'd never be anything other than *Joshy* to her. "Sure, Grandma."

She set out two mugs and started the coffee before sitting with him at the table. "You never told me how your date went last night. How'd Ms. Match do?"

"It was okay," he said with a shrug. In the light of day, he realized Samantha was nice but didn't light a spark in him.

Now was his chance to get out of having to use the matchmaker anymore. All he had to do was show his grandmother that he'd tried her idea and was ready to move onto something else.

"Joshy, okay is better than horrible. It was your first date. You need at least one or two more before you make a decision. No wonder your generation has trouble with relationships."

There were many things he wanted to say to her, but where to start?

She asked, "What was the girl like?"

Okay, I guess we're starting there. "Samantha was…fine."

"Fine? I need more than fine."

He tried to picture her in his mind, but Emma kept getting in the way. Emma? He frowned. Why did she keep popping up? He focused harder on his grandma's question. "Tallish, blond hair, blue eyes. She's a lawyer with crazy hours."

His grandmother frowned. "You haven't told me anything that wasn't on the matchmaker's form. Did you like her? Was she interesting? Is she a natural blonde? Funny? Someone you could see yourself having a relationship with?"

Again, Emma kept popping into his mind—the way her curls went every which way, how her mouth was expressive, how her eyes gave every thought away. He blinked. "I don't know. The date was a little weird, so we're going to try it again, just the two of us."

His grandma put her coffee cup on the kitchen table. "Just the two of you? How many were on your date?"

"It turned out to be a double date. Samantha brought her best friend and her boyfriend along." He frowned. "Her best friend is Emma Geffner."

Wide-eyed, his grandma leaned forward. "*Our* Emma?"

Our Emma? She definitely wasn't his. And he didn't want her to be his grandmother's, either. "The same Emma you sold your house to," he ground out.

His grandma's face brightened. "That's wonderful! She's such a nice girl. I'm glad she has a boyfriend. And if Samantha is her best friend, well, then she must be nice. Now we need you two to click, or you to click with someone else, and I can die happy."

"You'd better not die anytime soon," he said. "And since when do you care about Emma? Just because you sold our house to her..." Mentioning her name brought a bitter taste to his lips. Knowing she was going to inhabit the house he'd lived in, erase all the memories from it, made his entire body tighten like the strings of a violin.

His grandma gave him a look, and he groaned. Her looks always spelled trouble for him.

"Since when do *you* care about Emma?" she asked in return, her voice pointed, plucked eyebrows raised.

"I don't," he said. Even if a wave of emotions rolled through him every time her name was mentioned.

"Hmm." Her look was the same one she gave him when she caught him making out with a girl from youth group when he was fourteen.

"How attached to her boyfriend do you think she is?" she continued.

"How would I know? And why would I care?"

Now his grandma looked innocent. Too innocent. "Just curious." She drank the last of her coffee and rose. "I'm glad you're giving Samantha another chance. See, I knew Ms. Match was a good idea!" She walked out of the room, her light tread fading.

His grandma was full of good ideas. Those ideas, though, were not necessarily good for him.

Punching Ms. Match's number into his phone, he waited for her to answer.

"Anya? It's Josh Axelrod."

"Josh! How was your date last night? Have you filled out the feedback form yet?"

"That's what I wanted to talk to you about before I filled out the form," he said. "The date wasn't bad, but she brought along a friend."

Ms. Match's friendly tone morphed into something strictly business. "A friend? What do you mean, a friend?"

Josh gave her a quick rundown of the evening, and Ms. Match tsked in the background.

"Well, clearly I'm going to have to follow up with Samantha. I'm sorry about that. But I can promise you it won't happen again. I'd still like to get your feedback, though, so I can narrow down what you're looking for," she said.

"I'll send it to you as soon as we hang up, but maybe it's a sign I should let this whole matchmaking go. I mean, I'm grateful to my grandma, but—"

"Josh, I can understand your hesitancy, especially in light of how Samantha handled the evening, but I have to urge you to give her another shot. Unless the two of you completely hated each other, it's always a good idea to try a second date. That way, you can get past the awkwardness of a first meeting and get to know each other."

Josh sighed. "Okay, that makes sense. Can you give me her phone number?"

"Of course!" Ms. Match's voice pitched high with excitement. "I always wait until you've gone out the first time before handing over any personal information. But now that you've got that first date out of the way, I'm happy to share. And I think the two of you are going to hit it off."

He wasn't sure he'd classify them as hitting it off, but they didn't hate each other. "I think I need another date with her to determine that."

Ms. Match rattled off the phone number. "Of course. And don't worry, I'll make sure to follow up with her to go over the rules again. Good luck and don't forget to send me that form!"

"Did you hear that Rose is working for one of the big four accounting firms in New York?"

Emma cringed at her mom's question, gripping her phone a little tighter. It was too early for this conversation, Emma thought as she drove into town. She'd left the house before anyone was awake, or so she'd thought. Apparently, she was wrong.

"Yes, Mom, I did." Rose was their neighbor's daughter. Everything Rose did was blasted out to their entire social circle. At least her mother wasn't comparing Emma to her sister this time.

"You know, you could go to work for one of those firms. You've got your MBA, and you've always been smarter than Rose. Think of the salary you'd make and the security you'd have."

Emma parked her car and entered Isaacson's Deli. If she didn't know her mother better, she'd appreciate the compliment. But that compliment was a vehicle her mother used to question all of Emma's life choices.

Covering the phone, Emma placed her order before moving out of the way to wait. "I'm excited about the bookstore, Mom."

"But you don't know that it's going to be successful," her mom said.

"And Rose doesn't know that her firm won't do a round of layoffs, leaving her out of a job."

"You'd have a lot more security if you worked for someone else. Plus, the men you'd meet would be wealthy…"

Emma squeezed her hands into fists, her nails digging into her palms. Her parents' lack of faith in her was driving her crazy. Living with them made it harder. Thank goodness she'd be able to move out soon.

Her order was called, and she grabbed it. "Mom, I don't want to be late for my meeting. I'll see you later."

Hanging up the phone, she swiped her screen to check her emails as she walked out of the deli. With her sandwich bag tucked under one arm and her other hand holding her coffee, she ran smack into a body.

Her coffee landed at her feet, and she was about to lose her balance when hands gripped her upper arms, preventing her from landing on the pavement.

"Hey, watch where you're…" She met Josh Axelrod's gaze and gasped. "You!"

He frowned. "Me. But it's not my fault you weren't looking where you were going."

She gaped. "I know. I was surprised to see you."

"You mean run into me."

"Yeah, sorry," she said, not trying to hide the sarcasm. She bent to pick up her coffee cup. Wasn't a rabbi supposed to be…less rude? She searched for a trash can. "Did I get you?"

She scanned the seams of his light-washed jeans and his shoes. They seemed to be dry, and she sighed with relief.

She could only imagine the grief he'd give her if she stained his clothes.

He looked at his feet. "Luckily, no. I don't have time to run home to change." Moving out of the way, he tipped his head. "Are you okay?"

"Yeah, just moving too fast before caffeine and after my mother and clearly working with only half a brain. Which, now that the coffee landed on the ground, means it's not going to get better any time soon."

"Let me buy you a new one," he said. "I'm going inside anyway."

Her mouth opened. "Really?"

Stuffing his hands in his pockets, he nodded. "Or I can get one for myself, and you can figure out another way to get that caffeine jolt."

He had a point. "Thanks. Small black coffee."

"That's it?"

"What did you expect? A whipped concoction with more sugar than coffee?"

Josh shrugged. "I don't know. Something…more complicated."

"If I could, I'd inject the caffeine directly into my veins. All that other stuff gets in the way of the absorption."

He huffed, but the corners of his mouth quirked. "I don't think it works that way, but okay. Gimme a couple minutes."

She stared at his butt as he returned to the deli. Darn, that man filled out a pair of jeans. She blinked and reined herself in. She had no business being attracted to any part of this man. He was a rabbi *and* he was Samantha's match. Even if she doubted their compatibility, she wasn't about to cross any lines.

Her phone rang, and she smiled as she put it up to her ear.

Speak of the devil... "Hey, Sam. I was just thinking about you."

"Uh-oh, what did I do?"

"Nothing, but I literally ran into Josh a minute ago. He's buying me coffee because I spilled mine."

"Tell me you didn't get it all over him."

Emma flushed. Her clumsiness was well-known among her family and friends. "Nope, not a speck. A miracle, really."

"Good, because I think I like him."

Her stomach fluttered. "Are you sure?"

"Yeah, he's interesting. And he's a rabbi. How perfect is that? Didn't you like him?"

Emma glanced inside the deli to make sure Josh wasn't on his way out. "I mean, he's fine." An image of his butt in the jeans flashed through her mind, and she shut her eyes. "I... I'm not sure I see the two of you together."

"Did you spot any red flags?"

She replayed the conversations from the previous night. As much as Samantha might say she wanted a Jewish guy, she couldn't quite picture her best friend as the wife of a rabbi. Still... "I guess not."

Samantha's exhale echoed through the phone. "Good. He's significantly better than anyone else I've dated recently, and I'm thrilled he's a rabbi. That's cool! Hey, when he comes back, remind him to ask me out on a second date."

"Sam! How am I supposed to do that?"

"Oh, I don't know, how about, 'are you going to ask my best friend out again?'"

Emma kneaded her temple. "You know, you could ask him out."

"Not yet. I don't want to seem too eager."

"And my saying something won't make you seem too eager?"

"Oh, good point. Try to suss it out of him but don't be too obvious."

"Samantha!"

"Gotta run, Ms. Match is on the other line. Bye!"

Samantha disconnected as Josh returned with Emma's coffee.

"Did I hear you say Samantha?" he asked as he handed her a new cup. His face brightened with interest, and Emma's heated.

Was there a point to the conversation? She couldn't remember. "She called to… I have no idea why." *Not an outright lie.* She took the coffee from Josh and nodded. "Thank you for this."

"You're welcome. If you talk to her again, let her know I'll be calling her soon. Actually, tell her I've got to get a few things settled with my grandmother, so not to worry if it takes a few days."

Warmth spread through Emma's insides, and it wasn't from the coffee. Something about the way he cared for the older woman attracted her, which was ridiculous, because he wasn't her type. And he was interested in her best friend. She shook her head. Not doing that again.

"Will do. See you around." She waved and texted Samantha.

josh will call after he gets his g-ma situated

ty. apparently setting up a double date was taboo

oh no, I'm sorry. I didn't mean to get you in trouble

it's fine

Finished playing wingman and reinforced with coffee and bagels, Emma walked to the architect's office, trying to forget about Josh, his care for his grandmother and his sexy butt.

The receptionist waved her into the conference room, and her architect, Terrence O'Malley, all six-foot-something of him, rose to greet her.

"Emma, I think you're going to love what I've drawn up."

The large man with the booming voice ushered her into a seat across the conference table, spun his tablet around and slid it toward her. As he paged through his plans, he explained everything.

"The entryway will remain the same. To the right will be the adult book section, to the left the kid's section. The entire back of the first floor will be converted into a café and seating area. Since the kitchen is already there, it won't be as complicated to do."

He showed her the 3D renderings, and her pulse quickened. "I love this! And the bones of the house can stay the same."

He nodded. "Exactly. Then we move up to the second floor. There are three bedrooms and a bathroom, which we'll gut and turn into your new kitchen, dining room, powder room and living room."

"How hard will that be?" she asked.

He paused his presentation. "We're coming in on budget with everything I'm suggesting. Unless there's some unexpected surprise, this won't be a problem."

Emma sighed in relief. The business loan she'd taken out, plus money her grandmother had left her, were all she had to put into this project. She didn't want to fall in love with something Terrence suggested only to find out she couldn't afford it.

"And the third floor will remain the same, with minor updating. Three bedrooms, two bathrooms. All-in-all, there's plenty of room for you to live above the store, and if down the road you want to sell, you'll have an easy resale."

A nervous giggle bubbled beneath the surface. This really was going to work. "I'm excited," she said as she finished scrolling through the plans.

He anchored a hand on his hip and nodded. "I'm glad. I'll get the permits going, and we should be able to start at the end of the month."

"Which is perfect, since the Axelrods are moving out then." She rose and shook his hand. "Thank you so much for everything."

Leaving the architect's office, she couldn't help but sigh in contentment. The young girl who'd been called flighty, artsy and unpredictable possessed an MBA, a business plan, a building and a legitimate plan to turn an old house into a bookstore.

Even if her parents doubted her abilities, for the first time in a long time, Emma didn't.

Chapter Three

Swallowing the last of his coffee, Josh tossed the cup into the trash and entered the moving company's office. "Hey, I'm Josh Axelrod. My grandma hired you guys to move her, and I'm here for boxes."

The tattooed man behind the counter checked his computer and nodded, before scanning Josh with judgmental eyes. "You have a big enough car for all of them or do you want to make trips?"

Josh squirmed, somehow feeling judged and not liking it one bit. "I'm good. And if I need to make trips, I will." His Mustang wasn't exactly big, but how much space could boxes take up?

Josh followed the guy to the storeroom, where a pile of broken-down boxes sat, all labeled with Axelrod.

"These are yours."

Oh boy. There were a lot. He'd underestimated. "Can I move my car around to the bay?" Josh asked, pointing at a metal door that he assumed led outside.

The guy nodded, flicking the switch to lift the door. "Have at it."

Josh scoffed as he walked away. *Have at it*, implied he was in charge. Anyone familiar with his grandmother knew she was the boss. For all intents and purposes, Josh was the lackey.

He moved his Mustang to the large bay door. He didn't

object to helping his grandmother. She'd rescued him when his parents died, raised him and given him plenty of love. She was his only family. He owed her, no matter what she said.

He hated the march of time. His heart ached knowing moving was the necessary next step in her life, forcing him to contemplate his own life without her in it. Hopefully, though, not for a long time.

After he loaded as many boxes as would fit in his sports car, he honked the horn to let tattoo guy know he was leaving and drove home.

Midmorning in Browerville was bustling, and he looked around in wonder. It had been a long time since he'd been home on a weekday. Despite the winter chill in the air, young moms with strollers walked the sidewalks, maneuvering around businesspeople out for their morning coffee. Cars filled the streets, and shop doors opened and closed with customers rushing to do their errands.

Living and working in the city meant he mostly visited on the weekends, when the pace was different. As he approached the town square, he read a sign advertising the annual winter festival.

Maybe he'd see if Samantha wanted to go. Walking around among the food vendors and admiring the ice sculptures would be an easy opportunity to get to know each other better. And maybe, once he spent some time with her, he'd see how good Ms. Match's matchmaking skills were.

"Grandma! I'm home!" He entered the house and tossed his keys on the counter.

She stood in front of the open pantry, staring at the shelves. "You have the boxes? I want to donate the nonperishables to the food bank. There's no way I'll use all of this in the next month."

He kissed his grandma's cheek as he passed. "Great idea. I've got the boxes in the car. At least, some of them. There's a lot more when we run out of this stack. But maybe we should save the pantry items for later? We should start with the Hanukkah decorations and the things we don't use."

"You're right," she said. "By the time I need them again, I'll be all settled in. But the food donation was on my mind, and I didn't want to forget. Why don't you assemble the boxes and start distributing them? I'll go get the decorations."

"I'll take care of them in a second. I want to give Samantha a call first."

His grandma smiled. "Feel free to invite her to Shabbat dinner here if you'd like."

He did a double take. "Grandma, we haven't gone out by ourselves yet. While three people is better than four, I'd still like the chance to spend time with just her."

His grandma cackled. "I like giving you a hard time. Go call the woman before she decides you're not interested."

Jogging up the stairs to his room like a teenager first discovering girls reminded him of middle school. He'd been awkward and angry and hormonal. Not something he wanted to repeat. But dating while living with his grandmother for the next month was going to be…interesting.

He shut his door and pulled out his phone. Before he could second-guess himself, he dialed Samantha.

It went straight to voicemail. Disappointment surged, until he remembered it was a weekday, and she was working. Like he would have been if he hadn't taken leave to help his grandmother.

"Hey, Samantha, it's Josh. I enjoyed meeting you last night and wanted to suggest a second date, maybe at the winter festival next weekend. Give me a call when you're free."

He opened his email and called up the matchmaker's follow-up form. He answered the questions and sent it off to Ms. Match. Now it was time to help his grandmother.

* * *

Emma hit Order on her last batch of books, pushed away from her desk and stretched her arms overhead. "Ayiee," she squeaked as her vertebrae cracked.

"Problem?" Her mom peeked around the doorframe, basket of laundry on her hip.

"Nope, just sitting at the computer for too long."

"You should get outside. The cold air will do you good."

Emma glanced out the window at the winter-blue sky. "I have a lot to do."

Her mother stepped inside Emma's bedroom. "Fresh air will do you good. Go."

Why Emma, as a twenty-seven-year-old woman, was listening to her mother without question, was something she didn't want to think about at the moment. She rose, grabbing her phone and a heavy jacket to cover her white sweater, and left.

Her mother was right, not that Emma would ever admit that. Inhaling the bracing winter air did feel good. She stared at her childhood home for a couple seconds before walking down the street toward one of the paths that ran through the woods.

She'd spent far too long beneath her parents' thumb. Both her mom and dad were hard workers who believed nothing less than one's best was acceptable. Her older sister had thrived in that environment, always making the highest grades, achieving the top honors and basically doing everything their parents expected without ever seeming to mind. That included going to a top university, a top law school and getting a job at a top firm where she was on track to make partner any day now.

Emma was the rebel. She'd always put up a fight. If left to her own devices, she would have whiled away the hours reading, dreaming and doing whatever caught her fancy at the moment.

And yet, here she was, having done what her parents demanded and still about to launch her dream. Even better, she'd be able to move out of their home and above the bookstore, finally breaking the last of the cords.

She couldn't wait.

She followed the path as the sounds of civilization quieted and nature took over. The air smelled of snow, weak sunlight dappled the ground, and up ahead, squirrels skittered through the last of the snow. The path forked, and she followed the one to the right, which led to a park. It was pretty quiet, with an empty playground and deserted bike paths, although a few dedicated joggers pounded around the perimeter.

"Emma?"

The female voice interrupted her daydreams, and Emma blinked, trying to focus. "Mrs. Axelrod!"

The older woman wore a bright orange parka as she walked toward her. "How are you, sweetheart? It's nice to see you."

Emma gave her a hug. "I needed a break from ordering books."

"What genres are you ordering?"

"Romance, mystery, thriller, fantasy, women's fiction… and some nonfiction and children's books as well."

The older woman's expression brightened, and her cheeks flushed. "Romance? How spicy?"

Emma's cheeks heated. "I ordered a variety, but most are pretty spicy. I'd be happy to order you something…sweeter, if you'd like."

"Are you kidding? I love romances, the spicier the better." She leaned closer to Emma. "At this point in my life, the only spice I get is through reading."

Emma coughed, and Mrs. Axelrod patted her on the back, giggling.

"Well, I need to keep moving before my body stiffens up, and I have to call Josh for help." She winked at her. "I can't wait to shop at your store."

The older woman was gone before Emma was able to formulate an appropriate reply.

The difference between Mrs. Axelrod and her mother struck her like a punch in the gut. Her mother thought she spent too much time reading "nonsense." Mrs. Axelrod clearly was a fan of romance novels.

Emma nodded. She had one of her favorite series at home. Perhaps Mrs. Axelrod would like to borrow it. With a plan formulating in her mind, she rose and left for home.

Josh sat at his grandmother's kitchen table wrapping and packing dishes. He'd never paid much attention to the china his grandmother used, other than taking note of whether the dishes were for meat or dairy. Not until she'd decided to purge her belongings prior to her move. Suddenly, the silver-and-white floral patterns took on new meaning. They were the dishes she'd used for holiday celebrations.

He remembered Rosh Hashanah dinners with his parents, aunts and uncles, cousins and grandparents. Roasted chicken, brisket, noodle kugel and Jewish apple cake for dessert. He'd never left the table hungry, and he could still hear the voices of his relatives as they discussed current events, politics or which distant relative was dating a shiksa and whether or not it was a good or bad thing.

There was no way he could part with these dishes. He wanted to serve holiday meals on them to his own family someday and tell stories about the celebrations they'd served.

His New York apartment wasn't big enough to hold them, though. For now, he'd pack them away in storage and figure out what to do with them later. Someday, he'd have a bigger place to live.

"Am I allowed to sell *these*?" his grandmother asked, holding up a set of plain white dishes.

He nodded. "I don't need to keep your everyday dairy dishes. And honestly, I can't explain why I like these," he said, holding up a floral dessert plate. "I... I'm not ready to part with them yet."

With everything changing, his memories were the only solid things he had to hold on to, and he wasn't about to toss them, like old dishes, into a trash heap.

"Well, maybe your Samantha will like them."

"She's not my Samantha. I haven't even gone on a second date with her." Nor had she returned his call.

"That's why I want you to continue with Ms. Match. She set you up with one nice woman, and I'm sure she has plenty of others if you and Samantha don't work out."

He shuddered. "I wish you'd stay out of my dating life, Grandma."

She cupped his cheek. "I know. But I want you to be happy, and random women you meet in bars in the middle of a big city aren't necessarily going to be right for you."

He wrapped tissue around a dessert plate. "I don't pick up women in bars. Not usually, anyway. I use dating apps. And do you have any idea how many congregants from my temple in the city have invited me to dinner to meet their single daughters, cousins, cousin's daughters? They're as good as a matchmaker—"

His grandmother cleared her throat. "Are you serious with any of them?"

He shuddered. "Not at the moment."

"Well, then, stick with Ms. Match."

It was useless arguing. Instead, he nodded and kept wrapping. The doorbell rang, and he pushed away from the table to get it.

His grandmother's hand on his shoulder stopped him. "I'll go."

Her footsteps echoed through the empty hall. The front door squeaked as she opened it. "Emma, how nice to see you!"

Josh straightened, nostrils flaring. Wasn't it enough she would take control of his home in a month? Did she have to show up now, too?

"Josh, it's Emma," his grandmother said unnecessarily as they walked into the kitchen. "And she brought me books."

The wide grin creasing his grandmother's wrinkled face eased his annoyance and kept him from asking why Emma hadn't called first. Anything that made his grandmother happy was fine with him. Mostly.

He rose. "Hey."

His grandmother frowned. "That's how you greet a woman? No wonder you haven't found someone to settle down with!"

Josh's face burned, and he wished he could spontaneously combust right there.

Only the redness of Emma's cheeks gave him any sense of relief. At least she was embarrassed, too. "Hey," she responded.

He wanted to kiss her with gratitude.

Kiss her? No way. She wasn't his type.

Throwing her hands in the air, his grandmother muttered something about packing the books safely away where she'd be sure to find them the second she moved into her new apartment, said goodbye to Emma and left the two of them alone.

He cleared his throat before sitting again. "Wow."

Emma laughed. "Your grandma's a trip."

"That's one way of describing her," he said, shaking his head in disbelief. "What books did you bring her?"

"Romances. We ran into each other in the park and started talking, so I lent her one of my favorite series."

The air in the room evaporated. "Romances? My grandmother reads romances?" He buried his face in his hands. So many images he didn't want to entertain entered his brain.

Emma frowned. "Hey, romances are awesome."

He held up a hand. "I'm not knocking them. I promise. I just…she's my grandmother. The term, TMI, is too tame knowing she's reading about…you know." Great, now he sounded like he was twelve. "Never mind," he said. "The less I know, the better."

Emma walked toward the table, her eyes sparkling. "Are these your grandma's?" She picked up one of the floral plates. "They're beautiful."

"Yeah. I'm saving them for the future. What I'm going to do with them, I have no idea, but we served too many memories on them for me to let them go to Goodwill." Emma hadn't asked for details. He should keep his mouth shut.

"Lots of family dinners?" She sat next to him, perched on the edge of her chair.

He nodded. "Every Jewish holiday, whether it was the whole family or the two of us." His chest filled with nostalgia. He didn't know why he was telling Emma this or why the dishes took on such meaning. Maybe it was the moving on to another stage in life, at least for his grandma. "You probably think I'm nuts." His neck heated with embarrassment.

Emma shook her head. "Actually, I'm a little jealous. My memories of family get-togethers are filled with arguing over how I should be more like my sister. I don't remember much celebrating of anything, much less Jewish holidays." She turned her brown-eyed gaze to him and shrugged. "I always liked Hanukkah, though."

The last time he'd noticed her eyes, he'd thought them hard and unyielding. This time, they were soft and liquid.

He lowered his voice in sympathy. "That must have been tough."

She shrugged again. He thought she might be brushing off how tough it had been.

Before he could say anything else, his phone buzzed. "I'm sorry. It's Samantha." He turned to the side. "Hi, Samantha. Your friend Emma is actually here with me." He pressed the speaker button. "We were talking about dishes."

Great conversation starter, dude.

"Dishes?" Samantha's tone sounded skeptical.

Emma interjected, "Yeah, he's packing up his grandmother's things, and I was admiring them. They're beautiful."

Samantha cleared her throat. "That's definitely a you thing, Emma. You know me, I'm paper plates and takeout all the way. Much easier, especially if I don't want to mess up the kosher-not-kosher thing. Josh, I got your message. I'd love to go to the winter festival in Browerville. Saturday might be tough for me to get home because I think I have to work, but I should be able to make it home Sunday."

He hadn't pictured setting up a date with an audience, but it seemed par for the course with Samantha and Emma. And he wasn't about to let the opportunity slide. He turned the phone off speaker. "Sure, Sunday is fine." He firmed up the plans and said goodbye, then turned to Emma. "She said to give her a call when you can."

Emma nodded. "I should get going. I'm sure I'll see you around." She paused in the doorway. "Have fun at the winter festival."

For a brief moment, the urge to invite her along entered his mind, but he ignored it. She and her boyfriend had already gone on one date with them. He didn't want her on the second one.

Even if the room felt a little less bright after she left.

Chapter Four

"Hey, Sam, you wanted me to call you?" Emma said after leaving the Axelrods' home.

"You're alone?"

Emma gazed up and down the street. The combination of residential and commercial space meant you were never truly alone, with people entering and exiting offices inside converted Victorian homes, cars passing, and children playing in their yards. But she understood her friend's unspoken question—Josh wasn't with her. "Yes, I'm alone. Why?"

"Ms. Match berated me."

Emma paused with her car door open, her body halfway inside. "I'm sorry. What happened?"

"The matchmaker. She informed me that inviting another couple on a first date that she arranges is not allowed without prior permission. That doing it without warning the other party damages the trust she's trying to establish. And it makes her look bad."

Emma climbed fully into her car and shut the door. There was a part of her that understood that. "Hmm, while I get her point, I have a hard time imagining she'd yell at you. You're her client, aren't you?"

"I know, right? If I spoke to my clients the way she spoke to me, the partners would have my butt!"

"She yelled at you? That can't be good for client retention."

Emma loved her best friend, but Sam never liked being contradicted. As children, Emma was often the one who gave in to avoid an argument.

"Her tone was decidedly clipped. Did Josh say anything to you?"

"About the double date? No." He hadn't talked about anything relating to the other night.

"Well, he obviously said something to her."

"Sam, I wouldn't worry too much about it.

"Maybe Ms. Match was right. It's hard to get to know someone when other people are around."

"True, but lots of couples meet in group settings," Emma said. "It's not like Rob and I prevented the two of you from having a conversation."

Samantha agreed. "I think her nose is out of joint because I was leery of trusting *her*."

Guilt made Emma chew her bottom lip. "Which was kind of my fault. I'm sorry."

"It's fine. I needed to vent."

Emma tried to find the bright side. "He asked you to the winter festival. Clearly he wants to see you again." Her insides shifted as she spoke. He'd been a lot more pleasant today, but she still wasn't sure he was a great match for Samantha. No matter how enthralled Samantha might be with dating a rabbi, Emma wasn't sure her friend was cut out for a future with one. "Do you want to see him?" she asked. "I know you said yes when he asked you, but…"

"I'd like to see him again." Samantha sighed. "Crap, I'm being pulled into a meeting. Can we talk later?"

Emma said yes and hung up the phone. She yanked at her curls. This was her fault. She'd refused to let Samantha go out alone with Josh and now Samantha's matchmaker was angry. While Emma's motives had been pure—a woman couldn't be too careful going out with strange men—she probably should have stayed out of it. Or just insisted Samantha call her afterward. Or suggested something other than dragging Rob out to pretend to be a double date.

What if the matchmaker let her annoyance at Samantha affect the other guys she chose? Or what if Josh was upset and let his feelings color his opinion of Samantha?

Emma yanked open the car door, planning to drive to the house and apologize to Josh.

Except Josh wasn't the one she owed an apology to. Ms. Match was.

She pulled out her phone and Googled Ms. Match before she drove to the office a few blocks over.

The chimes over the door jingled as she entered, and a few seconds later, a woman close to her age—maybe a little older—with bright red hair swept in on a cloud of citrus perfume. Emma got serious fashion envy from her plum-colored pantsuit.

"May I help you?"

"I'm looking for Ms. Match," Emma said.

The woman stepped forward. "That's me. I'm Anya Rubenstein. Do you have an appointment?"

Emma stepped forward and held out her hand. "I don't, but I owe you an apology."

Anya frowned. "I'm listening."

"My name is Emma, and I'm Samantha Drucker's best friend. It was my idea to turn her first date with Josh Axelrod into a double date, not Samantha's."

The woman flared her nostrils. "Ah. You thought it would be more fun with a group?"

Emma bit her lip. "No, I was concerned about Sam's... judgment."

Ms. Match nodded, folding her arms across her waist. "I

appreciate your apology and how you're looking out for your friend, but I think you should stay out of this business and let me take care of Samantha's matchmaking. And safety. Understand?"

Emma swallowed. "Yes, ma'am. I'm sorry, again."

Ms. Match nodded, and Emma slowly backed out of the office. Somehow, that apology didn't make her feel any better. Hopefully, her apology to Josh would be more successful.

By the time she arrived home, her phone was buzzing with text messages. They were all from Sam. And none of them were pleased.

you went to ms. match?

r u crazy?

now she's more annoyed w/me because I got you involved

please stay out of it

How did all of this become such a disaster?

The next day, Josh loaded his car with bags of clothes his grandmother no longer wanted. How one woman owned so many outfits, he had no idea. Especially since she didn't go anywhere. He shook his head at the reflection of twelve large bags in his rearview mirror, put his car in Reverse and backed out of the driveway.

The Jewish Community Center collected gently used items to help those in need, and as he drove there, he blasted his music, trying to drown out his worries. Except some song about change came on and he groaned before turning off the music altogether.

Everything was changing. And he hated it. He didn't want to complain to his grandma and upset her, so he'd volunteered to take these bags, giving him a chance to escape and dwell in his sorrows for a bit before returning home to act like the same "Joshy" she expected him to be.

Turning into the JCC parking lot, he drove around to the loading dock. He backed his car up to the entrance before jumping out and looking around for someone to help him.

"Donations?" A man in overalls approached him.

Josh nodded. "Clothing."

The man checked something off on his clipboard before helping Josh unload the car. For a brief moment, the urge to take all the clothes, race home and return everything to the closets and drawers where they belonged overwhelmed Josh, making him stagger.

Emma could find another place to house her bookstore.

Except that the majority of these clothes hadn't been in style for thirty years. His grandmother didn't want them, regardless of whether or not she was moving out of their home. If he returned with the bags, his grandmother would see how much this was hurting him and prevent him from helping her.

Which meant she'd try to do all the moving herself.

Josh's guilt would kill him.

So instead, he brought the last of the bags into the loading dock, took the tax donation receipt from the man, waved and got back into his car.

Instead of driving home, though, he pulled around to the front of the building and entered the JCC. He'd attending this community center throughout the time he lived with his grandma, swimming and using the fitness center while his grandma attended classes or lectures. He signed in with Security and walked over to the reception desk.

"Do you have any short-term gym memberships I could

purchase?" he asked. "I'm here for a month." If only he could stay longer.

The woman behind the desk nodded. "We have a month-to-month gym membership for fifty-four dollars. You can use the weight room and pool and take three classes. You can also use the racquetball, tennis and pickleball courts."

Josh was going to get plenty of exercise packing and lifting and moving his grandmother. But a break from his grandmother—as much as he loved her—was the key to keeping his sanity intact. "I'll take it," he said.

He filled out the digital paperwork, posed for his identification photo and waited while everything was printed. After paying for the membership, he walked out.

As he was exiting, Rabbi Moskowitz of Browerville's Reform Synagogue, Temple Beth Kavod, entered. Her face lit up with excitement. "Josh, how are you, how's your grandma?"

He shook her outstretched hand. "I'm well. You know I'm a rabbi now, right?"

She gave him a huge grin. "I do. Mazel tov. Your grandma told me you're working in Manhattan."

"I am, although I've taken a month off to help her pack up the house."

"That's right. How's it going?"

He shrugged. "It's going." He wasn't about to talk out his feelings with his grandmother's rabbi.

Rabbi Moskowitz's eyes lit up. "You know, if you've got time, I'd love some help with the senior youth group. Their advisor is having some scheduling conflicts. Any chance you're interested?"

Josh paused. Working with kids was one of the things he liked best about his job—he was responsible for a lot of the teaching and activities for the younger members. "Sure, I'd love to help out."

"Fantastic. I think you'd be a perfect fit for us. And who knows, maybe you'll like it and decide to stay." She winked at him.

Give up his job in the city? He didn't see that happening, but he was certainly glad to volunteer while he was here.

"The teens are volunteering at the food pantry. Can you chaperone?"

"Sure."

She pulled out her phone, and they went over the dates and times of events occurring while he was in Browerville.

"Got it," he said. "Thanks."

And suddenly, a month he'd expected to be filled with loss—the loss of his childhood home, the loss of his grandma as the parent and him as the child—turned into something more meaningful. One he might actually look forward to.

He returned to his car, and once inside, he reached for his phone and texted Samantha. If he wanted to get to know her better, their conversations needed to be about more than setting up times to see each other.

how's your day going? You'll never guess what I did.

He waited a minute to see if she'd answer. When she didn't, he shifted into gear and drove to his grandmother's home, his mind alight with possibilities.

In the kitchen, a plate of brownies sat on the table, along with a note that she'd gone to the grocery store. He snagged a brownie, pulled out his computer and checked out the temple's website.

He'd attended the synagogue as a child, but now that he was a rabbi, he looked at it through a different lens. And he liked what he saw. The religious school and youth group were active, the temple organized social events for a variety of age groups, and it gave back to the community. For a small-town temple, they did a lot of good.

His phone pinged.

Samantha.

crazy busy. it's like everyone and their mother wants to sue somebody. What did you do?

Josh huffed. Samantha's job was surprisingly like that of a rabbi. Not the suing part, obviously, but the long hours, getting pulled in multiple directions and putting out a million small fires.

good thing they've got you. I volunteered to help out with our temple's senior youth group.

really? Why?

they needed help and I'm free.

better you than me.

Josh frowned. That wasn't the response he'd hoped for. Still, not everyone enjoyed being around teenagers. see you this weekend?

ha. if I live that long. RIP me

Sympathy welled within him. He'd felt like that lots of times, especially when he was working around the holidays. Congregants all thought their issues were the only thing Josh should focus on, which he understood to an extent. But juggling all their needs didn't leave much time for his own. And his current temple in the city left him to play catch-up with any issues the head rabbis didn't have time for, usually administrative issues or sermons for the less popular services.

Lately, he'd started to wonder if there was an area he could specialize in, rather than handling whatever the other rabbis didn't have time for. Something more fulfilling, like helping develop the next generation of Jewish adults.

Now that he was home, he also realized how important his family was to him, especially as he sorted through his grandma's things, most of which dredged up memories for him. He'd always loved and depended on his grandmother. But now, she was depending on him. He was honored to be able to help her and wished he could do more of it.

Even if along with all of that came fear and anxiety. Jewish teachings were clear on the mitzvah of taking care of the elderly. But what if he disappointed her? And could he support her as well from New York?

If he messed up anything with his grandmother…well, it wasn't like he could get a new one.

He turned on his music, inserted his earbuds and sorted through the boxes representing decades of his grandmother's life. He saved mementos for himself—a quilt she made, his grandfather's yarmulke and tallis, a book they'd read together… The rest he divided among the giveaway piles and things his grandmother wanted to bring with her in her move.

He frowned as he reached for a second brownie. When did he become so introspective? He savored the chocolatey goodness as he closed out of his emails. Maybe Samantha could relate. He picked up his phone but decided not to text her now. She'd said she was busy. The last thing she needed was him bothering her.

"Joshy?" His grandmother's voice carried through the hallway, slightly echoey as they continued to empty the house.

"In the kitchen!"

She walked in with a bag of groceries. He rose to help her, but she waved him back into his seat. "It's one bag. Enjoy your brownie," she said. "I'm playing canasta tomorrow at the JCC," she said. "Want to go to lunch afterward?"

He wiped his mouth on his hand, then sheepishly took the napkin his grandmother offered and patted his lips before answering. "Sure. What time will you be done with your game?"

"Should be over by twelve thirty. Maybe you can drop me off and pick me up so we only use one car?"

"Sure thing. And lunch can be my treat."

His grandmother's mouth stretched into a wide grin. "Treated by my grandson? Like I'd refuse."

Josh rose, kissed his grandma on the cheek and walked toward the stairs. "I'll be up in the attic packing if you need me. In the meantime, think of a good place to eat."

The following day, he met his grandmother at the front entrance to the JCC, waited for her to get in and fasten her seat belt and pulled out of the parking lot.

"Where are we going for lunch?" his grandmother asked, placing her handbag on her lap and holding it as if she expected it to fly out the window. He was driving a mile over the speed limit.

"You were supposed to decide," he said. "What are you in the mood for?" he asked, turning onto Main Street.

She looked out the window, scanning the storefronts and restaurants until she straightened and pointed. "There!"

"Where?" He scanned the area but didn't see any of the places his grandmother usually chose.

"Right here, Josh. Pull over or you'll miss it." She leaned forward, her eagerness to get out of the car palpable.

His grandmother never acted this way. He swung into the

first available parking space, and before he could turn off the car, his grandmother was out of her seat belt, door open, climbing out of the car. Still gripping her handbag.

What the heck?

He exited the car and slammed money in the meter, all while keeping an eye on the old woman who was racewalking down the sidewalk. "Grandma, wait!"

His yell was futile. She kept going as if she didn't hear him.

He frowned. Honestly, he wasn't sure if she actually couldn't hear him or if she was ignoring him. Finally he caught up with her in front of Tea Time. Her face was creased in a smile, her chest heaving with exertion.

"You want to eat here?" The shop sold tea and spices.

"No, silly, I want to go inside. We can eat later."

Josh's stomach growled in protest, but he followed her into the store. Although why she wanted to purchase more things when they were trying to pack up her house was beyond him.

A mix of herbal aromas filled the interior. He wrinkled his nose. Everything smelled like plants. Come to think of it, he didn't remember his grandmother drinking tea. Or if she did, it was the bag-from-the-grocery-store kind. He wandered over to a shelf and coughed at the price. For tea? Obviously, he was not the target customer.

"Emma, hello!"

His grandmother's voice carried across the space, and Josh froze in his tracks.

"Fancy meeting you here," she continued. "Josh, look who's here."

And now it made sense, at least partially. His grandmother wanted to see Emma. But why? And how did she know Emma was here?

He frowned at his grandmother, who shrugged her shoulders with fake innocence, before he turned to Emma and nodded. "Hi," he said.

She smiled. "Hi." Her smile softened some of his annoyance at his grandma's machinations.

"Do you love tea, too?" his grandmother asked Emma. "Their blueberry green tea is fantastic."

Blueberry green tea? Since when did his grandmother drink blueberry green tea?

"Oh, I like that one," Emma said. "I'm also partial to the rose hip and the chamomile."

His grandmother leaned toward her. "Buy all three," she fake-whispered.

Emma laughed. "Actually, they're not for me, although I might include something for myself. I need to buy in bulk for The Book Nook. I figure if I'm going to offer coffee, I need to offer tea, too."

At the mention of the bookstore, Josh's stomach clenched.

His grandmother nodded, making her gray hair flutter. "Absolutely right. You don't want to lose a book sale because someone doesn't like coffee." She turned toward him. "Joshy, isn't Emma smart?"

His face burned, almost bursting into flame when Emma covered her mouth, eyes dancing with merriment at the nickname. He and his grandmother were going to have to have a chat.

Before he could do anything but wish the floor would open so he could fall through it, the saleswoman came over and handed a ticket to Emma.

"We'd love to satisfy your bulk order," she said. "Mark on here which ones you want, we'll order them, and when you're ready, we can deliver."

Well, at least he wasn't going to have to accept packages for The Book Nook. Once again, his stomach growled. He looked around. Sometimes stores like these offered samples. Not that tea was going to satisfy his hunger, but couldn't there be food, too? If he owned a tea shop, he'd do everything he could to make his customers thirsty, including offering them food.

"...okay, Josh?"

Josh whipped around and focused on his grandmother. "Sorry, what did you say?"

She clasped her hands in exasperation. "I said, why don't you help Emma with her tea selection while I go sit over there?" She pointed to an overstuffed chair near the window.

Sit? If she wanted to sit, why didn't they go on to the restaurant?

Emma stood next to his grandmother, looking between the two of them like she was watching a ping-pong tournament.

"Uh, sure." He stuffed his hands in his pockets and followed Emma around the store.

"You're not much of a tea drinker, I guess?" she asked once they were out of earshot of his grandmother.

"I prefer coffee," he said. "But if you need help, I can try..."

She demurred. "I think your grandmother wants us to be friends."

"Friends?" Josh scoffed. "Maybe you should tell her about your boyfriend."

Emma returned the tin of tea she was sniffing to the glass shelf and frowned at him. "Boyfriend?"

"Yeah, the guy you brought on my first date with Samantha."

Her mouth opened. "Oh, Rob? No, we're not dating. He's a friend of mine I brought with me so it wouldn't be awkward."

"I've got news for you, Emma. That date was awkward."

She looked at the floor. Her curls covered her cheeks, but he thought her neck reddened.

A stab of remorse hit him.

"Yeah, I'm sorry about that," she said. "It seemed like a good idea at the time, but on second thought, probably not my finest moment."

Now his curiosity was piqued. "Why'd you do it?"

"I've never understood the appeal of a matchmaker." Emma ticked off the reasons on her hand. "And women can never be too careful when it comes to safety, even with a rabbi." She looked at him. "No offense. I was looking out for my best friend."

"None taken." The more he thought about it, the more he realized how scary it must be for women to meet men they didn't know.

They walked around the store as Emma noted on the ticket which teas she wanted.

"Actually, I agree with you regarding the matchmaker," Josh said.

"And yet you used one to meet Samantha."

"Only because my grandmother forced me to do it." He winced. "I meant forced me to use a matchmaker, not meet Samantha."

Emma snorted. "Forced you?" She looked toward the corner of the store, and Josh followed her gaze.

His grandmother sat in a chair, a cup of tea on the table next to her, sipping the hot liquid and looking innocent. Too innocent.

"I have a hard time believing a woman of her size or age could force you to do anything." This time, Emma turned her attention to Josh, and his face heated as she perused him from his face to his toes and back again. For a brief moment, he wondered if she liked what she saw but quickly dismissed the thought. He was dating Samantha.

"You'd be surprised how much sway someone I love has over me," he answered.

Now Emma's cheeks reddened, making him wonder what she was thinking. Before he could ask, she shook her head, curls bouncing.

"Good to know," she said. "I've got to get going, or I'm never going to finish my to-do list." She hurried away to the counter and handed her ticket to the saleswoman, her back firmly toward Josh.

He walked over to his grandmother. "Are you ready for lunch?"

She nodded, rising and taking his arm. "Let's go next door to the burger place." She walked with him to the door but paused outside on the sidewalk. "You made a hash of that, I see."

"A hash of what?"

"Your conversation with Emma."

"I don't know what you're talking about, Grandma. She was busy."

"Mm-hmm." She pulled against his arm, forcing him to start walking again or landing them both on the sidewalk.

I have a hard time believing a woman of her size or age could force you to do anything.

Emma's words echoed in his mind, and he looked toward the store, wondering if she had seen how his grandmother pulled him along.

But the store was empty.

"You're joining us for dinner Friday night, right?" Emma's mom posed the question to her later that afternoon.

"Um, I think so."

Standing in the foyer of the home she'd grown up in, she faced her mother who stood in the kitchen doorway. Her mom's lips pressed tight with disappointment, and Emma winced.

"I thought I told you about it when we made the plans with Alyse," her mother said. "You know how busy her schedule is. When she's actually able to make it here, it would be nice if we could eat as a family."

"I'm sure it's fine," Emma pulled her phone from her messenger bag, opened her calendar app and checked Friday. Rob—the guy Josh thought was her boyfriend but who was just a guy friend—had invited her for drinks at seven. She hadn't noted anything about a family Shabbat dinner, but she couldn't skip it.

Crap. She'd probably been annoyed at either her mother or her sister. As usual.

"No, um, it's there. I'll be there," she clarified.

"Excellent. I want us all together." Her mother walked away.

Emma leaned against the doorjamb and texted Rob.

can we make drinks late on Friday?

She gritted her teeth as she made her way up to her room. What she really wanted to do with her calendar was to check off the days until she wouldn't have to live here anymore. But that would be petty and immature.

Her mom wanted a family dinner. So what if her mother catered more toward her sister's schedule than her own? That was nothing new. In the Geffner family, Alyse was the favorite child, the one who could do no wrong. Emma had lived in her sister's shadow her entire life.

The good thing about shadows, though, was there were fewer chances to be seen. The less attention her family paid to her, the easier it was for her to do exactly what she wanted.

She'd done what her parents asked her to do—gone to college and gotten a business degree. Now she was following her own dream. And if her dream was as successful as she anticipated it being, she'd be able to surprise her family with how well she was doing.

If not? Well, her failure wouldn't make much of an impression. Either way, she could handle it.

What was more difficult to handle were the mood swings of one Josh Axelrod. And how he popped up all over the place.

Her phone pinged.

sure, 9:30?

She'd definitely need a drink by then, and her mother and sister couldn't object to her leaving.

perfect

She flopped onto her bed, feeling more like a moody teenager than a woman of twenty-seven years. Another reason to get out of this house.

The thought of her purchase and her dream coming true filled her with joy. Her breath came quickly, like little bubbles of excitement fizzing through her lungs.

Until Josh's face came to mind, and she groaned. He was not supposed to invade her thoughts.

She never should have gone with Samantha on her date. If she hadn't, she wouldn't be continuously bumping into the annoying man. She'd met him, and now she couldn't walk three feet in this small town without tripping over him. It was like coveting a new piece of jewelry only to suddenly see it on every person you passed. Josh was the same way.

Well, minus the coveting part.

It wouldn't be bad if his attitude didn't change more frequently than the weather. Sometimes he seemed happy to see her, and at other times, he acted like she was as appealing as a textbook he had to slog through.

Poor Samantha. Emma hoped he was more consistent with her.

If only there was a way to avoid him altogether.

That Friday, after she signed all the construction contracts and had a minor freakout over the amount of money she was spending, she rushed home to her parents' house, took a quick shower and jogged down the steps in time to meet her sister at the front door for Shabbat dinner.

"Hey, Alyse." Emma gave her sister a quick hug. "Nice necklace."

Alyse fiddled with the gold-and-diamond chain at her throat. "Thanks. I splurged with my bonus money."

"Darling," her mother gushed, sweeping into the foyer and pulling Alyse into her arms. "Good to see you." She examined the necklace. "I love it, and you totally deserve to treat yourself after your success. You're lucky to be able to do so." Wrapping her arms around both girls, she ushered Emma and Alyse into the kitchen.

"I love having my girls home with me," her mother kvelled. She turned and planted a kiss on Alyse's cheek. "It's not Shabbat without you."

Emma quelled the *what about me* she wanted to ask. As a child, she would have whined those three words immediately. In fact, she'd done just that often enough. And it did nothing except cause her parents to shush her at best or reprimand her for whining at worst.

Her mother let go of both of them as she went to stir the soup.

"Sorry," Alyse whispered.

Emma shrugged. Her parents always favored Alyse. Now that Emma was an adult, she realized it was because they understood her better. Alyse was the easy one, the one whose success showed itself in ways her parents understood. Knowing this didn't mean Emma's feelings weren't often bruised. But she'd figured out a way to look at the situation from a distance, so the bruises didn't hurt as much.

And she vowed to do things differently when she became a mom.

"No worries," she said to Alyse. The last thing she wanted to do was punish her sister for their parents' actions. In a louder voice, she said, "Tell me about this bonus of yours."

As the two of them set the table, Alyse gave an overview about the client she'd helped to land.

"Alyse, honey, it's good to be modest, but don't forget," her mother said. "You found the client to begin with and convinced them to use your firm. None of this would have happened without you."

Alyse ducked her head.

"Good for you, Aly," Emma said softly. "You should be proud of yourself."

"Of course she should." Their father entered the room, his booming voice filled with admiration. "She's doing a wonderful job."

He kissed them both, then their mom, before handing Alyse a bouquet of colorful carnations. "These are for you," he said. "Probably not as great as the bonus you got, but…"

"They're beautiful, Dad," Alyse said, giving him a hug. "Emma, tell me what's going on with The Book Nook."

"Wait, we have to light the candles," their mom said. "And say the Shabbat blessings. Alyse, since you're the guest of honor today, you light them."

Alyse's discomfort flashed across her face, but Emma smiled at her sister. Alyse *was* the guest of honor tonight. There was no reason for her to feel badly.

To distract herself, Emma placed a silent bet on whether her parents would bring the conversation around to the bookstore after they recited the Shabbat prayers.

She joined her voice with theirs chanting as Alyse lit the candles and again over the wine and the challah. They all sat at the table, serving each other soup, roasted chicken and noodle kugel. Emma ran her hand over the lace tablecloth her mom brought out for special occasions. It was beautiful, as was the special occasion china she'd used as well.

"So, Emma, your bookstore?" Alyse asked

Emma would have won the bet.

"The architect has the finalized plans and work is set to start as soon as the current owners move out."

"Isn't that going to make it hard for you to reach your opening day goal?" her dad asked.

She scoffed. "I can't exactly kick an old woman out of her house so I can make a date that I set in my own head."

"But shouldn't you have considered these kinds of things in your business plan?" her mom asked.

Alyse flashed Emma a sympathetic look across the table.

"I did, actually," Emma said. "I have multiple options, based on lots of variables." She squeezed her hand around the fork. "It'll work out as it's meant to."

Her parents exchanged a look. "A solid business plan shouldn't rely on karma or faith," her father said. "Not if you want it to be successful."

"Look at Alyse," her mom added, before Emma could respond. "She's successful because she doesn't sit around and wait. She goes after what she wants."

So do I.

"Mom, that's not fair," Alyse cried. "We're different people with different styles, but that doesn't mean one is better than the other."

Emma closed her eyes. She could kiss Alyse for standing up for her, but the last thing she wanted was a drawn-out argument that compared one sister with the other. Especially because there was no way Emma was going to come out of this in a positive light. Her parents wouldn't see her side until her business was up and running. And even then, it was going to be iffy.

"We would never say that." Her mother's mouth was wide with horror, reminding Emma a bit of *The Scream* painting. The black vertical-striped dress she wore certainly didn't do anything to dissuade the comparison. Emma bit her cheeks to prevent a smile from drawing any more attention to herself.

Alyse tipped her head to the side, a silent disagreement with their parents that her mom completely missed.

"However, we won't stand by silently when we think one of you is making a mistake or when one of you is doing a good job." At her father's words, her mother nodded.

Emma's stomach soured, and she pushed her plate away, no longer hungry.

"You're finished already, Emma?" her mother asked. "You hardly ate anything."

Swallowing every answer she wanted to give, she said instead, "It was delicious, but I'm not that hungry." She rose, taking her plate to the sink. "It's getting late, and I promised Rob I'd meet him for drinks."

"Even when your sister is home?" Her mother frowned, the same expression mirrored on her dad's features as well.

"It's no big deal, Mom," Alyse said. "Really."

They shook their heads in silence.

Her sister walked over and gave her a hug. "I'm sorry," she whispered.

"Don't be."

Rushing upstairs, Emma grabbed her canvas messenger bag, and escaped out of the house. Outside, the cool autumn air was a refreshing relief to the stifling judgment from inside. She climbed into her car and drove to the Gold Bar. On her way, she called Rob.

"Hey, I'm a little early."

"Rough dinner?" he asked.

"About as expected," she replied. "But I lost my appetite, and therefore, there's no reason for me to sit through it any longer. I'll meet you here."

"On my way."

She parked her car and walked into the dim room, admiring the gold-and-black motif. Her sneakers squeaked on the marble floor as she made her way to the end of the bar and snagged two seats.

"Emma!"

She turned and let out a relieved breath as Rob walked over and hugged her, before sitting on the barstool next to her. He flagged down the owner, Mo, and ordered two beers.

"What happened?" he asked.

"Well, let's say there was no Shabbat peace to the Shabbat dinner."

"Oof."

"I feel bad, because they don't realize they're putting Alyse in an uncomfortable position, too. I mean, I don't like being found lacking compared to my sister, but she doesn't like being the gold standard, either."

"Well, it's better than if she was all snooty about it."

Emma nodded. "True."

"Come on, let's drown our sorrows."

She held up her bottle. They clanked them together in a toast, before chatting about the progress of her bookstore.

"Now," she said, "what did you mean 'our' sorrows? What's wrong?"

He sighed. "I think Fiona and I are done."

Emma refrained from saying, *Thank God*, but barely. "Why?"

"She asked me to label the relationship, and she got upset when I didn't want to."

Emma was thankful for the darkness that hid her expression. She could have told him this was going to happen. He was a total commitment-phobe. "Did she break up with you?"

"No, but she's going to."

"You don't sound very disappointed."

He shrugged, the wool of his sweater drooping against his thin frame. "We've kind of run our course."

Which meant the chemistry wasn't as strong as he thought it was.

"I don't suppose you'd want to give it a go?" he asked.

She patted his arm. They'd always joked about how she was the one woman he'd never had sex with. And since they were both happier as friends—a foreign concept for him— she never refrained from giving him a hard time. "Josh actually thought you and I were a couple."

"From one double date?"

He cackled. "Cool. Speaking of, Sam and Josh? That's one couple that I can't see together."

"Really?" Emma's insides warmed a little. She couldn't see them together, either. "Why not?"

"Come on, they're nothing alike. Josh is a decent guy, a rabbi, and Samantha is—"

"Hey, that's my friend you're talking about."

He held up his hands in surrender. "I know. But she's way

more of a go-getter than he seemed to be, and they didn't have anything in common. You know how much she loves going to the theater and art galleries and expensive restaurants. I didn't get that vibe from Josh. And can you see her being happy on a rabbi's salary?"

Emma took another sip of her beer, and Rob moved onto talking about a big sale he was working on. Despite listening with half an ear, all she could think about was Rob's assessment of Josh.

Although she agreed that Josh and Samantha were different, she also believed opposites attracted each other. Even if she couldn't picture the two of them together for any length of time, especially with Samantha's schedule. But she assumed a rabbi's schedule was complicated, too.

She couldn't wait for the debrief on Monday.

In the meantime, who knew Rob was so perceptive?

Chapter Five

Josh let out a curse on Saturday morning when he read Samantha's text.

not making it home this weekend. Too much casework. Raincheck?

That's too bad. How about dinner next week?

I'll check my work calendar and let you know.

He tossed his phone on the bed and ran a hand through his short hair. Disappointment swirled. He'd been looking forward to getting to know Samantha better. Maybe she wasn't interested in him.

As the aroma of freshly brewed coffee swirled upstairs, he jogged down to the kitchen.

"Excited for your date?" His grandmother sat at the kitchen table, sorting through her utility tools and small appliances. "I don't suppose you'd want an apple corer?" She held up something that looked to him like a wheel with spokes.

"No, and I don't eat apples," he said, grabbing one of the last mugs in the cabinet and pouring himself a cup of coffee.

His grandma looked up and frowned. "That doesn't sound good," she said.

"It's not. Samantha texted she's hung up at work."

"On Shabbat?"

He nodded. "It's okay, Grandma. Not everyone can guarantee Saturdays off from work."

Sympathy showed in her brown eyes. "It must be tough to socialize when you're that busy."

It was one of the reasons why he hadn't dated much when he first started his rabbinic studies. Even now, he was careful to set expectations with friends and family so that he didn't disappoint anyone. Guilt always riddled him whenever he canceled plans at the last minute, causing him to second-guess his choices. But now that he was on the receiving end, well, he understood how his friends and family must have felt.

A bitter taste filled his mouth, unrelated to the black coffee he'd drunk.

"You should ask our Emma to join you instead."

He choked, and only by sheer force of will did he keep his coffee from spurting out of his mouth or nose. He swallowed, cleared his throat, and took a deep breath. "Emma? Why?" The idea didn't sound as bad as it should, and guilt flooded through him. He was interested in Samantha, not Emma—and they were best friends.

"I can give you her number."

"I'm going to stay here and help you pack instead."

His grandmother glanced out the window. "It's a beautiful day outside, sunny and cold. Perfect for the winter festival. I'm not keeping you indoors."

His mood soured further, and he checked his watch. It wasn't yet ten o'clock, and his day was already going down the drain. "Grandma, we don't have a lot of time to get everything packed before I leave, regardless of the weather. And I'm not asking Emma to the winter festival. It's too weird with her being Samantha's best friend."

They sorted through cabinets and drawers in silence for a few minutes. Then his grandmother's voice almost made him drop a salt shaker.

"What about asking Ms. Match for other options?"

He juggled a bit and saved the avocado green ceramic. He swallowed, trying to figure out the best way to express his disdain for the matchmaker. "I don't think I have time for that right now. Plus, I want to give Samantha a shot."

He clenched his teeth, hoping she'd move onto something else.

"Pfft, it's not going to take us that long to pack everything up."

Keep your mouth shut, keep your mouth shut, he told himself.

"Although I'm glad you're not one to make hasty decisions about your love interests, it might be beneficial to broaden your horizons. You know, in case you and Samantha don't work out."

His brain hopped from *love interests* to *broaden your horizons* to what the heck was his grandmother doing? "I'm good, Grandma, but thank you. Do you want this?" He held up a small flower vase, one that she'd kept on her windowsill for as long as he could remember.

Her eyes welled.

In panic, he rushed forward. "It's not a problem, Grandma, it's small, it can easily travel with you."

She patted his shoulder and took it from him. "It was my mother's," she said. "It doesn't look like much, but every Friday night, my father would pick my mother a daisy from the nearby field for Shabbat. And every week, she'd put it in this vase on her windowsill so she could look at it as she did the dishes."

Josh's heart twinged. Such a simple gesture, yet it affected his grandmother and him, to this day. "You have to save it," he said, his voice rough.

"And someday, I'm going to give it to you."

"I'm not sure how many fields of daisies I'm going to pass, Grandma."

"It's not important whether or not you fill it, Joshy. It's important to remember the little things."

The little things. His mind was overloaded with all the big things—work, his grandma, his life. He didn't understand how one small vase was going to help him with any of those things, but he did understand the sentimental value of the vase. Instead of arguing, he nodded and packed it away in the Keep box.

A couple hours later, and the kitchen was mostly packed—at least the parts they didn't need between now and move-out day. He rose, stretching to relieve his cramped muscles, and helped his grandmother to her feet.

He gave her a kiss on the cheek and loaded his car with pots, pans, dishes and appliances his grandmother didn't need. He threw on his winter jacket, grabbed his keys and drove toward the donation center.

Browerville was crowded, with lots of people walking to or from the town square for the festival. Dads with kids on their shoulders, faces painted like winter fairies, the moms carrying bags of donuts. As Josh waited at the traffic light, he tapped his hand on the steering wheel and strategized the best way to get to the donation center.

Twenty minutes later, when it should have only taken eight, he pulled into the parking lot, grabbed the boxes and brought them inside. Armed with a receipt and a warm feeling from helping others, he stood next to his car.

He'd been looking forward to walking around the winter festival with Samantha.

His stomach growled.

Okay, stomach for the win.

He thrust the receipt in his pocket, left his car where it was and walked the fourteen blocks to the winter festival.

Immediately upon entering the town square, his spirits lifted. There was something about the atmosphere that turned a dreary January day into something magical. To his left, a display of ice sculptures sparkled in the sun, to his right were tables for decorating snowflakes. Snow cones were for sale at the far end of the green, which was decorated with fake snow and twinkle lights. Powdered sugar donuts and hot cocoa were situated in the center. Crowds surrounded the facepainting table, and across from it was a craft table for making and decorating small wooden sleds. And all the way in the back, horses snorted as they waited for passengers to ride in their sleighs.

"Kind of appealing, isn't it?"

He spun around at the voice, inhaling sharply when he recognized Emma. "You've got to be kidding me," he muttered.

Her humorous expression fell, and a pit of regret formed in his stomach. She turned away, and he followed.

"I'm sorry," he said. "That was totally uncalled for."

She shrugged him off. "It's fine. I didn't mean to disturb you."

"It's not fine, and you didn't."

She raised an eyebrow, disbelief etched on her face. "Yeah, right."

He took a deep breath. "My mood is because of my grandma, not because of you. I responded poorly. Please forgive me."

She looked like she wanted to walk away, but instead, she remained where she was. "Weren't you supposed to be here with Samantha?"

He stuffed his hands in his pockets. "She had to work. Once she canceled, I wasn't going to bother coming."

"But you're here," she said.

He patted his stomach. "I couldn't resist the donuts."

At that, she laughed. "Don't let me keep you." When Emma laughed, her face brightened and her eyes sparkled, making her just as appealing as the donuts he'd come for.

"Join me?" he asked.

She bit her lip. "I wasn't planning on coming, but I wanted to hand out postcards about my bookstore."

"It's like it was bashert or something," he said.

Again, she laughed, and again, he was drawn to her.

She shrugged. "I can't resist the donuts, either."

"Ah-ha!" he crowed. "Come on, now you have to join me."

"Wait," she said. "You didn't tell me what happened with your grandma to put you in a mood."

He swallowed before answering, aware he needed to be careful how he spoke. "When Samantha canceled, my grandma suggested I ask you to come. But you're Samantha's best friend. And my grandma doesn't seem to get that." *And I can't figure out my emotions when I'm around you.*

"Plus, you don't particularly like me."

"What?" He'd never known someone so blunt—or honest—before, and he didn't quite know what to make of her. Most people couched their words and feelings carefully around rabbis. Even young, modern ones like him.

She remained standing where she was, several paces away, silent. Before he could question her further, his stomach growled. Apparently the sound was loud enough for her to hear, because she gazed at his midsection and bit her lip, her cheeks reddening.

Great. Just great.

"You've never been hungry before?" He folded his arms across his chest, waiting to hear what she'd say.

"Everyone gets hungry." She stared at him as if something was growing out of the top of his head.

He refrained from running his hand through his hair to check. He didn't want to give her the satisfaction. Although if he were honest with himself, he was enjoying this back-and-forth they had going between them. "Good, let's get something to eat. And for the record," he added, "I don't dislike you."

Emma scoffed. "Wow, that's a ringing endorsement. No wonder you're using a matchmaker."

He'd leave that comment for later. Because he could tell he'd stepped in it. "I was repeating what you said earlier. I like you. Okay?"

"Marginally better, but it still needs work." She started walking toward the donut table. "Coming?"

Pausing for a beat, he caught up to her.

He waited with her in line to get their donuts. When it was their turn, he ordered powdered sugar donuts for both of them and pulled out his wallet.

"You don't have to pay," she said.

"Consider it penance for what I said earlier."

She turned her brown eyes on him, her long lashes framing them, and a jolt of electricity slammed into him. She licked her lips. "Thank you."

Busying himself with paying for the donuts and grabbing napkins gave him a chance to break whatever connection her look forged. He handed her a napkin and her donut.

She brought the donut to her mouth and paused. "Wait, do you need to recite a blessing or something?"

He shook his head. "Reform rabbi here. Eating a donut at a festival doesn't require any blessing ahead of time." He took a bite to show her, chewed and swallowed before continuing. "Although these are so good, we might have to give a prayer of thanksgiving afterward." He winked.

Emma took a bite of her own donut, powdered sugar rimming her pink lips.

Hastily, he took another bite. At least his hunger pangs would stop.

"Too bad Yom Kippur is over," she said, "or you could atone for your sins."

Her dry humor amused him. "Lucky me."

"Oh, I want to check out those mini sleds for the bookstore," she cried, pointing at the craft table filled with sleds, paint, glitter and fake snow.

"And maybe some snowflakes," he suggested. He pointed to the neighboring table, which displayed knit snowflakes in a variety of colors and styles. "Come on."

He'd never given much thought to holiday decorations, but suddenly, Emma's desire became important to him. "Do you like these wooden sleds or the metal ones?" he asked. When she didn't answer, he picked up the first wooden one he saw and held it in one hand. "This one?" He returned it to the table, grabbed a metal one and held it up. "Or this one?"

She bit her lip before he put the second sled down.

"One of each it is," he said. "Now you have to decorate it."

"No, wait," she said. "The metal one isn't as pretty, and I'm afraid it's going to rust. Just the wooden one."

He watched her pick up a wooden sled and reach for blue and green paint. He stood next to her, admiring her concentration as she painted the sled, adding powdered snow and writing *Whee!* in white lettering.

Her face brightened. "Now I need it to dry." She turned to him. "Do you want to make one for your grandma?"

"Not this time." He grabbed some cardboard to transport

the wet sled. "But how about we check out the ice sculptures?" He looked around at the kids running from one to another, oohing and ahhing over some of the characters that were carved from blocks of ice.

"Look at those," he said, pointing to two dogs that looked as if they were chasing each other.

Emma walked over to them, giggling. "They're like Fred and Ted."

One of the carved dogs was a mastiff, the other a yorkie. *Talk about opposites.* "Or Oscar and Felix," he added.

"Lucy and Ethel."

"Bert and Ernie." He'd raised his voice louder than he'd intended, caught up in the fun of the moment, and the children around him stopped mid-whatever they were doing.

"Bert and Ernie!"

"Bert and Ernie!"

One by one, all of them yelled, "Bert and Ernie!" creating chaos all around him.

When he caught Emma's gaze, tears of laughter streaked down her cheeks. She leaned forward. "I think we might have started a riot."

He nodded. "Should we make a run for it?"

Her eyes sparkled, reminding him of the brown sugar crystals his grandmother sprinkled on her linzer bars. "I don't know, seems kind of cold to rush away from adorable toddlers."

He leaned over and whispered in her ear, "I was thinking more about the potential for angry parents when they see that I helped cause a scene."

She shook her head, her curls bobbing. "Who the heck gets angry at Bert and Ernie?"

Their nonsensical argument charmed him. He hadn't had this much fun with Emma before. In fact, if you'd asked him if he *could* have fun with Emma, he would have said no. Yet, here he was, not wanting to leave.

"Should we decorate snowflakes?" He pointed to a table set up with paints and glitter.

"No," Emma said. "I think I'm going create something at home." She looked up at him. "The thought of all that glitter in my car…"

"Oh yeah, I remember one time in Hebrew school, we decorated dreidels for Hanukkah, and my grandma's car was covered with it."

"Exactly," she said.

He leaned toward her. "I've got to confess, all those little kids screaming kinda scared me. I'll take moody teenagers any day."

He'd said it to make her laugh, and pleasure coursed through him when she did. The sound was deep and throaty, and he couldn't help the smile that crossed his own face.

"Well, we should probably move out of here." Carrying her sled, she led the way, and he happily followed her.

Emma looked at a sleigh led by two horses. "I remember begging my parents to go for a ride on that when I was a child."

He followed her gaze. The horses snorted white steam in the cold air. A ride with Emma, snuggled up with her under a blanket? His body tightened with desire, despite his mind telling him it wasn't a good idea. They were supposed to just be friends. He was a rabbi, expected to set a good moral example. But something about the wistful tone in her voice made him unable to listen to that advice. "Want to go?" he asked.

Surely one ride can't hurt.

Emma bit her lip, hesitating, as if acknowledging the warning his mind had tried to give. She swallowed, looking between him and the sleigh. Moments ticked by, and then she nodded.

They stood in line at the entrance, waiting their turn for an available horse-drawn sled. Finally, two horses returned, pulling a gold-colored wooden sleigh up to where they stood. The horsy odor combined with the pine smell of the nearby trees filled his nostrils as they climbed in.

"Here you go," Emma said as she held up part of the blanket.

He sat next to her, their thighs touching. Heat travelled up his leg and he moved to give them more space as guilt sliced through him.

With the flick of the whip, the horses trotted off. The sudden movement pushed Emma into him, and he wrapped his arm around her to keep her steady.

Yeah, to keep her steady.

Another flash of guilt, and he let go of her. People's voices called from within the park, but they were alone in the sled. He glanced at her, admiring her red cheeks, bright eyes and curly hair. The vanilla scent of her skin tickled his nostrils.

There was something compelling about Emma, a pull that drew him closer than he should be. A breeze kicked up, mussing her curls. One caught on her lip, and without thinking, he reached a finger out to brush it away. The soft skin of her cheek tickled his fingertip. Her brown irises changed to amber. Her lashes fluttered. She sighed, and her warm breath made clouds in front of them. He released her curl, watched it spring back, and resisted the urge to push it behind her ear.

She stared sideways at him, lips parted, for four beats of his heart as it pounded against his ribcage. On the fifth beat, as he was going to bend closer, she turned away, out of his reach.

"No," she said, voice husky.

He blinked, reality crashing around him once again. Although alone in the conveyance, hordes of people surrounded them in the park. Not where he wanted to be when he kissed her.

When?

He was supposed to want to kiss Samantha.

He leaned back with a brief nod. He had no idea what he was doing. But he needed to put physical distance between him and Emma, and that was impossible in the sleigh.

Finally, the horses pulled up and their ride ended. Josh helped her down and took a step back. He inhaled. Disappointment sliced through him. His stomach clenched.

What would have happened if they'd kissed? He couldn't risk letting his mind go there. Josh was about to make his exit when Emma spoke.

"Look at the hot chocolate bar," she cried, pointing across the green.

He followed the length of her arm and smiled. He loved hot chocolate, even if his body temperature was warm enough to make him sweat after spending time next to Emma.

But friends could enjoy hot chocolate together.

"Want some?" he asked.

She nodded, and relief that she didn't want to leave washed over him. Together, they walked over to the booth.

"Five dollars per cup," the volunteer said. "And half goes to charity. We also have make-your-own snow cones for the same price" She handed them a brochure about the Browerville Food Pantry.

Emma turned to Josh. "What a great way to support a worthy cause."

He nodded. "I'm going to stick to hot chocolate."

"Me too." Emma scanned the menu posted on a cute chalkboard sign. "Now we have to choose our flavors."

While she looked at the options, Josh looked at her.

He loved how seriously she was taking her order. Cocoa had always been a favorite of his, but Emma was acting as if her choice mattered.

If he were honest with himself, he was starting to like a lot of things about her. He cleared his throat, as if somehow, he could dislodge Emma from the hold she had over him. He was supposed to be getting to know Samantha. He was supposed to hold himself to a higher standard as a rabbi.

"I want dark chocolate with cinnamon, no whipped cream," Emma said.

"I'll have the milk chocolate with whipped cream and chocolate shavings," he added. He shooed Emma away as she tried to pay.

"I've got this," he said.

"You got the donuts earlier," she protested.

He handed his money to the volunteer and turned to Emma. "Before was an apology. Now it's a mitzvah."

She snorted. "A good deed?"

"Yeah, to support the food pantry."

She rolled her eyes. "You've got an answer for everything, don't you?"

He shrugged. "I *am* a rabbi, you know."

"This was fun," she said. "I haven't been to this festival in years."

"Me neither," he said. "I think the festival started when I was in high school."

He looked at Emma. "You graduated a year after me, right?"

"Me and Samantha," Emma said.

Samantha.

Her name blunted his enjoyment.

As Emma reached for her cup, he pulled out his phone to

see if Samantha had texted. The blank phone screen made him sigh, and he pocketed it again.

"I'll have to see if The Book Nook can participate in some way next year," Emma said, as she took a sip. "Mmm, this is good."

His neck tightened at her mention of the bookstore, and he grunted. He didn't want to talk about The Book Nook, or next year, when his life, his home, his grandma, would be different. He'd rather focus on his hot chocolate.

"So is this," he added.

"You don't think that's a good idea?" Emma asked. "The Book Nook participating in some way in the festival?"

"I didn't say that," he said.

"No, but you're 'hmm' was less than pleased."

She got that from a grunt? "I think you're reading into things," he said.

Shaking her head, she tossed her cup and stuffed her hands in the pockets of her jacket. "You get a tone and a look whenever we talk about the bookstore."

"But we haven't talked about it today."

Emma smiled. "And until right now, you didn't use that tone or have that look."

He scoffed. No way could she identify his ambiguous tones and looks. She barely knew him. "Anyway, is there anything else we haven't done here?" He didn't want to get in an argument with her. The day had been too much fun.

She inhaled. "No, I think we covered most everything. Don't you love the smell of snow?"

And like that, his mood lifted. He'd never known anyone like this, and if he weren't in the middle of pursuing Samantha, he'd let himself fall for Emma. Especially because he was starting to think she *got* him. But falling for her wouldn't be fair to either of them, especially since they were friends. If only he'd gotten to know Emma first.

She stopped beneath a fir tree decorated with fake silver icicles. Lifting her chin, she pointed toward the edge of the green. "I'm parked over there," she said.

He turned in a slow circle, not wanting the afternoon to end. "I'm the other way."

She took a step forward and their bodies were mere inches apart. His arms twitched, aching to give her a hug. Friends could hug, couldn't they?

Before he could stop his mind from spinning out of control, she wrapped her arms around him and gave him a quick hug. And just as quickly, stepped away, her eyes a storm of emotions.

"I'm glad we ran into each other," she said.

And before he could say anything else, she walked away.

Walk away, walk away, walk away. The words echoed in Emma's mind as she left the winter festival. Josh's gaze bore into her back. She wouldn't be surprised if she found a bruise between her shoulder blades later. Her blood sizzled and all she wanted to do was run to her car, but he'd know how his warm body made her skin tingle and her pulse hum in her ears, and there was no way she'd admit to that shame.

He was matched with her best friend.

Best friends didn't poach boyfriends. Or potential boyfriends. Or matches, no matter how improbable the match might seem.

Best friends didn't inhale the scent of the man as they hugged him. Heck, best friends didn't hug the man, period.

Especially when, the more time they spent together, the more interesting he seemed.

She swallowed, searching the line of parked cars for hers.

Where was it? She didn't remember the walk from her car to the winter festival taking this long. If she didn't reach it soon, she might be tempted to turn around, find Josh, and ask him if he'd felt anything when they'd hugged.

Or sniff him.

Because no man should smell that good. Spicy, clean and... "Ugh, stop!"

She jumped, not expecting to have said that out loud. A family walking along the sidewalk her turned to stare at her, and she waved, wishing she could hide behind a fir tree.

Finally, after what felt like long enough to have walked to New York City, she found her car, right where she'd left it. Only once she was inside, doors locked, did she let out her breath and try to calm her racing heart.

She was either desperately out of shape or...nope, she was sticking with desperately out of shape. Time to sign up for the gym, hire a personal trainer, anything to keep her heart-rate and her lungs at whatever optimum point they needed to be so she wouldn't have this crazy reaction when she walked across the town green to her car.

Emma banged her head against the seatback. "No, no, no. This is not happening."

She was not about to fall for Samantha's guy—again.

The first time it happened, they'd been in fourth grade. Jeremy Olgerson had the longest lashes she'd ever seen. He sat between Emma and Samantha—the teacher didn't allow friends to sit next to each other—and he owned the coolest pencil case. It was camo colored on the outside with compartments on the inside. He also owned a pet turtle named Seymour and the most popular video game system. Emma was in love.

Unfortunately, so was Samantha, and Samantha had announced it first. Sam followed him around on the playground, asked him questions about her homework, and declared to all who would listen that he was her boyfriend.

But when Jeremy invited Emma to play his video game with him and meet Seymour, Samantha felt betrayed. She'd given Emma the silent treatment for a week, only relenting after Emma apologized and gave her a new package of stickers and a sparkly hair bow.

The second time it happened, and Emma couldn't believe it happened again, was when they were in high school. Samantha's crush, Elliott, asked Emma to the prom.

Emma didn't want to go to prom. She found the guys her age too immature. But as the newspaper editor, she'd gotten to know the sports editor over the year. One day, she'd opened the file he had sent her only to find that he'd created a promposal instead. Shocked, she'd told him how sweet it was. He'd assumed her compliments were a yes, and she hadn't wanted to crush him. Slogging her way home, Emma knew she had to tell Sam about the promposal before her friend heard from anyone else, even if Sam would be devastated. By the time she got home, Samantha had already heard and was livid.

To be fair, Emma had offered to correct Elliott's misunderstanding and skip the prom, but Samantha told her not to bother. Privately, Emma thought Samantha got satisfaction out of Emma's discomfort. Even more privately, Emma thought she deserved Samantha's anger and more. Especially because after the prom, when Elliott drank a little too much, he'd made Emma uncomfortable with his sloppiness, and it was Samantha and her prom date who jumped in to rescue her. As Samantha had said, "Best friends forever."

Emma had spent a lot of time analyzing her behavior and came to several conclusions. One, Emma was clueless when it came to guys.

Two, Samantha's friendship was more important to her than any guy.

Three, no matter how different she and Samantha were, their bond weathered any difficulties.

And so, any time she and Samantha were doing something, Emma made sure that Samantha knew how loyal a friend she was.

Which was why she needed to completely nip this attraction-thing to Josh in the bud. No more thinking about him and no more hanging out with him alone. As she pulled up to her house, she glanced at her phone on the seat next to her.

She should call Samantha and let her know she'd bumped into Josh at the winter festival. It's what she'd do if she'd gone to the event with any other person. It was only natural she'd tell her about Josh.

She picked up her phone and let it rest in her palm. Its weight added import to the task. She needed to be aboveboard and make sure Samantha understood she was not trying to poach Josh. And Samantha needed to hear about it from her first. Because if Josh mentioned it, Samantha would wonder why Emma didn't tell her. And questions might start. Questions she most definitely didn't want to answer.

With a deep breath, she dialed Samantha's number.

Maybe she wouldn't pick up.

"Hey, Em."

No such luck.

"Hey, Sam. How's work?"

"Crazy. I'm taking a quick break now, before diving back in. I'll probably have to work tomorrow, too. I was supposed to see Josh today and had to cancel."

Perfect opening.

"Yeah, he told me. I ran into him at the winter festival."

"Was it fun?"

"It was. The ice sculptures were cute, though. There was a castle with turrets and flags."

Samantha sighed. "I have to call Josh to reschedule, and I have no idea when I'm going to be free. I hope he doesn't think I'm avoiding him."

"I didn't get that feeling from him at all. He knows you're busy."

"Great, I'll shoot him a quick text. Chat later!"

Emma hung up and relief surged through her. The last thing she wanted was for Samantha to be angry with her. As for Samantha texting Josh…

She stayed seated in her car, turning it over in her mind. Josh was a nice guy, and she didn't want Samantha ignoring him. She was glad Samantha was texting him. It probably meant they'd reschedule their date.

Her throat seized. She swallowed, trying to banish any emotion other than acceptance. Which wasn't an emotion, but she'd worry about that later. Because right now, a lot of other emotions threatened to develop—jealousy being the biggest.

There was nothing she hated more than jealousy.

Taking a deep breath, she exited her car. Sitting around moping wasn't going to accomplish anything. She reached into the back seat and grabbed her sled.

"Hello?" she called as she walked into the house. No one answered. Once again, a flicker of relief flashed. She wanted a chance to savor her time at the winter festival and get her thoughts in order before she dealt with her parents.

Grabbing a pencil from the junk drawer, she sketched some winter decorating ideas for The Book Nook. Next year she planned to decorate the entire store. For now, she'd try out a few things on her family's front porch. She walked outside and put her sled next to the front door, arranging it this way and that until she found the perfect angle and returned inside.

Five minutes later, her parents walked into the house.

"Love the sled outside," her mom said, kissing her cheek. "I moved it slightly, though, so it's at a better angle. Have a nice day?" her mom asked as she started to prepare dinner.

Emma nodded. "Yes. I've got inventory to order. Call me when you need me?"

Her mom waved her away, and Emma retreated to her bedroom. Instead of thinking about Josh and Samantha, she was going to bury herself her in setting up her dream. She was close enough to taste it, and she was too busy for a relationship.

She'd convince herself of that…somehow.

As she searched online for the books to order, she stared longingly at the romance titles. *Love Gamble*. She ordered five copies, wondering what the odds were that she'd find someone compatible with her hopes and dreams. Her parents wanted her to marry rich and build a successful career. But she didn't want a life ruled by long hours and judged by dollar signs.

The Altar Arrangement. She ordered another five copies of that. She'd love to get married and have a family. But not quite yet. She still wanted to enjoy her freedom. That didn't mean she didn't want to meet someone and spend time together, though.

Blue Collar Billionaire. Adding it to her shopping cart, she nodded. Exactly. She wanted someone who worked hard, but understood real life, too.

She pushed away from the computer. This was crazy. Why was she comparing herself to book titles or characters in a romance novel?

Maybe *she* should use a matchmaker.

Okay, clearly, she was losing it. When the time was right for her to seriously consider getting married, if she hadn't met someone organically by then, maybe, *maybe* she'd consider using Miss Match. But now? No way.

In an effort to change the trajectory of her thoughts, she searched the mystery catalog instead.

Running Out of Time. She ordered five copies. *Find Him*. Emma practically burst out laughing. *Identity Crisis*.

"Okay, I'm done," she muttered, pushing herself away from her desk. Yes, she needed to get work done, but without a clear head, she was useless. A quick look at the yoga schedule over at the JCC reassured her. If she changed fast, she could make it. And then, she was going to focus her energy on the store. Not on men, and certainly not on a man who was possibly going to be her best friend's boyfriend.

And the next time she sat down to order books, she was going to look into the self-help books. It was probably safer that way.

Josh adjusted the neck of his sweater as he got ready for his date with Samantha, his hands sweaty. He was picking her up at the train station, taking her to dinner and dropping her at her parents' home afterward. He couldn't wait to spend some time alone with her, getting to know her.

During the three days since they'd texted and arranged these plans, he'd spoken further to the matchmaker. At the time, he'd had hesitations and expressed them to Ms. Match.

"What if I'm forcing this?" he asked. "I'm not sure we're right for each other." He couldn't help thinking of Emma as he held the phone to his ear.

"Josh, the point of this next date is to find out if you and Samantha are compatible," Ms. Match said. "Hesitation is normal."

"Are you sure?"

Being around Emma was easy. And he never thought of Samantha when he was with Emma.

"Yes, Josh, I am. The two of you matched originally and both of your follow-up forms show promise. I'm not saying the two of you are bashert, we won't know that yet, but give her another chance. Worst case, if you don't hit it off, I'll gain a better sense of what the two of you are looking for in your next match."

He'd breathed a sigh of relief when he hung up. Ms. Match made sense. So, he'd researched restaurants to take Samantha to and planned everything for the date they should have gone on the first time. And in between, he'd made huge strides in packing up his grandmother's things, as well as arranged with a friend of his to crash in his apartment for the rest of his time in Browerville.

Leaving only stolen moments for him to think about Emma. He expelled a breath. He wasn't going to let Emma's infectious laugh or her witty comebacks invade his thoughts any further.

Grabbing his keys, he jogged downstairs.

"Grandma!" he called.

"In the living room," she answered.

The room was cleared of her things. The mantel, where she'd kept family photos, was bare. The large display cabinet filled with family mementos, precious china figurines and her dreidel collection was empty. Only the furniture remained, and the movers and Goodwill would handle those things.

She sat in the corner of a sofa reading her book. She looked up and smiled when he entered. "You look handsome."

"Thanks. I'm going to pick Samantha up for dinner. I'll probably be home late. You're all packed for tomorrow?"

He swallowed past the lump in his throat, hating the idea of her moving into the assisted living facility. Yet it was safer, especially now that there were so many things to maneuver around in the house. It was better she wasn't here for the last of the packing.

And maybe, once she was settled in her new place, he'd have an easier time adjusting.

"Just my last-minute unmentionables. What about you?"

"Same." He leaned over and kissed her cheek.

"Love you, Joshy."

"Love you, too."

Ten minutes later, he pulled into the train station parking lot and glanced at the clock on the dash. Three minutes until Samantha's train was due. He turned on his music, anticipation sliding along his spine. Ms. Match had set them up. Therefore, she must have seen something in their profiles to indicate they'd be good together. He couldn't wait to find out what it was. Embody's "Be Cool" ended, and he looked at the clock. He frowned. The train was supposed to have arrived. He climbed out of his car and walked over to the tracks. As if somehow, the train could have arrived without his knowing.

He scanned the random people on the platform, not expecting to see Samantha, but just in case.

An announcement crackled over the intercom: "Train from New York City on track two in three minutes."

He looked at his phone. They were cutting it tight if they wanted to make their reservation. He tapped his phone again, in case he'd missed a text from Samantha. Not that she could control train delays. But he sighed at the absence of a text.

Finally, the train whistle echoed down the line, and he turned toward it, the light of the train slowly coming into focus.

He stepped back and waited for the train to stop.

Samantha was the first person off the train. She waved as she stepped onto the platform, her red trench coat flapping in the breeze. An image of Emma with her wild curls distracted him, and he ran his hand over his eyes, trying to dislodge the picture.

"I'm sorry," she said, walking up to him.

He leaned forward and kissed her cheek. "Not your fault," he said, holding out his arm to guide her to his car. "We'll have to rush to make our reservation, though." He reached for her work bag and slung it over his shoulder. "I'm glad you were able to make it."

"Me, too," she said as she climbed into the car.

He shut her door and jogged around to the driver side. "I'm glad you like Indian food," he said, pulling out of the train station. "I've been wanting to try this place, and my grandmother isn't into spicy foods."

"I like them."

She looked out the window as they drove along Main Street. "It's funny," she said. "I grew up here, yet I never think about coming here for dinner." She nodded toward the variety of places they passed. "There are an awful lot of new ones to choose from, though. I'm sure we'll be fine with getting seated."

He hoped so. The restaurant was new and had received a lot of great reviews. Although Browerville was known for its eclectic restaurants and stores, Masala was a new Indian restaurant, and he'd been dying to try it. As they drove to the opposite side of town, they passed the Gilded Age, Tuscan Delight, Isaacson's Deli and the Lotus Blossom.

"If only there was a good sushi bar," she said, her voice wistful.

Josh frowned. "Sorry, that's the one food I'm not a fan of."

"I could eat it every day."

"The Lotus Blossom is supposed to be good," he said, as he pulled over and maneuvered into a parking spot.

"It's fine," she said. "I've tried it once or twice. But once you're used to sushi in New York, it's hard to come home."

They approached the restaurant, white arches and large windows breaking up the brick facade. A sign hanging over the front door said Masala in gold lettering.

Josh held open the door and followed Samantha into the dimly lit restaurant. Mouthwatering aromas of cinnamon, garlic, cumin and ginger greeted them.

"Hi, I have a reservation," he said to the hostess. "Josh Axelrod."

The hostess scanned her list, frowned and studied it more intently. "I'm sorry, I don't have anyone by that name," she said. "Can you spell it?"

He swallowed, his neck heating. He'd made the reservation as soon as he and Samantha arranged their date. He spelled his last name, looking over the counter to see if he spotted it.

But he didn't.

Embarrassment and annoyance flared, making a trickle of sweat slide down his spine.

"Are you sure you made a reservation?" Samantha asked.

"Positive." His voice was clipped, and he took a breath before looking at her once again. "Sorry. Yes, I called and spoke to a man who answered the phone."

Samantha nodded.

"I'm sorry, but there's no reservation." The hostess turned and scanned the dining room before turning to him. "And as you can see, we're packed."

"Is there anywhere you can squeeze us in?" His voice rose in desperation. What a way to ruin a date.

"Let me check," she said and walked away.

Samantha touched his arm. "We can go somewhere else," she said. "There are plenty of restaurants."

She was right, and he appreciated her flexibility. But *this* was where he'd wanted to take her. It was unique and good and they did a fancy dessert presentation he thought she'd love.

The hostess returned, a dismayed look on her face. "I'm sorry. We have no tables available for at least two hours."

Josh turned and led Samantha outside. "I can't believe they lost the reservation."

She shrugged. "It happens. There must be another restaurant we can find."

The first time he met her, she'd given off the impression of having high standards. He was glad she didn't seem to be holding this mistake against him. He tried not to beat himself up about it as they walked up and down the street, scanning menus and peeking inside windows.

Josh pointed to an Italian place, but Samantha wasn't in the mood. She suggested Korean, but there were no available tables. He was about to suggest the Gold Bar—his stomach was growling and anything would be better than continuing to wander—when they passed a pizzeria. It wasn't creative or unique, but it also wasn't crowded. Heat, garlic and music greeted them as they entered.

Josh scanned the dining area and chose a table toward the back. "I promise I owe you a much better dinner, but let's make do with this," he suggested, taking her coat and handing her into the booth with a flourish and a smile.

"I'm so hungry at this point, I could eat an entire pie myself."

His mood brightened. "Excellent. Tell me what you like on your pizza, and I'll put in the order."

Josh ended up ordering a salad pie and a half meatball, half sausage pie before snagging a basket of garlic knots and bringing them to the table.

"Thank goodness," Samantha exclaimed, diving for the

basket. She ripped one open and stuffed part of it into her mouth.

He did the same, groaning in satisfaction. "I could probably eat this entire basket," he said.

"Same."

"Sorry again about the confusion," he said when he'd sated the raw edge of his hunger.

She glanced around the pizzeria, her glance bounding from the brick walls to the white curtains and the red paper place mats. She shrugged. "It happens." Her voice dropped.

He couldn't put his finger on it, but something in her tone hinted at disappointment. Although, to be fair, he was disappointed, too. Masala was a great restaurant.

"So, when we went out the first time, you mentioned you divide your time between here and New York?" Josh asked. He wasn't quite sure how often she came here, and her location would definitely affect how often they could get together.

She nodded. "My dad keeps an apartment in the city on the Upper West Side for when he has to work late, and when he and my mom want to go see a show. If I have to work late, I stay there, too. Otherwise, I come home. Lately, though, I've been spending more and more time in New York."

"That apartment must come in handy," he said. "My apartment is in Murray Hill."

"Ugh, that's hard to get to unless you take the bus," she said. She held up a hand. "Sorry, I didn't mean for that to come out wrong. The 'ugh' was for the transportation issues, not for your apartment."

She blushed, and her uncertainty surprised Josh. She'd come across so confident the last time they'd gone out. It was unexpected and…nice. He was starting to understand why she and Emma were friends.

He swallowed and focused on the woman in front of him.

"No harm. I take the bus a lot. Or walk. And there are subways there, they're just not always the most conveniently located."

Samantha scrunched her face, reminding Josh a bit of a rabbit, the movement brief. "I'm not big on public transportation," she said. "My office covers transport costs if I'm working late, and friends and I usually rideshare at night. I think it's safer."

Might be safer, but Josh could only imagine how costly it must be. What would Emma do if she were in the city?

Stop!

"Probably true," he agreed. "Honestly, I'm starting to enjoy not having to worry about a subway or bus while I'm here. It's nice to have the freedom to hop in my car and go where I want."

Samantha shook her head. "Not me," she said. "If I could live in the city full-time, I would."

"If you're using your parents' apartment, why don't you?"

She scoffed. "My parents and I don't get along at all. Life is much easier if we're separate as much as possible. I use the apartment while they're here and come here when they're not."

Josh clenched his muscles, trying not to react to her blunt statement. He scanned her expression for sadness or hurt, but there wasn't any that he could see. "I'm sorry." He couldn't imagine not getting along with his grandmother.

"Don't be. It's finally a solution that works. Otherwise we fight all the time. And in the meantime, I'm saving up for a nice place in the city. I'd been hoping to convince Emma to move in with me and share an apartment, but she's a small-town girl. And now that she's got the bookstore here, well…" Samantha shrugged.

A small kernel of disappointment lodged in his stomach.

When he returned to Manhattan, that would be the last he'd see of Emma, probably. "No other potential roommates?"

She shuddered. "God, no. I'd rather live on my own."

The waitress brought their pizzas to the table, and after each of them took a slice and a few bites, Josh continued the conversation. "What do you like to do in your free time?" he asked.

"Well, to be honest, I don't get a lot, what with my job and all," Samantha said. "But when I have time, I love the art galleries, clubs, museums and concerts. It's another reason I don't like to spend too much time here. There's much more to do in the city. I don't think I'll ever get bored."

Josh thought about the evenings he'd recently spent hanging out with his grandmother. Would he still be able to when she moved? In his mind, he rolled his eyes at himself. She was moving, she wasn't leaving. Still, he vowed to make sure he dedicated time to spend with her.

"Do you ever miss the quiet, though?" he asked. "I mean, I love that there's always something to do in the city, but slowing down sometimes is nice, too."

His mind drifted to some of the days spent packing up the house. Sure, packing was hard work, but quietly talking about memories attached to the objects they wrapped and boxed and donated filled him with warmth. Emma's presence hadn't bothered him as much as he expected.

He choked as her image popped into his mind.

"Are you okay?" Samantha pushed his water glass toward him, and he took a large gulp.

"Yeah, thanks. I choked on…air?"

She smiled. "As far as missing the quiet…" She stared off into the distance.

Josh took the time to study her. Something cracked slightly in her polished demeanor. Was she less confident than she appeared? And if so, why? But he still didn't know her well enough yet to ask, and the cracks he'd spotted glued themselves back together.

"Too much quiet gives me too much time to think," she said, her smile not quite reaching her eyes.

His chest ached with sympathy for her, even if he couldn't pinpoint the reason.

"Plus," she continued, "I can never sleep when I'm home. I need noise in the background."

Josh commiserated with her. "I totally get that. For me, it's the first couple days that are the hardest. But I think I'm starting to get used to it."

There was something soothing about the slower pace here. It wasn't a huge difference, but there was more privacy and fewer people around to shove through. Fewer congregants watching his every move. Even if his grandmother knew everything he did.

"Better you than me," she said.

They each took another slice of pizza. Samantha's eyes brightened.

"This all tastes good," she said, folding a slice of the meatball pie in half. "I'm not sure which I like best."

"I'm glad you're enjoying the pizza."

She looked at him over the slice. "Oh, don't get me wrong. It's not nearly as good as Indian food, or for that matter, pizza in the city, but it will do in a pinch."

Something in Josh snapped. "Look, I'm trying to make the best of a situation and still get to know you. I don't think it's necessary to mention how this date is second or third rate."

"Whoa." Samantha put her slice on her plate, wiped her mouth and held out her hand. "I'm sorry. I didn't mean to insult you. I wasn't talking about the company or the date. You're a good guy, and whether or not Masala lost our reservation, you pivoted pretty well. I'm glad we're spending time together. But I can't help if I'm a food snob."

Slightly appeased, he decided to bite the bullet. "What else are you a snob about?" Usually, he preferred to take his time delving deeper into everything, whether it was work or a date. Finessing out information tended to yield better, more well-rounded results. As a rabbi, it was a skill he'd learned. But things with Samantha had been off-kilter from the start, and he wasn't about to lose an opportunity to find out once and for all if they were compatible.

"I have high standards," Samantha said. "I like quality clothing, excellent food and people who treat me well. And I don't think there's anything wrong with that."

"Not at all," Josh agreed. "I don't begrudge you any of those things. Especially the part about being treated well."

Samantha nodded and continued to eat her pizza.

"However," he continued, "I'm not sure you and I have the same standards when it comes to material things, especially when I'm on a rabbi's salary. I'm less concerned with labels, and I love a good dive if it's got good food. I don't need all the trappings to impress me."

"I don't think there's anything wrong with that, either," she said. "And I truly admire your honesty." She took a deep breath. "And I want to be honest with you, too," she said, wiping her lips. "I don't know if you remember from our last date, but I'm dedicated to my career. I'm not looking for a guy to support me while I stay home and raise kids."

"You mean the date where you brought reinforcements?" Josh gentled his voice as he said it, but since they were being honest, he didn't think there was any reason to sugarcoat things.

Samantha had the decency to blush. "When Emma suggested it, I initially thought it was a bad idea, but her reasons were valid, so I agreed. From your perspective, though, I can see it probably wasn't the best idea. I should have at least warned you. I'm sorry."

Josh's stomach dropped. He wasn't sure what surprised him more, the fact that it was Emma's idea or that Samantha apologized.

"Wow, that's two apologies in the same date," she said. She looked around the pizzeria. "You must think I'm horrible."

"It takes a good person to admit when they're wrong. I give you credit for knowing what you want, going for it and apologizing when you make a mistake. Emma's lucky to have you as a friend."

"Thank you."

"For the record, though," he said, "I have no intention of forcing any partner to quit her job."

"But you want children. Family is important to you." She leaned forward, looking him directly in the eyes.

He could only imagine how good she was at her job. Family was everything to him. "Yes," he said. "And yes."

She fiddled with the place mat in front of her. "We might have a problem. I don't want them. I'd be a terrible mother."

He paused, thinking back to her profile. She'd stressed the importance of her career, but he didn't remember a "no-kids" comment. Of course, he hadn't specifically said he wanted them, either. "I respect your choice and your honesty," he said, his voice quiet. "But can I ask why you think you'd be terrible? I can't imagine you being terrible at anything."

Samantha froze, and to Josh's horror, her eyes filled with tears.

His heart pounded against his ribs. *What the heck?* He didn't mean to make her cry.

His fear must have shown on his face, because she reached across the table and took his hand. "That might be the nicest thing anyone has ever said to me." Her voice wobbled, but at least she was smiling now.

He thought he was safe from tears. Maybe. He squeezed her fingers and waited her out.

"The truth is, I'm not close with my family. My parents are successful people from a business perspective, but they probably shouldn't have married, and they definitely should never have had me. I throw myself into my job because that's what I've seen them do from the second I was old enough to be aware of their actions."

His heart bled for her. No matter how many tragedies he'd experienced in his life, he'd never suffered from a lack of love.

"Luckily, I love my job, and I'm good at it," she said. "That's where my focus is. While I'd love a relationship, I have no interest in children."

Josh thought about the profile Ms. Match sent. "How come you didn't say that on the matchmaker form?"

"I could swear I did," she said. "Unless I missed it? I remember filling out the form while on a break from work. If something came across my desk while I was in the process, I may have missed something."

It made sense to Josh, but he was frustrated all the same. He rose, ready to pay the bill and leave. "Well, I do appreciate your honesty," he said. "And I wish you lots of luck in the future."

She smiled. "Thank you. You, too."

They hugged before paying the bill at the counter and leaving the pizzeria.

"Can I drop you at the train?" he asked.

"I'm spending the night with Emma, actually."

"Let me drop you off."

Chapter Six

"How was your date?" Emma asked as soon as she opened the door for her best friend. As Josh's car reversed out of her driveway, she resisted craning her neck to get a last glimpse of him.

Samantha sighed. "Well, let's see. My train was late. We missed our reservation. And we ended up at the pizza place."

"Yikes," Emma said.

"Oh, and we're not going to see each other again."

A spark of hope ignited in her chest. "Oh no! Why not?"

"We're different. And the kids thing is a deal-breaker."

Emma wasn't surprised. She'd never thought the two of them were right for each other. Sam needed a high-powered alpha guy, someone to take charge and treat her well. Josh, was not Sam's type at all.

He might be mine.

Emma pushed the thought down, deep down, where she'd hopefully forget all about it. "I'm sorry. I hope you're not too disappointed."

Samantha shrugged and dropped her overnight bag on the floor.

"Well, I've got ice cream and wine here," Emma offered, "my parents are out, and we've got the house to ourselves for at least another couple of hours."

Samantha sank onto the living room couch. "Sounds perfect."

Emma left her in the living room and fetched a container of triple chocolate fudge truffle and two spoons, plus two wineglasses. "Which goes better with chocolate ice cream, red or white wine?" she called from the kitchen.

"Red," Samantha said, "but we can do both."

Emma grabbed the two bottles and settled on the opposite end of the living room couch from Samantha. She poured them both from the red, leaned against the couch cushion and took a big sip. "Are you going to talk to the matchmaker?" she asked.

"I'm supposed to give feedback each time we see each other, so yes." Samantha shrugged. "But to be honest, I'm not sure I'm going to continue to use her."

"Why not?"

Samantha took another sip of her wine. "I don't know. I'm not sure what I want to do. But I know Josh isn't the one for me."

"He is pretty focused on family," Emma said. "You should see all the things he's saving for his own one day."

Emma smiled to herself. She and her sister stored boxes of things they were saving for their kids at some point, but she'd always thought that was a "female" thing. Listening to Josh and Mrs. Axelrod discuss the history of some of their possessions warmed her heart and allowed her a glimpse into Josh's softer side.

Shaking her head, Samantha stared off into the distance. "I don't understand why people are such pack rats," she said.

"You don't like looking at things from the past and hearing stories about them?"

Samantha pinned Emma with a look. "My parents don't

do that, remember? I doubt they've saved anything of theirs, much less mine. Unless, of course, it's worth a lot of money."

Emma reached for her friend's hand and squeezed. "How about we watch a movie?"

Samantha nodded. "Can we skip the romcoms, though? I'm not in the mood."

"And no horror for me."

"After all these years, I still can't convince you to try one?" Samantha asked, grabbing the remote and flicking through some movie choices. "Even a campy one?"

"You sound like—" Emma clapped her hand over her mouth.

Samantha turned. "Like who?"

"No one. Never mind. I will never give in to horror. How about a comedy?" Emma's words tumbled over one another as she frantically tried to cover her almost-slip.

Samantha handed her the remote. "Fine, find a comedy. But who were you comparing me to?"

What kind of a friend was she if she constantly brought up Josh? Never mind that she couldn't stop thinking of him. This wasn't the time to talk about him with Samantha. If it ever was.

But her face heated, and Samantha stared at her over the rim of her wineglass. "Like who?"

"Josh." Emma let out a deep breath. "I'm sorry. I don't mean to keep bringing him up. I'm sure you're disappointed that the two of you didn't match, and the last thing you need is me mentioning him, and I promise not to do it again."

Samantha's eyes were narrowed to slits.

Emma swallowed. "It's like when you go to a funeral and you can't help saying the wrong thing," she added in a thready voice. *Girl, shut up.*

Samantha placed her wineglass on the maple coffee table,

rose and straightened her shoulders. "It's not bringing him up that's a problem, Em."

Emma took a deep gulp of her wine. Based on Samantha's posture, there was more. Much more. And Emma was going to need the wine. "No, I suppose it's not," she said.

"Are you falling for Josh?"

It was always tricky when Samantha questioned her. The woman was born to be a lawyer. And no matter how long Emma knew her, how often she'd experienced the questioning, how many pointers she gave herself, she always fell into the same trap. Samantha's quiet volume and friendly tone lulled her, Emma's body and brain relaxed, until her best friend went in for the kill.

"He's your match, not mine," Emma said.

"But you've been spending a lot of time together."

"I'm moving into his home, dealing with his grandmother, and I live in Browerville. It's impossible not to run into each other."

Samantha studied her, and Emma tried not to squirm.

"You've enjoyed your time with him, though."

Emma nodded. She hadn't done anything wrong. "He's a nice guy. We've had fun. But I've always known you were interested in him—and he, you—and I've never crossed the line. There's nothing wrong with your best friend liking the person you're considering dating." She paused. "As a friend."

She pushed aside all thoughts of how close to *anything but a friend* she'd gotten.

"And now that he's available—or will be as soon as I contact Ms. Match—are you going to go after him?"

Emma frowned. "Go after him? You make me sound like some predatory animal and not your best friend."

"Who in the past has often fallen for men I'm interested in."

Replacing her wineglass on the table in the exact center of the table, Emma turned to Samantha and folded her arms. "*Often* is a little bit of an exaggeration. And *men* is, too, frankly. What we did as children shouldn't count. And I've apologized."

"Yet you still spent time with Josh."

"Which you knew!" Emma ran her hands through her hair, the curls knotting around her fingertips. She winced. "I think this is a stupid argument, Sam. You said you're not interested in him, that you're going to tell Ms. Match it didn't work out."

"You're right, it's the first thing I'm going to do tomorrow. But I think out of loyalty, you should avoid him," Samantha said.

"Completely?" Emma's mind spun. How exactly was she supposed to avoid the man?

Samantha nodded. "Yes. You say you don't go after the men I'm interested in. So don't."

Emma leaned forward, resting her elbows on her knees. "I don't know what happened or when, but I feel like we've entered some alternate universe. How exactly do you think I can avoid a man who lives in the building I'm currently renovating? And you said you're not interested in him. Since when did you become jealous of me?"

Samantha's eyes widened in shock. "I've always been jealous of you, Emma, but this has nothing to do with jealousy."

Emma's throat thickened. "Jealous of me? Why?"

"You have family who loves you."

Emma nodded. She couldn't deny that, even if she and her parents rarely saw eye to eye. "You're right," she said. "But you're my best friend, and I love you, too. I'd never do anything to hurt you."

Samantha sagged. "I know. Please promise me you'll avoid Josh as much as possible."

"This makes no sense, Sam."

"I know. And I can't explain it. But I need you to do this for me."

Emma rose and strode to the sliding doors overlooking her backyard. She and Samantha had spent hours out there as children, playing on the swing set that still sat in the corner. It probably wasn't safe to use anymore. She sighed. "I'll do my best, okay? But I can't help it if we run into each other while he's moving, and I'm renovating."

Samantha nodded. "Thank you."

"I think I'm going to skip the movie and go to bed," Emma said. "You've got my sister's room, as usual. Let me know if you need anything."

As she climbed the stairs, she wondered when *her* needs would factor into anything.

The next morning, Josh was packed and ready to move his stuff to his friend Ari's apartment, where he'd stay for the rest of his time in Browerville, when his doorbell rang.

A man with a work belt around his waist stood there.

"Can I help you?" Josh asked.

"I'm here to measure for bookshelves," the guy said, holding out his card.

Josh frowned. "Can you hold on a sec?" He pulled out his phone and dialed Emma, silently thanking his grandma for having her number. He didn't give her a chance to say anything but spoke as soon as she answered. "Did you send someone over to measure for shelves?" He swore under his breath. "Sorry. Hi, it's Josh."

"Oh crap, he's early." Emma said. "I did, I'm sorry, he was supposed to arrive this afternoon when I was there." She paused. "And hi, Josh."

His annoyance at the uninvited workman disappeared as Emma's voice washed over him. A sliver of joy wedged its way between his ribs into his heart at her response to him. She hadn't given him a hard time for not saying hello. She'd responded in kind.

He rubbed his forehead with his free hand and looked over at the man in the doorway. "I've never heard of workmen being early before." He chuckled. "I'll let him in. Want to tell me where he should start? And how are you?"

"Thank you. He's got the plans. There's nothing you need to do. I'm on my way. Oh and, Josh?"

"Yeah?"

"I look forward to having a conversation in the right order when I see you."

She hung up before he could say goodbye, and Josh put his phone down ruefully. She'd given him a taste of his own medicine.

A zing of excitement ran through him. She was coming over.

Looks like Ari is going to have to wait.

He turned to the workman. "Come on in."

Once he'd made sure the workman knew which rooms he needed to measure, Josh retreated to the kitchen for coffee. He'd been amazingly coherent for seven in the morning, but he'd barely managed not to offend Emma. Caffeine was a must. He plugged in his grandma's ancient percolator, missing his top-of-the-line espresso maker from his apartment, and grabbed the last three mugs.

Make that four. In addition to his grandmother and the workman and himself, the way to this woman's heart was a caffeine drip, and although Josh shouldn't be interested in Emma's heart, offering her coffee would never be a bad thing.

As the water dripped and the steam hissed, his inner voice chastised him. *You sure you're not interested in Emma's heart?*

He shook his head, hoping to dislodge the annoying thought. Emma was not his match. She lived here in Browerville while he lived in Manhattan.

Before he could list the myriad reasons why he wasn't interested in her, his doorbell rang again.

"Emma, dear!" his grandmother said. She must have just come down the stairs if she answered the door so quickly. "How nice to see you," she continued.

Josh entered the foyer.

"I believe Josh made the coffee and, oh, there you are!" His grandmother turned to him. "You did make the coffee, right?"

"It's almost ready," he said. He smiled at Emma. "Hi, come on into the kitchen."

Emma's expression was frazzled. Kind of like her hair, with her curls every which way. Like she'd rolled out of bed a moment ago.

He swallowed. *Nope, not going there.*

"Let me check in with Ralph," Emma said. "He's the workman who showed up. At least, he's supposed to be?"

Josh nodded. "Relax, it's him. And he's in there." He pointed to the living room.

"Thanks." Emma rushed away.

He and his grandma walked into the kitchen.

"You did make coffee for everyone, right, Joshy?"

"Four mugs, grandma. Don't worry."

She patted his cheek. "And not a travel one in sight."

Josh frowned. "Huh?"

"Well, last time Emma was here, you couldn't wait to shoo her out the door. But you used actual mugs this time. We're making progress."

He wished he could glare at her. If she were one of his buddies, he'd have lots of words to say. But this was his grandmother and none of those words were grandma-approved.

Instead, he rolled his eyes. "The last four mugs we have left. They're going right into this bag as soon as we're finished."

His grandmother reached for one and poured coffee into it. "I'll take this to Ralph and leave you to serve Emma."

Was it his imagination, or did his grandmother stress the word *serve*? He watched the older woman strut out of the kitchen.

Josh grabbed his and Emma's coffee and went in search of her.

His grandmother winked as he walked into the living room, and the three of them, Ralph included, faced him. For some reason, he started to sweat.

"Black coffee," Josh said, handing Emma the cup.

Her fingers brushed his, and he wanted to grab her hand and not let her go. But he'd spill the coffee, probably burn himself or worse, her, and have an audience to boot.

Emma turned to Ralph. "You're all set in here?"

He nodded, and she inclined her head toward the kitchen. "I'll be right back."

Josh wasn't sure who she was talking to, so he followed her. He'd swear his grandmother chuckled.

"You remembered how I like my coffee."

He stuffed his hands in his pockets. "I did."

Her gaze softened, and she said nothing, quietly sipping her coffee. The silence was nice.

"When does your grandma move officially?" Emma asked after a few minutes.

"Tomorrow. And I'm moving in with a friend of mine. Thanks again for being flexible with us."

Emma shrugged. "Of course. You look less than thrilled, though."

He leaned against the counter and looked at Emma over the rim of his coffee cup. "There's a part of me that wants to physically throw you and the workman and everyone else out of this house, lock the door and keep my grandma in this place forever."

Emma's eyebrow raised. "I'm not a fan of physical maneuvering of any sort."

He took a gulp, wiped his mouth and set his cup on the table. "For the record, neither am I. Which makes this struggle harder. Because rationally, I know my grandmother needs to move into something that's easier for her to handle. I love her. I don't want her to suffer, and I certainly don't want her to sacrifice anything else for me. But that doesn't stop the irrational side of me from hating every second of the change."

The words poured out of him, and with them, all the emotions surrounding them. His throat tickled with grief and embarrassment. His temples ached from shame and anger. And yet, the weight in his chest lessened from sharing with this woman. Even if she was the last person he should share anything with.

As a rabbi, he was used to being on the receiving end of confessions. This side of the aisle was different…but nice. Maybe it was due to who he was confessing to.

Emma's mouth turned down in sympathy. "I'm sorry for my part in all this." She looked around, arms wide.

And for the first time, he didn't blame her. "It's not your fault," he said. "My grandmother was determined to sell. Trust me, that woman is a force of nature. Don't let her size fool you."

Emma's laugh was infectious, and he joined her for a moment. "You're lucky to have her."

"I know," he answered. "And seriously, if this place needed to go to anyone, I'm glad it's you."

"Even if I'm making changes to it?"

He took a deep breath while he thought about her question. He hated change. But in this case? "Actually, I think it might be better that you're making the changes." His voice lowered as he considered each word. "You've got a vision. Maybe a passion. And I'd rather see this place filled with love, even if it's different from the love that I experienced growing up here."

A cry from the other room interrupted his train of thought. Together, he and Emma rushed into the other room.

Ralph was helping his grandmother sit on the bottom of the stairs.

"What happened?" Josh's heart leaped into his throat as he scanned his grandma for injuries. If she'd fallen down the stairs, he'd have heard it, or he'd see evidence of it, right?

"It's nothing, Joshy," she said, cradling her knee.

"Ralph?" Emma asked.

Josh had forgotten she was there.

"She slipped on the bottom step," the workman said.

Josh's eyes widened. "Grandma, let me take a look at you. You could be hurt."

His grandmother reached out a veined hand and grabbed his forearm. Her grip was still strong, but seated below him like that, she looked frail. "Joshy, I'm okay. I tripped."

"But I heard you cry out all the way in the kitchen."

"That means I have strong lungs." She winced as she moved her leg.

His gaze immediately focused on her injured limb. "Let me see," he said, kneeling in front of her and lifting her pants leg. Her pale skin showed every vein, as well as a large bruise forming on her shin. "We should call an ambulance, Grandma. You might have broken your leg."

"No way," she said. "All I did was trip."

Emma stepped forward. "Mrs. Axelrod, you might be right that an ambulance isn't necessary, but Josh also might be right, and the sooner you get your leg checked out, the better everyone will feel. How about we drive you to urgent care? No sirens, but no head in the sand, either."

Josh stiffened as his grandmother and Emma stared each other down. And he did a double take when his grandmother gave in.

"Okay," his grandma said.

He glanced sideways at the curly-haired wonder next to him. How did she do that?

"Go get your car," Emma whispered to Josh as he remained in place trying to figure out what the heck was going on.

He startled. "Right." He patted his pockets in search of his keys, turned and rushed to move his car close to the front door.

Ralph, who was a big guy, carried Josh's grandma to the car, with Emma opening doors and clearing their way.

Once Josh was sure she was settled as comfortably as she could be, he turned to Emma and Ralph. "Thank you."

"No problem," Ralph said. Pointing behind him, he added, "I'm going to finish up inside if that's okay."

Emma nodded, surprising Josh for a moment, before he realized she was just as able to give permission as he was. It was her house, after all. He looked at his grandmother, tiny in his car, and swallowed.

"Go take care of her," Emma said, her voice soft. "I'll make sure everything is locked up here after Ralph finishes what he's doing. Text me how she is and let me know if there's anything you need. I can always bring something by afterward."

It took him a minute to realize she was talking about his grandmother's things, like a sweater or pills, rather than something intangible for him, like her comforting presence. And when he did, his neck heated. He was selfish, and his grandmother was paying the price.

"Thanks," Josh said and jogged around to the driver's side. "You ready?" he asked his grandmother.

She nodded. "But are you?"

Emma watched Josh's car pull away with Mrs. Axelrod inside. A pit of worry sat in her stomach, twisting strands tighter and tighter until she wanted to curl up in a ball. Mrs. Axelrod was sweet. Her face lit up each time she saw Emma. She'd loved Emma's ideas for the house, and she'd suggested a few of her own. Seeing her wince in pain was awful.

Emma walked into the house to find Ralph. "You're finished with the living room?" she asked, entering the dining room.

He nodded. "A few more in here, and I'm on to the den. I'll be all finished in about fifteen minutes."

Emma nodded. "Thanks for your help with Josh's grandma."

"I hope she's okay."

Emma did, too. She was starting to care for the woman. But it wasn't just Josh's grandma who worried her. It was Josh, too. They'd reached a thaw in their relationship, a sense of ease and humor permeating it. Emma liked it.

Samantha's words echoed in her mind. Didn't matter if she liked it. Emma couldn't do anything about it. No matter how much she might want to.

And that was the problem. How could she betray her best friend for a guy? She couldn't. That was all there was to it.

She walked around the empty rooms, trying to picture how everything would look painted with bookshelves filled with books, cozy seating areas and a small café.

But all she saw was Josh in every room—packing his grandmother's things, serving Emma coffee, chatting about family.

No matter how attracted to him she was, he couldn't be hers. She needed to focus setting up The Book Nook.

"All right, I've got all the measurements I need," Ralph said, interrupting her thoughts. "I'll get back to you with the final costs and delivery date."

She thanked him and walked him to the door. Pushing it closed behind him, she turned and scanned the foyer.

This would be renovated into the sales area, with the staircase removed and a new entrance for her living quarters moved to the back. She pulled out the paint swatches she kept in her bag and imagined the foyer in a pale yellow with black-and-white tiles on the floor.

Although she'd promised Josh she'd lock up when Ralph was finished, she wanted to take five minutes to walk through the rooms while no one was here.

To the right of the foyer was the living room, and behind it was a sunroom. She planned to paint both of them a pale green. The shelves Ralph was building—floor to ceiling plus a bunch of low ones that would divide the room into genre sections—would be a light oak, and she'd found a patterned carpet in blue, green and cream. The sunroom would have low shelves and comfy cream-colored sofas, along with some plants to soften the vibe.

At the back of the house was the kitchen, which didn't need much work. She'd add a few small tables and chairs and a coffee bar, and she'd use the same pale yellow of the foyer in here. On the other side of the house, the den and the dining room were to be painted a light blue. The blue, green and cream carpet was going to go in here, along with the same types of shelving as the living room. Some well-placed ottomans and some low shelving to again divide up the genres was all that was necessary.

Emma could finally picture it coming to life. Except the

thrill—the flutter of her heart, the zing in her veins, the buzz in her ears—was missing. In its place was a thick throat and a knot in her stomach.

She was worried about Mrs. Axelrod, and she regretted leaving Josh to deal with it on his own.

Pacing the foyer, she rattled off all the reasons why it was silly of her to worry. "Josh has been taking care of his grandmother for years. She's old but strong. She was barely injured. It's not like she tumbled down the full flight of stairs. Or had a heart attack, God forbid." Emma paused, saying a silent prayer just in case.

"Everything is going to be fine. You'll only get in the way. They don't want you there. No matter how strange it feels to be here when they're there, it's the right thing to do. You're not Josh's girlfriend or a member of the family. You're the woman who bought their house. Nothing more."

Except, Josh's gaze had been filled with fear. And Mrs. Axelrod looked tiny. And most important, Emma was a good person.

She couldn't ignore their crisis. When her own family had an emergency, she was the first one to offer to help, though her parents never seemed to think she could handle anything. Certainly not as well as her sister.

She groaned. Now wasn't the time to catalogue all the times her family hurt her feelings. Now was the time to act.

Throwing caution to the wind, she double-checked all the other doors were locked before stepping outside, locking the front door and jogging to her car. As she sped through traffic lights and wound around cars that had no business driving at the speed of a snail in the middle of the day—didn't they know people had places to be?—she berated herself.

"He's not going to want you there."

She repeated those seven words over and over until she'd shifted into Park on the side of the urgent care.

"Dumb, Emma. This is a dumb idea," she muttered as she walked inside and scanned the waiting room.

It was full, but there was no sign of Josh or Mrs. Axelrod. Did that mean they'd come and gone, or were they in the examining room?

Straightening her shoulders, she walked to the window and tapped on the glass. The frosted glass door slid open, and a man with a buzz cut held out an intake form.

"Hi, I'm a friend of the Axelrods. Can you tell me if they're in an examining room or if they've left?"

He frowned at her, and for a second, Emma wondered if she should take the intake form from his hand. But she plastered her sweetest smile on her face and hoped for the best.

"They're in an exam room, but I can't give you more information than that," he said.

"Thank you."

All of the chairs in the waiting room were filled. She leaned against a wall in a corner and waited. Despite all her arguments to the contrary, she couldn't make herself leave. She needed to see if Mrs. Axelrod was okay. And as for Josh? Well, she needed to see if he was okay, too.

She scrolled on her phone for the next twenty minutes, keeping an eye on the door and an ear out for the sound of their voices.

"This way, Grandma."

Josh's low, modulated voice made Emma drop her phone. Its muffled clunk as it hit the carpeted floor made him turn to her.

"Emma? What are you doing here?"

She picked up her phone and walked forward. "I was worried."

Something flickered in his gaze.

"Emma, how sweet," Mrs. Axelrod said. She elbowed Josh. "Isn't she sweet?"

Josh's face reddened. "Yes. She is."

Emma's insides flip-flopped, and she turned her focus to the older woman. "How are you, Mrs. Axelrod?"

"I'm fine, honey. Just a bad bruise. And they want me to use this ridiculous cane." She held up the offending metal cane with four rubber-tipped ends as if it were a pair of smelly gym socks.

"Grandma, you have to use it," Josh said. "At least for a few days."

Emma tapped her finger to her lips as an idea blossomed. "You know, we could decorate that. Make it festive for spring or add bling to emphasize your sparkling personality…"

The laugh that burst from Mrs. Axelrod satisfied Emma like nothing else. "Ha! Can you imagine me with a blinged-out cane?" She looked at the metal before walking slowly with Josh out the door of the urgent care. "I was hoping not to show up at my new place with this, but I guess it can't be helped."

Emma squeezed her shoulders as Josh opened his car door. "Didn't you say you had friends who already live there?"

The older woman nodded. "Yes, Carol, Brenda and Diane all live there."

"Well, I suspect they'll be glad to know you're not seriously hurt, and they won't care what you show up with. And the rest of the women might be jealous if we outfit that cane just right."

Mrs. Axelrod looked at Josh. "Joshy, we need to stop at the craft store."

His look of dismay made Emma chuckle. Still, she took pity on him. "Better idea," she said. "How about I go to the craft store and buy a few things while Josh takes you home?"

She looked at her phone. "It's past noon, and you two must be starving."

The look of relief on Josh's face warmed her. Come to think of it, many things about Josh warmed her. But that thought would have to save for another day. A way-far-in-the-future day.

"That's a great idea," he said. "Let's go home and eat, Grandma." He turned to Emma. "Have you eaten?"

She demurred. "Don't worry about me."

"Emma, you can't skip lunch, honey," Mrs. Axelrod said. "Joshy, make sure you stop for something for her as well."

"I'll take care of it, Grandma," he said, shutting the car door. He fiddled with his key fob as he turned to Emma. "Never threaten a Jewish grandma with skipping a meal."

Emma held up her hands in surrender. "I promise I'm fine, but do what you need to do to keep the peace. I'll see you later." She needed to get away, before she did something stupid, like hug him goodbye.

"Oh and, Emma?"

His voice slowed her steps, and she turned around.

"Thank you for coming here. I appreciate it."

So many thoughts struggled to be heard, and every single one of them clogged in her throat. Things like, *I needed to make sure she was okay. I needed to make sure you were okay. I needed to see your face.*

And she couldn't say any of them. Instead, she nodded, before turning blindly toward her car to pick up the craft materials.

Chapter Seven

Josh needed more eyes. He kept one eye on his grandmother, unconvinced she wasn't faking how okay she was and prepared for her to fall over in agony. The other eye he kept trained on the front door, waiting for Emma. For the first time, he actually wanted her to be here, and there was no way he was delving into that right now. Not when he also needed to come up with something for lunch when their fridge was empty.

"How about I order deli sandwiches?" he asked.

"Whatever you'd like, Joshy."

He peered at his grandmother. "You're okay? There's nothing wrong?"

"Just because I say whatever you want doesn't mean there's a problem. My leg is sore. It's supposed to be sore. But otherwise I'm perfectly fine." She pinned him with her bright blue gaze. "Now stop staring at me."

He looked at his phone as he called up the app. She was right. "Okay, grandma."

The kitchen was silent as he placed their order. He glanced at the empty stove. They'd prepared lunch together thousands of times. He was going to miss this.

"Getting old is a part of life, Josh."

His grandmother's voice cut through the silence and made him freeze.

"I know," he said.

"Life has cycles, and it's perfectly normal to move from one to the next."

He swallowed. "Doesn't mean I have to like it, though."

"I know," his grandma said, "but the Torah tells us old age is considered a virtue and a blessing."

"I don't want to lose you." Josh sank into the seat next to her, no longer hungry.

Her expression softened, and she reached for his hand. "You're never going to lose me in here." She pointed to his chest. "Or in here." She pointed to his head.

He shut his eyes.

"And if you spend all your time with me fighting every change, every decision I make about where and how I want to live, you're going to ruin the time we have left, which, by the way, I hope will be decades, and regret it later."

"I know you're right," he said.

"What's that?" She cupped her hand to her ear. "I'm old, and I can't hear you."

His grandmother's hearing was better than his. "Very funny."

"I got you to smile, though."

"True. But I'm not sure how not to do this." He waved his hand in a vague gesture.

His grandmother opened her mouth to respond as the doorbell chimed. She leaned forward. "That must be Emma."

He rose, his pulse quickening. He opened the door and stared at her. Her curls were wild, and his hand ached to touch them. Her vanilla scent, which reminded him of the hamantaschen his grandmother made for Purim, wafted around him, making all his concerns lessen.

"Come on in," he said, stepping away from the door. "Did you leave any craft materials at the store?"

Her laughter warmed him. "I like options. Plus, I have your deli order."

"Bless you."

He turned but not before seeing her cheeks flush. "Grandma, Emma's here," he called. "With lunch."

"Emma! Join us. Joshy, make room."

Emma placed her bags on the counter and gave his grandma a hug. He loved how the two of them cared for each other. He'd resented it at first, but it was hard to keep fighting against something that was obviously right.

"Mrs. Axelrod, here you go." Emma handed over her sandwich.

"Thank you. And you should start calling me Muriel."

Emma frowned. "We'll see."

"What is *we'll see*? *We'll see* is what you say when you don't want to commit to something. Not with a request to use my given name."

"Grandma, give her a break." Josh made sure everyone's lunch was settled before glancing at the craft bags. "Emma, what did you bring?"

The look of gratitude Emma gave him made up for the glare his grandma shot his way.

"I have ribbons, press-on jewels in all sorts of colors, foil also in lots of colors, decoupage glue and colorful fabric. The saleslady was trying to convince me to get twinkly lights, but I figured that was something I should check with you about first. I wasn't sure how much of an entrance you wanted to make, nor what vibe you wanted to give off."

His grandmother burst into laughter. "Twinkly lights? What am I, a walking menorah? No, I think I'll pass on those. Smart, Emma."

As Emma and his grandmother alternated between eating their sandwiches and pouring over the crafts in the bags, comparing colors and visions, Josh studied Emma.

He'd given up his resentment of her. It was impossible with someone so warm and friendly. Heck, if anything, he admired someone so devoted to a friend that she'd tag along on a date to make sure said date was safe. He might not approve of her methods—or appreciate them when he was said date—but he understood the purpose. Although not the same thing, he'd do anything for those he cared about.

Sun slanted through the window, illuminating a smattering of freckles on Emma's nose. He'd never noticed them before. What else hadn't he noticed? She spoke with her hands, which flitted around as she chatted with his grandmother. Her nails were short and gave off "capable" vibes. He liked that.

He was starting to think he liked a lot about her. The question was, did she like him?

At that moment, she looked up, caught him staring at her and smiled. One of her teeth was slightly crooked and a dimple punctured her cheek.

The floor dropped below him. His grandmother and lunch and her cane faded into the background. Like a movie, Emma zoomed into focus. The blood rushed in his ears.

Was this what it was like to fall head over heels for someone?

"Joshy, are you all right? You look a little green."

His grandmother's voice brought him back to the present, and he blinked. "I'm fine, Grandma."

Fine, if fine was falling for the wrong someone at the most inopportune time.

"Want to see what we've decided on?" Emma asked.

He didn't give two hoots about a decorated cane, but Emma was the one asking, so of course he did. "Sure." Thank goodness she seemed to accept as normal his total lack of knowledge when it came to arts and crafts, though he sat at the same table as them.

Emma held up pieces of green fabric threaded with gold, silver and rose. His grandma had piled silver and gold press-on jewels.

"We're going to wrap and decoupage the fabric around the cane and intersperse some jewels for a little added bling."

"Pizzaz," his grandmother said. "If I have to be old, I might as well be fabulous."

"You've always been fabulous," Josh said. He was no schmuck.

"Good answer," she said, winking at him. Turning to Emma, she continued, "Okay, show me how this is going to work."

There was nothing for Josh to do. They didn't need him. He should finalize the last-minute packing. Or check in with his senior rabbi to make sure there wasn't an emergency he needed to handle. Or check in with Rabbi Moskowitz about the youth group activity. Or confirm the timing of tomorrow's movers.

But he didn't want to do any of those things. He wanted to stay right here with his favorite person in the world, and the woman he was quickly falling for.

Even if the matchmaker was probably going to yell at him.

He sat and watched as they attached the fabric and jewels. When the art project was finally complete, his grandma took the cane and examined it from all angles before placing it on the ground and testing it out.

"Still works," she said with a grin. "And much more fashionable." She lowered her voice. "Don't tell anyone, but I might actually like this thing."

"Wonderful!" Emma cried, clapping her hands.

Her joy was infectious, but more important, her compassion for his grandmother was electric.

"Let's see how it works now that it's decked out," Josh said.

His grandmother rose and walked the length of the kitchen. "What do you think?"

"I think you're going to have all the other residents begging you for help tomorrow," he said.

"Or begging to use it when I'm finished with it," she said.

"That, too."

"Let me help clean up before I relax," his grandmother said.

"Don't worry about anything," Emma responded. "We've got it covered, right, Josh?"

Josh nodded. "You okay on the stairs?"

His grandmother nodded, but still, he walked with her into the hallway to make sure. She took it slow but turned on the landing. "Go spend time with Emma," she said with a wink.

Was he that obvious? For once, he didn't care. After making sure his grandmother made it to the top without incident, he returned to the kitchen.

Emma was just about finished cleaning up.

"Sorry to have left you with the mess," he said. He rushed over to the table to help her.

"Don't be sorry, you were helping your grandma."

She reached for the same length of ribbon as Josh did, at the same time, and their fingers tangled. Josh flexed his hand as heat flashed up his arm. He looked at Emma, but she'd turned her face away. He couldn't see her expression, just the clenching of her hand into a fist. He swallowed and continued cleaning up the craft supplies.

Emma picked up the bottle of glue and screwed the top on. Josh maneuvered around her to grab the garbage bag and bumped her hip. The still-open bottle of glue fell from her hands.

"Watch out!" he cried, and lunged for the bottle.

He missed, and his hand landed in a splotch of glue on a paper plate.

"Ugh," he cried, pulling the paper plate off his hand. Spinning around to go wash off the glue, his hand connected with Emma's.

She inhaled, and the two of them stared at their connected hands. A moment or two passed in silence. All he could think about was curling his fingers through hers and holding on tight. What would she do if he did?

Her skin was paler than his. The freckles that splashed across her nose also dotted the back of her hand.

He looked up into troubled brown eyes. She bit her lip, and he pulled his hand from hers. The slight sucking sound, under normal circumstances completely unnoticeable, echoed in the silent kitchen.

This was ridiculous. Without another word, he strode to the kitchen sink, turned on the faucet and scrubbed his hand. Soft laughter from behind alerted him to her presence, and he exhaled. He reached for a paper towel and dried his hand before turning around.

And once again, entered her space.

He'd known she was there. Her low laughter had tickled his eardrums and made him smile. Yet, still, he was unable to avoid her.

She sidestepped and stumbled, and he reached out to steady her. Gripping her upper arms, he held on to make sure she regained her footing. Somehow he ended up pressed against her body, her back against the counter, his face inches away from hers. Her long lashes fluttered as her eyes widened.

His pulse raced, and a longing to take her in his arms enveloped him. But a voice whispered in his brain, reminding him that trapping her was not the way to go, no matter how attracted to her he might be.

With a start, he backed away, holding up his hands. "Sorry." His voice sounded gravelly in his ears.

Emma remained frozen in place, leaning against the counter.

"Emma?" he asked.

Her mouth opened, and her tongue darted out to wet her lips. He couldn't look away. This was all wrong. He and Emma weren't supposed to be a thing.

He was still committed to working with the matchmaker.

He was only home for a few more weeks.

Her brown eyes darkened. She licked her lips again.

He groaned. She was killing him.

So was uncertainty.

He faced two options. He could make an excuse and flee. Or he could kiss her.

Emma stood in Josh's, soon-to-be-her, kitchen, pressed up against the counter where she hoped to serve pastries and coffee to book lovers, and stared into Josh's impossibly blue eyes. The heat emanating from those midnight orbs burned through her.

She should duck under his muscled shoulders and escape. He was off-limits. She'd promised Samantha nothing was going to happen between the two of them, and though she didn't agree with Samantha's demand, Samantha was her best friend. And you made sacrifices for your best friend. Especially if you had a history of "borrowing" said best friend's love interests.

Except Emma hadn't counted on Josh melting away every reservation toward him she possessed. He was caring and compassionate. Strong and vulnerable. Plus, he was sexy as hell.

His spicy scent surrounded her. The pulse in his neck entranced her. His breath against her cheek taunted her.

Everywhere his body touched hers—and in this position, his body *was* everywhere—tingled. She bit her lip, and his gaze narrowed. She licked them, and he groaned.

It wasn't just her.

Relief washed over her, making her giddy. Need swooped in, wiping away everything but a desire to kiss him.

She rose on tiptoe as he lowered his head. Their mouths met, softly, gently, agonizingly slowly. She sighed and wrapped her arms around his neck, pulling him closer. Her eyes fluttered closed. He ran his fingers through her hair, and she hummed as tingles of desire skittered along her spine.

Kissing him was the sweetest drug, and she wanted more. Their mouths moved in tandem, and she lost track of where she ended and he began. Their breath mingled, and she sighed against his mouth.

What could have been days later, he pulled away, resting his hands on her shoulders. She struggled to focus, and when she was finally able, he was smiling.

"That was even better than I imagined." The pitch of his voice rumbled in her belly.

She reached up to palm his cheek, sliding her hand down his chest. His heart pounded against her hand, solid and fast. Smiling, she met his gaze. "I think I agree. But I might need a repeat to verify."

The corners of his eyes crinkled. "I've never known you to be unsure."

She shrugged. "There's a lot you don't know about me."

Josh's gaze heated. He hooked his thumbs through her belt

loops on either side of her waist, his hands caressing her hips. "I'd like to find out more," he said.

"What about Samantha?" She fluttered her hands, clenching and unclenching her fingers with nerves.

Josh frowned. "What about her?"

"She's my best friend, and I don't want to do anything to hurt her."

He took her hands in his and brought one to his mouth. He kissed each finger before placing her hands on his chest again. As if he wanted her to touch him, to feel his heart beat. "She and I agreed we're not a match. And while I still have to follow up with the Ms. Match to officially let her know, I'm sure Samantha has already done so. And if she hasn't, we both agreed. There's nothing that says either one of us can't move on."

Emma swallowed, her promise to Samantha echoing in her brain. But this wasn't like other times, when Samantha was interested in someone. She'd passed on Josh. Nothing Emma did would prevent Samantha from finding her own happiness.

"Okay," she said. She'd talk to Samantha later and explain how she felt.

The smile Josh gave Emma blinded her. Emma couldn't help but return it.

"I'm helping my grandma move into her new place tomorrow," Josh said. "But would you want to go out tomorrow night? We could go to a movie or check out one of the local bands. There might be a home football game at the community college."

"I feel like you're throwing spaghetti at the wall to see what will stick," Emma said. "I'm happy to do anything with you. The workmen are descending tomorrow at one. Once they're set up, I'm free."

"How about dinner and a movie? I could pick you up at six."

Emma nodded. "If you don't mind picking me up from my house. I don't want to crowd the workmen."

"It's a date," Josh said.

He leaned in to kiss her again before pulling away far too quickly from Emma's point of view.

"I'll see you tomorrow," he said.

"Tomorrow."

Her phone rang as the door snicked shut behind Josh.

"Hi, Alyse." Her voice was still breathless, her mind on her upcoming date and that kiss.

"Oh, am I interrupting something?" her sister asked.

Emma shook her head. "It's fine. What's up?"

"I wanted to hear about the bookstore."

Emma blinked, trying to turn her focus from the hot rabbi she'd kissed to the bookstore she was developing. After a beat, she filled her sister in on the latest news from the contractors and her plans going forward.

"It sounds amazing, Em."

Awe shaped Alyse's tone, and for the first time in a while, Emma let pride build in her soul. "Thank you."

"No, I mean it. I'm impressed. I can't wait to come and browse."

"I'd love you to," Emma said. And realized she meant it.

"Okay, I've gotta run, but keep me updated, okay?"

Emma hung up and hugged herself. Maybe, maybe, she was finally going to make it.

The Marble House's iron gates and large sweeping drive led to several brick-and-stone buildings situated among trees, gardens and lush lawns. To the left, groups of people practiced tai chi. Others did yoga. Seated to the right beneath a portico, people played mah-jongg and canasta while others stood at easels painting. Bike trails wound through the property, and several people rode large three-wheelers. Others were walking together, deep in conversation. And in the distance, tennis and pickleball courts were packed with people.

It was a thriving community of active older adults who appeared happy to be there. But Josh couldn't get rid of the pit in his stomach, no matter how hard he tried.

He gripped the steering wheel, following the moving van to the building farthest from the main one as his grandmother stared eagerly out the window.

Pulling up to the building, Josh parked the car but remained motionless. He wasn't ready.

"Come on, Joshy. I've got the key. We have to let the movers inside."

She was right. Dawdling wasn't going to help anything. But climbing out of this car was going to set the next phase of her life in motion. And all he wanted to do was make life move backward. Not too far, because the last thing he wanted to relive was the death of his parents. But maybe a couple of years.

Unfortunately, time travel still wasn't real. And as much as he hated what came next, his grandmother was excited. Her face was filled with joy and anticipation. He didn't have the heart to take that away from her.

"I'm coming," he said.

He climbed out of the car, joints aching, feeling old enough to move here himself. His muscles only hurt more as the day wore on and he helped his grandma move in and unpack.

If he'd thought packing up the big house was hard, unpacking was worse, because he couldn't leave boxes around for later. They'd get in the way, or his grandmother would take it upon herself to do it. No, he needed to get her unpacked today.

"The apartment is nice," he said.

His grandmother opened her arms wide. "Look how light and airy it is. I'm glad we picked this model."

On the second floor of the four-story building, the southern exposure let in lots of light through the huge bay windows in the living room, bedroom and kitchen. The white walls and pale gray carpets were neutral, as were the gray-and-white-flecked sofa and black lacquer dining set that came with the apartment. His grandmother's favorite pieces of furniture from her house—her bed, a red easy chair and ottoman, and a large bookcase—plus the colorful accessories she'd brought along, made the place homey and vibrant.

Even if it wasn't the home he wanted her to live in.

He straightened his shoulders. Enough. He couldn't fight time. And he wasn't going to win this battle. Somehow, he needed to figure out a way to make the best of it.

His grandmother hummed some tune he didn't recognize. She bustled about from one room to the other, adding knick-knacks and tchotchkes, straightening things just so, and welcoming her friends who stopped by to say hello.

It reminded Josh of freshman move-in day in the dorms. He stifled a snort as Sophie popped her head in.

"Yoo-hoo!"

"Hello!" His grandmother rushed over and gave her a hug. "Joshy, you remember Sophia Adler?"

He held out his hand. "I do. How are you?"

"I won three hands at mah-jongg. Figured I'd better leave before anyone yelled at me, and when I remembered your grandma was moving in today, it was the perfect excuse."

"Three?" his grandmother asked. "You'll be lucky if they let you play again."

Sophie shrugged. "Eh, Doris runs the group, and I supported her Hanukkah party idea last year. She'll give me a pass, as long as it doesn't happen too often." She toddled farther into the apartment, squinting. "Looks good, but whoa it's bright."

Josh's grandma nodded. "I know, I love it."

Turning to Josh, Muriel pointed a bright red pointy manicured nail at him, and he resisted, barely, rubbing his chest. "You need to hang pictures on the wall and curtains to make it homier and less bright when friends visit." She looked like she was about to say more, but she glanced down and spotted the cane. Her mouth opened. Her bent back straightened almost enough to add additional height to her tiny frame.

"Your cane!" Sophie's voice, which rasped with some age-related threadiness before, bellowed with new-found strength.

As his grandmother stood in the center of the room, Sophie toddled around in circles around her. If she didn't slow down, she was going to get dizzy, and Josh was going to have to help her get up off the floor. Not what he wanted to do after lugging boxes all morning.

"Holy Moses, that is a work of art!"

His grandmother angled her cane this way and that. "Thank you. Josh's friend Emma helped me."

Josh whipped around toward his grandmother at her emphasis on the word *friend*. He frowned, but she wasn't looking at him. He cleared his throat, but she didn't turn.

It was as if she were ignoring him.

"Ohhh, do you think she'd be willing to teach a class?"

Josh almost choked on air. Forget his grandmother. Emma? Teach the residents to decorate their canes? In a class?

It wasn't that he doubted her ability. Clearly, she'd helped his grandma whip up something admiration-worthy, if Sophie's reaction was to be believed. But she was opening up a bookstore and her time was limited.

He wasn't ready to share her.

"We'll ask her the next time we see her," his grandmother said. "Right, Josh?"

He didn't want to ask Emma if she'd teach his grandmother's friends how to decorate their canes. He wanted to ask her to spend more time with *him*, not his grandmother, and certainly not the random old ladies in this place.

But his grandmother elbowed him in the ribs.

"Ouch."

He turned to her as he rubbed his side. She looked at him with the sweetest expression on her face. But he wasn't fooled in the slightest. He'd grown up with that woman, and her looks could be deceiving. Especially when she was displeased with him. She'd present one face to the outside world, but he saw through it to the flutter of her lashes, the twitch of her eyebrow and the shape of her lips when she gave him the smile that meant *do what I'm saying*.

He caved, at least for appearances' sake. "Right, Grandma. I'll talk to her about it the next time I see her." *And tell her not to do it.*

Sophie clapped her hands. "Wonderful! I'll tell Maureen, our social director, and get her to put it on the calendar."

Abraham, Isaac and Jacob, no. Absolutely not.

"That might be a little premature," he said, trying his hardest to keep his voice even. "She's got a lot on her plate, and I'd hate to commit her to something before asking her."

His grandmother's friend nodded toward his phone. "Do you have her number?"

His breath froze in his chest. All he could do was nod.

"Great, why don't you call her?" Sophie suggested.

Call her. "Now?"

"Well, if we want to get her on the social calendar, we need to get a move on. And trust me, when the other ladies see this cane, there's going to be a clamor the likes of which this place hasn't seen since Morty threw his back out with his Elvis impersonation." She placed her hands on her hips. "He was doing the famous Elvis hip wiggle."

Josh ran a hand down his face, unsure of whether he wanted to laugh or cry. What he did know was he didn't want to see Sophie wiggling her hips. He caved. "I'll call her."

Pulling out his phone, he searched for her contact information, tapped her name, and hoped she wouldn't answer.

"Hi, Josh." Her rich voice soothed him.

"Hey." He glanced up to two sets of eyes—his grandmother's and Sophie's—staring at him. "Your cane decorations are a hit here."

She hummed. "I'm glad."

"They'd like you to come and teach a class how to do it."

She sputtered. "I'm sorry, what?"

"Doesn't that sound like fun?" He did have an audience.

"Your grandma is right there, isn't she?"

"Yep. She showed her friend, Sophie, who loved it."

"It's fantabulous," Sophie shouted. She moved as if to take the phone from Josh's hand, but he took a step away.

"Oh my. Um, tell her thank you, and I'll, um, figure out my schedule and let her know."

"Perfect." He lowered his voice. "I'm sorry."

"Don't be," she said. God, he loved her voice It played around all his edginess, softening the rough spots and heating the icy shards of anxiety until they started to melt away. "I love that your grandma is happy and that everyone admires her cane. It'll make it easier for her to use it."

"Well, I don't know about everyone, but Sophie certainly does." He'd walked away from the women, who had started chatting about an upcoming lecture series. "Look, you don't have to do this. I know you're busy getting The Book Nook ready. They didn't give me any choice but to call you, but I can easily get you out of it if you want. Trust me, this isn't an I-can't-say-no-to-a-rabbi request."

She huffed a breath over the phone. "I figured as much," she said. "Seriously, don't worry. We can talk more about it tonight... I assume we're still on for tonight?"

"Absolutely." The thought of seeing her tonight was like a breath of fresh air. It gave him something to look forward to, reminding him that life wasn't ending. It was changing for everyone, but maybe in a good way.

"Good," she whispered.

He couldn't help the smile her response caused.

"Now go help your grandma, and I'll see you later."

Chapter Eight

Emma stared out her parents' living room window at the driveway waiting for Josh's car to arrive. She was early, but she couldn't help it. Her excitement had built all day, making the clock drag as she ran around the old Victorian, directing workmen and overseeing the transformation.

His phone call scared her at first, thinking he was canceling. And then his concern for her time touched something deep inside her core. All of which made her eager for his arrival and resulted in her getting ready twenty minutes early.

Now, she waited.

"You look pretty," her mom said, walking up behind her and placing her hands on her shoulders, before adjusting Emma's curls.

"Thanks." Emma smoothed her purple sweater with a cowl neck.

"He's going to come to the door, right?"

Emma shook her head, making her gold hoop earrings bang against her neck. "No, Mom. When I see him, I'll run outside."

Her mom frowned but remained silent.

Luckily, a car slowed before pulling into the driveway, giving Emma an out. She grabbed her jacket, forgoing her usual canvas messenger bag for a small clutch, blew her mom a kiss and raced out the door.

Josh was halfway out of the car when she slowed on the walkway.

"I would have come to the door," he said, opening her car door for her.

"Not necessary," she said. "You don't need the third degree from my mom and dad."

He reversed out of the driveway and drove into town. "I'm a rabbi. I can handle it. Besides, it's nice that they care," he said.

She paused, about to give a flip answer. Deep down, she knew her parents cared. Obviously. "You're right," she said. "I wish they'd show that care in a positive, rather than negative way."

"You don't think they'd approve of you going to dinner with me? Most Jewish parents would be thrilled their daughter was dating a rabbi."

He pulled into a parking spot in the back of La Traviata and turned to her. His expression was solemn, and the air between them was heavy, like everything going forward depended on this answer.

"My parents aren't like most Jewish parents," she said. She held out a hand. "Oh, don't get me wrong. They'd probably think I won the lottery. But it's always a competition for them between me and my sister, and they're always focused on my success rather than my happiness."

She followed him into the restaurant and, after he gave the hostess his name, followed him again into the glassed-in courtyard. Twinkly lights crisscrossed the ceiling above them. Sparkly snowmen sat at the bases of the trees, and silver linens covered small round tables.

The hostess handed them small chalkboards with the daily menu written in white chalk.

"This is adorable," Emma said. "I love how seasonal they are."

"I'm glad you like it. And as for your parents," Josh said, "some people aren't able to make the distinction between success and happiness. For them, it's the same thing."

"Is it for you?" she asked.

He exhaled. Small votive candles in the middle of the table freckled his face with light and shadow. "I used to think success would determine my happiness," he said. "And then I started working for my synagogue doing a variety of tasks and rituals and counseling all kinds of people, and I realized that there were different ways of defining success."

She liked his answer. "Being a rabbi satisfies you?"

"More than I ever expected. I feel good at the end of the day knowing I'm helping people. I can look at myself in the mirror and be proud of what I'm doing."

They paused to place their orders.

When the waitress left, Josh leaned on the table, folding his arms. "I'm sure your parents are proud of you for starting your own business."

Emma shrugged. "I don't know. I don't think they're convinced it will be successful. Neither am I, for that matter, but nothing in life is guaranteed, and at the end of the day, I want to enjoy what I do."

Josh nodded. "How did it go today?"

She thought about saying fine, glibly washing over all her worries. But something about the way he looked at her, the pitch of his voice when he asked, made her hesitate. Was that his rabbi look, or did he focus on everyone that way? Maybe she was a little raw from discussing her complicated history with her family.

Or maybe she just liked Josh and wanted to be honest with him.

"It was overwhelming," she said, her voice shaking a little. She took a sip of wine before breathing deeply. The evening air, cool and perfumed with the scent of garlic and herbs from the kitchen, filled her nostrils. "The contractor was barking orders and asking me a million questions, the workmen descended like ants on honey, and I suddenly realized that I was in charge." She shrugged. "I mean, I know I'm in charge, but it hit home. Like, if I make a mistake, it's on me."

Josh reached across the table and took her hand. He squeezed. His hand was warm, his grip firm. In the candlelight, dancing shadows hollowed out his cheeks.

The waitress returned with their food, but still he held on. Part of her thought they should move out of the waitress's way, but the woman didn't seem to care. Maybe she was used to this.

Emma wasn't, but she could be.

When the waitress left, Josh ignored his food, focusing on Emma instead. "It's scary, isn't it?"

The acknowledgment lifted a weight off her shoulders. She couldn't ever admit her fear to her parents. They'd use it as another reason why she should do something else. Her sister, who meant well, would try to step in and show her all the ways she could do it better.

But Josh understood, and for the first time in a long time, Emma had nothing to prove.

"Terrifying," she said.

"I know it's not the same, but when I agreed to help out Rabbi Moskowitz, a similar fear overwhelmed me. Like, what if she's dissatisfied with me? This is the synagogue I grew up in, and there are people who know me there. What happens if my New York synagogue gets upset and fires me?"

Emma nodded. He was right, it wasn't exactly the same, but it was close enough. She exhaled. "You understand. And

I feel pressure for everything to be perfect." Like her family was waiting for her to fail so they could say *I told you so*.

He squeezed her hand again before letting go. "You're human," he said. "I am, too. Give yourself some slack. Nothing has to be perfect. You're going to mess up. We all do. The key is how you recover."

She blinked tears away and focused on her plate. "Thank you," she said, after swallowing a bite of food. "I needed to hear that."

They spent the rest of dinner talking. Emma marveled at the ease with which they moved from their jobs to books they'd recently read to trips they wanted to take and onto more serious topics like religion and dreams for the future.

"I didn't grow up religious," Emma said. She twisted her hands in her lap. "Is that a problem for you?"

He looked at her, a soft expression emanating from his blue eyes. "Why, because I'm a rabbi?"

"Yes."

"Are there things you like about being Jewish?" he asked.

She nodded. "I like the food and the holidays."

"Me, too," he said. "I like how helping others is built into the religion, and that it's flexible enough to accommodate lots of people in lots of ways."

She'd never thought about it that way. "I do, too."

"I don't think you have anything to worry about," he said.

The more Josh talked and listened, the more attractive he became.

Emma bounced her knee beneath the table, her heel tapping against the brick patio. She wanted him. She didn't want to get ahead of herself, but she wanted a relationship with this man.

"Where did you go?" he asked after they ordered dessert. "You disappeared for a second."

He'd noticed? She swallowed. Delving deep into the truth was working with him; she wasn't about to backtrack now.

"I was thinking about us." She looked at him, expecting him to recoil or grow anxious. Wasn't that what was expected after such a short time?

But as usual, Josh waited patiently for her to continue. His blue gaze was steady, his broad shoulders relaxed. "What about us?"

She leaned forward. "I like you. And I want us to explore a relationship together."

"I feel the same way," he said.

She warmed, unable to stop the smile that appeared on her face. But she paused. "What do we do about Samantha?"

Now he reacted, his frown showing confusion. "I don't see why we need to worry about Samantha."

"I don't want her to think I'm stealing you."

"Stealing me? I kind of like the idea that you two think I'm a catch, but there's no stealing involved."

Emma shifted in her chair. "We kind of have a history. Or at least, I do…" She explained the previous examples, which only grew in her mind the more attracted to Josh she became.

"I don't think what you did was horrible," he said. "Nor do I think you owe her an explanation now."

"I'm not sure she agrees."

"That sounds like something she needs to address on her own. She and I didn't work out. You and I like each other. I think we should explore what's going on between us. But it's early, and we have plenty of time."

"You're returning to New York, though, right?" she asked.

He nodded. "I am, but that doesn't mean I can't come here regularly. It's only a short train ride away. And you're going to be busy with The Book Nook."

She swallowed. "Am I crazy for starting a relationship with you now?"

He shrugged. "Maybe a little? But it's a good crazy. And no more than I am starting one with you when I don't live here."

She covered her face with her hands, but he pulled her arm away. "How about we don't jump ahead? We like each other, right?"

She nodded.

"We want to keep seeing each other, right?"

Again, she nodded.

He rose, came around the table and sat next to her. "We should kiss to seal those two things."

She raised an eyebrow. "Oh, really?"

Now it was his turn to nod. And before she could react, he reached his hand around the nape of her neck and pulled her to him. Their lips met. He tasted of red wine and garlic and bread. She sighed, and he deepened the kiss, his tongue making a gentle swipe in her mouth before he pulled away. His breathing was a little off.

"You don't know how much I wish we weren't in a restaurant right now," he said.

"Oh yes, I do."

His embrace filled her with need and made all her fears fade into the background. However, there were other people in the restaurant, and she didn't want to put on a show.

Josh returned to his seat, and after paying the bill, they left, walking to the theater. He wrapped his arm around her waist, pulling her up against his side, showing the entire world they were together.

Her body warmed, and her pulse hummed in her ear.

She loved it. Now that the sun dipped beneath the tree line, streetlights and the glow from windows lit their way. Up ahead, the movie marquee with its running white lights, black lettering and old-fashioned red velvet curtains outlining the ticket booth beckoned.

They stood in line waiting to purchase their tickets. Emma rested her head on Josh's shoulder. He squeezed her tighter for a moment, making her sigh in contentment.

"What are you thinking?" he asked, leaning toward her.

"I like this."

He angled his body and kissed her nose. She wrinkled it, and he caressed her cheek. "I like this, too."

Once inside the theater, they bought popcorn and Junior Mints and looked for seats.

Josh started down the aisle, but Emma balked.

"No, I don't want to sit there," she said. "It's too close."

"Close? It's halfway between the screen and the back."

She shook her head. "It still feels too close."

With a shrug, he backed up and chose an aisle three rows closer to the back.

"No, that's not right, either," she said. "It's got a weird glow from the exit sign."

He looked at her askance.

Emma bit her lip. "You think I'm crazy, right?"

He opened and shut his mouth a couple of times before speaking. "I think you should be in charge of where we sit."

With a nod, she chose an aisle two rows farther back, and two seats slightly left of center. "See, this is perfect for lighting, and based on the angle of the screen, we'll have the best view."

Without a word, he sat next to her, grabbed her hand and kissed her fingers. "Whatever you say."

"Promise?"

He settled in and offered her popcorn. "Yes."

Emma sighed in contentment as the credits rolled. She'd curled into Josh for at least the last half of the movie, thanks to the shape of the seats. Though a movie hadn't given them a chance to talk, their intimate positions kept him top of mind for the entire movie. Every hitch in his breath, every huff of laughter, every startled reflex felt as if it came from her. Now, as the lights in the house rose, she pulled away, immediately missing the warmth and solidity of his body next to hers.

"You enjoyed it," he said as he stretched.

She smiled. "I did. So did you."

"Very true."

He laced his fingers through hers, and they followed the crowd out of the theater.

The cold January temperature made Emma shiver, and Josh pulled her closer to him. She could get used to this. And then, he leaned over and kissed her. Heat ignited within her. He wrapped his hand around the nape of her neck, his fingers disappearing into her curls. His kiss was firm, confident, and when he pulled away, she wanted more.

"I like this," he said. "I like us."

"Me, too."

"Want to come with me on an adventure tomorrow?"

She frowned. "What kind of adventure? And is it something I can work around the bookstore?"

"I'm chaperoning some teens at the food pantry. Rabbi Moskowitz needs some help, and since I'm home, I agreed. Come with us?"

"What do you mean, you're chaperoning?"

"The senior youth group's advisor has some scheduling conflicts, I ran into the rabbi at the JCC, and she asked if I was available. It'll be fun."

What would be fun was spending time with Josh. Teens? She remembered those years, and she wasn't sure she wanted to repeat them. Still… "Okay, what do I have to do?"

He hugged her to him and resumed walking toward the

car. "I'll pick you up at eleven and drop you off afterward. All we have to do, other than organize food donations and serve lunch, is make sure all the teens stay alive."

Her eyes widened.

He patted her shoulder. "I'm joking. It's going to be fun. Trust me."

At his car, he took her hand and swung her to him. He placed his palms on her cheeks, warmth sliding to her toes. Leaning forward, he kissed her once again.

This rabbi could kiss. He tugged on her bottom lip with his teeth, and when she opened her mouth, he slid his tongue inside. She sighed, pulling him closer, and their tongues danced as prickles of excitement and desire raced up and down her spine. The cold January air was no match for the heat as he wrapped his arms around her. He paused, and their breaths mingled. His heart pounded against her chest. Or maybe it was hers. She couldn't tell. She just knew she liked it. She liked him.

This time when he pulled away, his chest rose and fell, and his cheeks were ruddy. "If we don't stop now, I'm not going to be able to…" His voice was hoarse. "And living at my friend's apartment… I'm not sure what his plans are or where there's space—"

She placed a hand over his lips as regret and understanding warred within her. "My parents are home, or I'd suggest my place." She shut her eyes. "God, I can't wait until I can move into my own apartment."

He tipped his head against hers. "So, rain check, until we can figure things out?"

She nodded. "Rain check."

The next day, Emma sat on the porch of The Book Nook waiting for Josh to arrive. She'd never been a youth group kid, and she didn't know what to expect. She certainly didn't expect the van that showed up in her driveway.

Josh leaned out the window. "Hey, pretty lady, want to help distribute food?" He waggled his eyebrows at her, and she rushed over to the front of the van.

Climbing inside, she leaned over to kiss him hello, but he pulled away, tipping his head toward the kids in the back of the van. The edge of his kippah caught her eye.

Right. He's working.

"Everyone, this is Emma. Be nice to her and don't scare her away. Emma, this is everyone. If they give you any problems, I'll take away their phone chargers."

Emma's cheeks heated. She'd been so focused on Josh, she hadn't realized the teens were already in the van. How embarrassing. She turned to them, smiling at their eye rolls and groans. "Hi, nice to meet you all."

"Are you his girlfriend?" one of the boys asked.

Her heart seized at the unexpected question. Then again, teenagers were blunt, so she shouldn't be surprised. "Well, I'm a girl, and I'm his friend," she said, looking sideways at Josh.

"You're a woman, not a girl," one of the girls said.

"Very true," Emma said and smiled at her. "I appreciate the respect."

"And that wasn't an answer," the girl continued.

Josh called out, "Okay, guys, give her a break." To Emma, he whispered, "Sorry."

Another five minutes in the van, and Emma knew all the names, what music they liked and how many more mitzvah points they needed.

"What are mitzvah points?" she asked the group as Josh pulled into the parking lot of the food pantry.

"Our youth group is divided into three teams. We compete for mitzvah points. What we do determines how many points we get. At the end of the school year, the winning team gets a pizza party."

"Cool," Emma said. She turned to Josh. "Do you help them out often?"

"This is my first time."

Emma raised her brows in surprise. He didn't act like this was his first time. As they all climbed out of the van, Josh greeted each teen by name. His easy posture and gentle teasing made all the teens respond. He was clearly a natural with them.

He pulled her against him as the teens walked toward the front door. "Girlfriend question later?"

She nodded.

Inside the food pantry, they were directed to the storage room, where several large boxes were filled to overflowing with cans of food.

"Okay, guys, it's time to organize," Josh said.

They spent the next fifteen minutes placing nonperishable food on the shelves.

"You can't put green beans next to the cake mix," one of the boys said to his friend, giving him a light shove. "Geez, don't you shop?"

Emma shook her head as the boy rearranged the organizational faux pas.

Josh hefted large boxes and moved things for easier reach. The muscles beneath his sweater bunched and rippled, and Emma couldn't help staring. She'd gotten a hint of them when he hugged her, but this was different. This was seeing them in action.

She fanned herself before returning to her task of sorting cans of fruit by size and variety, slightly afraid of getting on the boy's bad side.

When everyone finished sorting and organizing the nonperishable food, they entered the cafeteria. Emma watched as Josh assigned each of the teens a task to help the pantry get ready for the lunch crowd. Somehow, he got them not to mind the hairnets and gloves they were required to wear.

Something low in her belly tugged at her. He'd be a great dad. Blinking away the thought, she put on her own hairnet and gloves and got in line to help serve soup.

By the time they were all in their places, the doors opened and the sound of patrons' shoes squeaking on linoleum floors filled the room. All the kids chatted as they served the soup, sandwiches and sides, fruit and dessert.

Josh stood at the opposite end of the table, but somehow, each time Emma looked over toward him, she met his gaze. He winked, and heat ran through her.

After the last patron pushed his tray through the lunch line, they packed away the food, cleaned up the tables and returned to the van.

"You all were fantastic," Emma said once everyone was seated. "I was impressed."

The teens' faces lit up.

"You were pretty good, too," one of the boys said. "Although you were a little stingy with the French fries."

She laughed. "I eventually got the hang of it."

They pulled up to the synagogue, and all the teens climbed out of the van. As the last one left, he turned to Josh. "You should make her your girlfriend. She's cool."

Joy bubbled up in Emma's chest.

Josh's cheeks reddened. "Thanks for the advice, Adam."

He started the van and drove toward Emma's home.

"Thanks for coming today," he said. "I liked having you here."

"I'm glad you asked me. It was fun. And meaningful."

He turned to her, pride straightening his posture. "Yeah,

it was, wasn't it?" He reached for her hand, and held it for the next few minutes until he pulled up in front of her house.

"This is me," she said.

He nodded and climbed out at the same time she did. They stood in the driveway, toes an inch apart. He reached for her hand again, and she squeezed.

"So, about what Adam said…"

Emma smiled, anticipation making her giddy. "The girlfriend question?"

"Emma!"

Samantha's voice made Emma turn around.

"Sam!" Emma dropped Josh's hand and pulled away from him. "Hi." Her breath puffed in the cold night air.

Samantha's gaze narrowed. "Josh. What are you… Are you two together?"

Josh stepped forward as Emma's throat clogged. "I didn't realize you were in town," he said.

Samantha folded her arms over her chest and looked between the two of them. "I didn't know I needed to give you warning."

Emma stepped forward. "Sam—"

"Yes, Emma and I are together." Josh took a step closer to Emma, his body heat rolling off of him in waves.

Samantha's face reddened, and she shifted her gaze between the two of them. Betrayal and hurt flashed.

Emma swallowed, wishing she was anywhere but here.

"I thought I asked you to avoid Josh," Samantha said.

Visions of previous encounters with Samantha's former boyfriends flashed through her mind—giggling with Jeremy over his pet turtle; flirting with Elliott at the prom.

Josh stepped forward. "You and I aren't together, Samantha," he said. "We agreed we weren't right for each other.

Only after that did Emma and I realize we *were*. What does it matter if Emma and I date?"

Samantha whirled toward him. "You don't understand. Stay out of it."

"Sam, come on. This doesn't make sense," Emma said.

"If you were my friend, it wouldn't matter whether or not it made sense," Samantha said, tears welling in her eyes. "You'd stay away from him because I asked."

"And if you were *my* friend, you wouldn't have asked that in the first place," Emma retorted. *This is ridiculous.*

Samantha stood in front of them, chest heaving. "I guess we're not friends anymore." Without another word, she spun around and stalked off.

Emma's stomach dropped, and bile rose in her throat. "Sam!" She shouted, but her friend disappeared down the street.

"Let her go," Josh said, his voice quiet. "Give her time to cool off."

"I can't let her go," Emma cried. "I have to talk to her. We've been friends forever. I'm not about to let some guy come between us."

The words fell out before she realized what she was saying.

Josh winced, before making his face a mask.

"I'm sorry," she said. "I didn't mean for it to come out that way."

"It's okay," he said, but his voice sounded funny.

It wasn't okay. And Emma didn't know how to fix any of it. Their relationship was too new, the words were too fresh, and her emotions were too raw.

Instead, she watched Josh climb into the van and pull out of the driveway. The longer she stood there, the more impossible it seemed that she would be able to fix anything. She wanted to apologize to Josh, but she also wanted him to understand her loyalty to her friend, and she didn't know how to justify both. If only he'd turn around.

If only Samantha had never seen them.

Instead, Emma walked alone into her house.

"How was the food pantry?" her dad asked.

She jumped, not expecting him to be waiting for her. The interior smelled smoky, and past her dad's shoulder, flames danced in the fireplace. "Um, good. I'll see you later."

She ignored his quizzical look and trudged upstairs, not wanting to talk to him about what happened. She doubted he'd understand. Josh hadn't, and he was much more understanding than her dad.

The steps squeaked beneath her feet, and she shut her door with a click, each sound reverberating in her ears and giving her a headache.

She tried calling Samantha, but the call went straight to voicemail. She tried texting.

Can we talk?

Emma stared at her phone, waiting for Samantha to respond, but there was nothing. The text didn't switch to Read.

Her best friend was ignoring her over a guy.

Hunching over on herself, she sat on the bed, her foot tapping with anxiety. The entire situation was ridiculous. Why was she letting her best friend dictate who she could date? Why was she letting a guy come between her and her best friend?

She thought about her lifelong friendship with Samantha—all the sleepovers in this very room, giggling and shrieking as they watched movies; the homework and teachers they complained about, commiserating together when their parents told them to tough it out; comparing notes on guys they dated and alerting each other to potential red flags that the other was blind to.

It was meant to be a friendship to last a lifetime.

Yet for some reason, Sam was setting unreasonable boundaries, and Emma didn't understand why.

She checked her phone in the hopes that Sam had responded, but there was silence. She tried calling her again, and once again it went straight to voicemail.

Emma burned with anger. How could her best friend think that because a matchmaker paired her with Josh, once the two of them decided it was a bad match, Emma couldn't date him?

Emma liked Josh. She was attracted to him. She wanted to pursue a relationship with him. Did Sam think she was going to mark him as off-limits though neither he nor Sam were interested in each other? Did that mean that any name on the matchmaker's list was permanently off-limits to Emma?

Her stomach churned. She never should have agreed to stay away from him. And more important, she shouldn't have made Josh feel she was choosing friendship over him. There might be a time that she'd have to make that choice, but today wasn't it. And no good friend would force her to do so.

She paced the confines of her room, her heart pounding. She needed to call him and apologize. But when she dialed his number, it also went straight to voicemail.

Her eyes burned. Staring at the wall of her childhood bedroom plastered with posters of the Foo Fighters and Red Hot Chili Peppers, she saw her budding relationship with Josh fizzling out like a Shabbat candle when the wax was almost gone.

She gave an ironic huff. Josh would appreciate the metaphor.

She wasn't about to let him go. Not without a fight.

Emma pulled out her phone and texted him.

I messed up today. Let me buy you breakfast tomorrow and fix it.

She stared at her phone screen, obsessively tapping it in time to the beat of her heart while she waited for his response. He might have turned off his phone, but he must have seen his screen flash with a message, right? Weren't rabbis always on call?

She sighed with relief when his response lit up her screen.

Ok

Thank goodness.

Josh stood outside the Caffeine Drip as the morning rush passed him and waited for Emma to show. She'd hurt him last night with her pledge to stick with her friend over him. Not that he didn't understand the importance of a lifelong friendship, but her treatment of him wasn't fair. And if they were going to have a relationship together, he needed her to know how she'd hurt him.

He spotted her bouncing curls before the rest of her, bundled in a jacket and scarf, and despite his unhappiness and confusion, he smiled. There was something about those curls that he couldn't resist.

"Hi," she said, biting her lip and gripping her messenger bag until her knuckles whitened. "Thank you for agreeing to this."

"I'm glad you texted," he said.

They entered, ordered their coffees and found an empty table at the back. Sipping his brew, he let the caffeine hum through his veins. After a sleepless night filled with worries about Emma and his grandma and all the changes he was going through, he needed the boost more than usual.

His eyes were gritty, and the noise of the popular coffee shop added to his discomfort. But nothing was going to make him leave until he got some answers from Emma. "So," he said.

"I owe you an apology," she answered.

"An apology, maybe. But I think I'd prefer an explanation."

She nodded, expelling a breath. "Samantha and I have been friends forever. We've both dealt with tough times with our family—her more so than me—and because of that, we've relied on each other when no one else was there to help us."

Josh's chest swelled with sympathy. "I understand tough times," he said. "That's what my grandmother's been for me."

Emma nodded. "Again, out of the three of us, you included this time, my life has definitely been the easiest. Samantha's parents had no business having children, and you lost your parents as a child—I can't imagine what that was like. In comparison to the two of you, my role as the screwup in my family doesn't compare. But at the time, I needed Samantha's support as much as she did mine."

He took a sip of his coffee before speaking. "You know, this doesn't have to be a competition of who suffered through the most difficult upbringing."

"I know that, but there are definite differences and I feel like that needs to be acknowledged."

"Okay," he said.

"In a lot of ways, it's been me and Samantha against the world. We've always been able to count on each other when everyone else might have failed us. Therefore, when she asked me to stay away from you, I said yes without thinking. Without thinking whether or not her request was fair to you or to me."

He leaned forward on the table. Her remorse made her

beautiful mouth frown. Her brown eyes remained glued to his. As hurt and confused as he'd been—as he still might be—he also admired someone who owned up to her faults. And a part of him understood her motivation.

"I think I get it," he said. "I don't like it, but I understand it. And honestly, as much as I don't like it, I can see why you'd support her, someone who has always been on your side. It's scary to move onto someone new."

She nodded. "Especially when we don't know where we'll be in the future." She held up her hand. "I'm not asking for commitment. It's way too early, even for me. We're in the exploration phase of a relationship, and I don't want to rush that. I'm saying that if we compare the two, in theory my loyalty should lie with my best friend."

He swallowed. "Should?"

She gave him a small grin, one that hinted at her sparkle deep inside. "Should," she nodded. "But after I got home, I started thinking about Samantha's demand. I don't fully understand why she made it, but it isn't fair. It leaves us in this limbo where no one is sure of anything."

"I've got to admit, I don't understand her demand, nor do I like it much," he said. "It's not like she and I are going out. We both agreed we're wrong for each other. It would be different if she thought we might work and I didn't."

"I know. And I've tried calling and texting her to find out what's bothering her about the two of us, but she hasn't answered." Emma sipped her coffee and pushed her hair out of her face. "The silent treatment isn't like her. At least, not with me."

"What do you want to do? Because I like you, and I'd like to see where this goes. I know you said it's too early to label anything, but I would like to think of you as my girlfriend. At the same time, I've got to be honest here. I don't want to compete with your best friend. It takes too much energy and makes me doubt myself and you. You've got a choice to make. I hope you make the right one, but I can't force it."

Emma spun her coffee cup in a circle before meeting Josh's gaze. "I'm not the sad little girl any more, wondering why my parents always side with my sister. I love Samantha, and she'll always be my best friend. But I've gotten used to following my dreams without other people's approval. While I do want to talk to Samantha and find out what happened, I also want us to move forward. I like the idea of 'girlfriend.' If you'll still have me."

Appreciation warmed Josh, and happiness made him unable to rein in the grin that creased his entire face. He reached for her hand, the first time he'd touched her since last night. As their fingers entwined, a jolt of recognition ran through him. He'd missed the feel of her. It was like the first time he'd wrapped tefillin when he was a bar mitzvah boy. As he'd wound the leather straps around his arm and recited the prayer, knowledge of what he was now allowed to do made him realize what he'd been missing.

Though he didn't engage in that religious practice often—and he certainly hoped he'd be holding onto Emma way more often than he wrapped the phylacteries—the feelings that ran through him were similar. Connection. Hope. Faith.

"I will most definitely have you," he said.

He pulled her forward and kissed her across the table. Her lips were soft, her breath warm, and she mewed as the kiss deepened. But all too soon, reason returned, and he pulled away.

"I'm sorry about you and Samantha," he said, breathless from their kiss.

Her eyes sparkled and her hair was a little mussed. Just

as he liked it. "Thank you." She lowered her voice. "I wish we weren't here."

"Me, too," he said. "I have an idea. Come with me?"

She nodded, and he took her hand and led her out to his car.

"Where are we going?" she asked.

"My friend's apartment."

Emma frowned, but Josh put a hand on her leg. "Trust me?"

"I do."

Those simple words made his chest expand.

Once inside Ari's apartment, he led Emma to into the living room.

"No one's here," he said. He reached for her hand.

Emma looked around. "No roommate?"

"He's at work until five." He took a step toward her and caressed her cheek.

"No grandmas?"

Josh shook his head. "And no parents."

Emma leaned into his palm. "There's no noise."

"No construction workers, either." He clasped the nape of her neck and drew her to him. The kiss in the coffee shop had been tender and brief. This one he drew out, nibbling on her bottom lip until she opened her mouth. Their tongues danced, and she pressed her body against his. He hardened and pulled away.

"Do you want this?" he asked.

She nodded. "Yes. I want you."

"You're sure?"

He took her hand and led her to the extra bedroom he was using. He shut the door behind them and muttered a curse. He couldn't believe he was unprepared.

Drawing her to him, he pulled her into a hug. "Give me a second. I have to see if Ari has any condoms."

She stepped away. "Don't worry about it. I do."

His eyes widened. "Really?"

She opened her messenger bag and pulled one out. "I'm not stupid enough to go anywhere unprepared."

"I love that about you," he said, as he unbuttoned his shirt.

Emma removed her sweater. His mind buzzed with appreciation and he took a few moments to watch her. Her creamy skin begged him to touch her. Unable to resist, he drew her to him, trailing kisses across her collarbone, over her shoulder and up her neck as his hands roamed her body.

She took a step away, and he paused.

"Am I moving too fast?" he whispered.

"No." Her fingers tickled his chest as she finished unbuttoning his shirt. "You're not naked enough."

He started to say something, but his words died in his throat as her hands dipped inside the waistband of his jeans. His stomach leaped at the contact.

Moments later, they were both naked and lying together in bed. He stared into her eyes, drowning in their chocolatey depths. She touched him, and his skin burned at the contact. His heart pounded against his ribs. He couldn't stand the space between them. Wrapping his arms around her, he drew her close, reveling at the skin-on-skin contact.

When he didn't think he could stand it a second longer, he whispered in her ear, "I need the condom."

She pulled away before pushing him against the pillows and trailing kisses across his chest.

"Emma," he said.

"Shh."

He grabbed the sheets and fisted his hands as she rose next to him and slowly unwrapped the foil.

When she touched him, he bucked his hips. Once sheathed,

he grasped her upper arms and pulled her on top of him. "I need you now," he said between gritted teeth.

She straddled him, lowering herself, all the while keeping her gaze locked on his.

God, she was beautiful. He waited for her to set the pace and once she was settled, she leaned over and kissed him. Their bodies moved as one. Need built in him until he wasn't sure how much longer he could last. He touched her, wanting her enjoyment to peak. When he thought he couldn't hold out much more, she gasped his name, her body shaking and her muscles pulsing around him. His release came only a second or two later, and she collapsed on top of him.

His pulse pounded in his ears, their bodies were slick with sweat, and he couldn't tell where her body started and his stopped.

They were one, and he'd never been more satisfied in his life.

He drifted in the hazy afterglow until she eventually moved off of him. He pulled her close, and they lay together in sleepy wonder.

When his eyes opened again, he stared straight into Emma's face, her cheeks flushed, her lips curved.

"That was…" he said.

"Incredible," she answered.

Joy ran through him. "I'm glad we agree," he whispered, brushing a lock of hair off her face.

She bit her lip. "Maybe we should try it again, though, to make sure. I mean, make-up sex is always earth-shattering, I think we should find out if regular sex is as good."

He pulled her toward him once again. "Anytime, anywhere," he said.

She rested her chin on her hand, elbow leaning into the pillow. "What are your plans for the rest of today?"

"Ha," he said. "Actually, as much as I'd love to spend the entire day with you right here, at some point, I have to check on my grandma, make sure she's settling in and help her to unpack."

Emma nodded.

"However," he said, "if you need help with anything, let me know."

"I'm at that point right now where I don't know what I need." A worried look crossed her face.

"Ah, you've reached overwhelm."

"Reached? I think I've been there from the start."

He shook his head. "Well, you've hidden it well. I'm impressed. Trust me, when I'm overwhelmed, everyone notices."

She studied him. "I can't picture you overwhelmed."

"Ha! During my first year as a brand-new rabbi, I was charged with leading the monthly youth services. I must have written and rewritten every service at least eight times, printed out reams of paper with my sermons, only to change them and have to reprint them. I actually broke the temple's office printer four times that year."

"Impressive," Emma said.

"Anyway, I was stuck in front of my computer for so long, my head ached and my hair was a mess from my pulling it all the time. Actually, I'm surprised I didn't get a bald patch or two. My kippah was permanently crooked. I didn't walk anywhere, I ran. One of the senior rabbis pulled me aside one day and told me I needed to manage myself better or I was going to cause concern among the congregation, which would get back to the temple board and the rest of the senior rabbis."

"Seriously?"

Josh nodded. "Apparently, showing how overwhelmed I was wasn't inspiring confidence in anyone."

Frowning, Emma leaned forward. "That's ridiculous. I

mean, I'm not saying you shouldn't be aware of the impression you give, but rabbis are human, too."

He shrugged. "We are, but shh, no one is supposed to know." He winked. "Anyway, my point is that you're going to do fine. Trust me."

"I'm gonna lean into your trust for the moment," Emma said, before rolling over. "And as much as I'd love to stay here with you, I have to get to the store."

His stomach clenched at the mention of *store* instead of *home*.

"Call me later?" he asked after they'd dressed. He walked her to the door of the apartment, drew her to him and kissed her. Her body against his, the sound of her breath, the taste of her lips made him want to stay in this place for as long as possible. Especially because earlier this morning, he'd thought he lost her.

But too soon, she pulled away. Their hands remained entwined as she stepped over the threshold, their arms stretching out until he had no choice but to let go.

But this time, unlike last night, he knew where they stood.

Chapter Nine

Emma returned to The Book Nook to a cacophony of raised voices, whining power tools and sawdust and paint chips everywhere. She gingerly stepped over the threshold, trying simultaneously to stay out of the way but still observe the progress. The front two rooms were empty of people but filled with drop cloths, ladders and supplies. As she went deeper into the building, a flurry of curse words greeted her.

"Hello?" She raised her voice over the din, and the room went silent.

Her contractor, Jim, came forward. "Emma, perfect timing. We have a problem."

Her stomach dropped. "What kind of problem?"

He led her into the kitchen, and her blood froze. What was once a warm and homey kitchen now looked like a war zone. Dry wall buckled, the sink sat in the middle of the floor, water puddles warped the hardwood floors and the humidity in the room made her curly hair frizz.

"What happened?" she asked, aghast.

The contractor pointed to a gaping hole in the wall separating the kitchen from the dining room. "Long story short, thanks to the cold snap last night, the pipes burst. It's caused a significant amount of damage and is going to need a massive amount of repair." He sighed. "Basically, what we thought we could save by using the existing kitchen, we're going to need to spend to fix the problem and replace everything."

He continued to explain what happened and the fix required, but all Emma could focus on was how far over budget she was going to be.

And she couldn't afford to go over budget.

She grasped at anything she could think of. "What if we rip out the kitchen entirely and make the entire ground floor a bookstore?" She could always hook up a coffee maker or two to the wall and bring in pastries from a local bakery.

"With the amount of repairs necessary to make this space safe and usable, you're still not going to save that much money."

Crap, she'd still have to spend money she didn't have. Her temples throbbed like the hammers the construction team used. "The inspector didn't catch the faulty pipe?" she asked.

"Unfortunately not."

She rubbed her forehead, wishing away the ache, the water and the extra problems that were quickly accumulating. "Can you draw up an estimate of repairs and some options of what we can do? I've got to call the insurance company."

He nodded. "I'll do it myself and have the guys work on the other rooms in the meantime."

"Thank you." Her mind spun in a dozen different directions, none of them good. She couldn't go to the bank to ask for a bigger loan. They'd given her as much as she could get with her credit rating. Part of her wanted to ask Muriel if she'd known about this, but without a doubt, the woman was blameless. This could have happened to anyone. Unfortunately, this was bad luck.

She had a little extra cushion in her bank account. She'd have to hope the kitchen repair was smaller than anticipated and that the insurance company would cover it in time for her planned opening.

Forty-five minutes later, she'd spoken to her insurance company and was trying to figure out how she'd find the money for the deductible, much less handle the blown timeline. As a brand-new customer, she didn't have the history with her insurance company to make them willing to dole out money on faith. And when she'd applied for insurance coverage, she'd only been able to afford the option with the highest deductible. Which meant she couldn't afford to fix this on her own.

Jim found her upstairs in Josh's old bedroom. It was the quietest room in the house. Plus, it made her think of him, and that brought a much-needed smile to her face.

By the expression on Jim's face, however, she wasn't going to smile much longer. "The fix is going to add an additional twenty thousand to the project."

"That much?" Emma's chest constricted. No amount of math—girl or otherwise—was going to make that money magically appear in her bank account.

"At least," Jim said. "And probably more."

He handed her his tablet with the cost breakdown listed, and her hopes plummeted.

"What about only the must-dos?" she asked.

"These *are* the must-dos."

Emma collapsed against the wall. "I don't have the money for the deductible, much less this," she said. "I need time to make arrangements." Though she had no idea what those arrangements were.

Well, that wasn't true. She had one option, an option so horrible, she didn't want to consider it. She needed time to come up with something else. *Anything* else.

"I get it," he said. "But don't wait too long, or remediation costs are going to go up." He left Emma alone.

Temples pounding and stomach roiling, Emma moved blindly downstairs to the back door and exited out onto the patio. When she'd originally seen the flagstone outdoor space, her mind conjured adorable iron tea tables with bright-colored table linens in the warm weather and potentially heated igloos in the colder weather. Now, as she stood in the backyard inhaling deep shaky breaths, she only saw potential for lawn rot, broken flagstones and lawsuits.

If her contractor hadn't just broken the bad news to her, she'd be inclined to think she'd spent too much time with her sister, the brilliant family lawyer. And while Alyse wasn't the cause of Emma's thought train, she definitely was one of the destinations.

There must be another way.

Her mind raced, her feet matching the pace of all the ideas that zipped through her mind. But none of them would work. Another loan? She'd maxed out. The lottery? She didn't play.

She sighed before pulling her phone out of her pocket. She gritted her teeth as she punched in the number and listened to the phone ring.

"Emma, darling, how are you?"

"Mom, can I come talk to you and Dad?"

Entering their house twenty minutes later, she rehearsed a million different ways to ask the dreaded question. She disliked all of her options.

"Emma, we're in here!" her mom called from the living room, and Emma followed the sound of her voice.

She wiped her sweaty palms on the thighs of her jeans, entered the room and kissed both of her parents. Sitting across from them, she curled her toes inside her sneakers to keep from tapping her foot.

"What did you want to discuss with us?" her dad asked, exchanging a look with her mom.

"The Book Nook."

Their expressions flattened, as if they were trying to keep their thoughts to themselves. But she'd heard enough of their arguments to know what they were thinking, even if they said nothing.

"What about it? Are the previous owners giving you a hard time?" her mom asked.

"Not at all, the Axelrods are wonderful."

"You're lucky," her dad said. "That was pretty risky giving them extra time to stay in your building. What if they'd damaged something?"

"It was all in the contract, Dad. They were responsible for any damage they caused. But everything turned out fine." She made a fist in her lap.

Her mom's gaze tracked the movement. "And?" she asked.

"The cold snap last night froze one of the pipes, causing a huge leak in the kitchen."

Both her parents gasped. "Oh no. Was there a lot of damage?" her mom asked.

Emma nodded. "It's going to cost at least another twenty thousand dollars, which I don't have."

"Emma, how many times did I tell you to leave yourself a cushion?" her dad asked.

"Even aside from this business venture of yours," her mother added, "you always need a financial cushion to protect you in an emergency."

The weight of their combined disapproval sucked the air out of the room. The attempt to remain calm, speak rationally and breathe overwhelmed her.

"I do have a cushion. I also have insurance. But I'm still short the money I need to pay the deductible, much less redo the kitchen. And the longer this takes to repair, the farther back my opening day goes, which means the longer it will take for me to generate income."

"That's why you have to prioritize what you do," her dad said. "Maybe this is a sign you've bitten off more than you can chew. Start small. You don't need a kitchen for a bookstore."

"I did prioritize," Emma countered. "Even if I leave it empty, I still have to repair it."

"Start small," her mom repeated. "Skip the upstairs and live here. If your bookstore is a success, you can use the money you make to fix the kitchen and renovate the upstairs floors."

Emma tried not to let her mom's use of the word *if* offend her.

Her dad nodded. "That's right. Maybe speak to your sister about how she budgets her salary. I'm sure she can give you a lot of useful pointers."

Tension raced along Emma's spine. Of course they wanted her to talk to Alyse. What would a day be like without Emma the screwup being compared to Alyse the golden child? As she thought this, a niggle of guilt interrupted. Her sister didn't like the comparison any more than she did.

"Maybe she can." Emma forced out the admission, if only to stay on her parents' good side. "But what I do need is help with the financing."

Her mom pursed her lips. "I don't think Alyse has the money to help you, Em. With all of her responsibilities, the last thing she should have to do is bail you out."

As if Emma had committed a crime punishable by law.

"What about you and Dad?" Emma asked. The question scraped her throat raw, reminding her of when she'd come down with strep as a child. "Is there any way you could loan me the money? I'd pay you back as soon as I started to make a profit, before I pay back the bank."

Both of them immediately shook their heads.

"Out of the question," her dad said. "There's no guarantee this business venture of yours will work. It's already run into a setback. We can't risk our life savings, especially since there's a good chance you won't be able to pay us back for years, if at all."

Emma sat there, filled with disappointment. "I can't believe you don't have faith in me," she said. "I'm your daughter."

"Lending money to family or friends is never a good idea, sweetheart," her mom said. "It puts burdens on the relationship that can't be overcome."

"But my business plan is solid, the insurance is going to come through, and I'll be able to pay you back."

"And what happens if The Book Nook fails?" her dad asked. "You'll have to pay the bank back first, not us, no matter how much you might want to. And with what money? No, I'm sorry, honey, but I think you need to revise your business plan and remember to read the fine print. Make it smaller, more manageable for someone like you who's never done something like this before. You need to protect yourself."

Why did they always identify the negatives when talking with her? With her sister, they encouraged her to reach for the stars. But with her, they constantly pointed out all the ways she could fail.

Were they right?

She rose, unable to continue a pointless conversation. "That's it, then," she said.

"Emma, don't be like that," her mom said. "I wish you could understand that we're only looking out for you. We don't want you to bite off more than you can chew."

Emma paused in the doorway, her heart pounding. "And I wish you had more confidence in my abilities. You've never stopped by to see my store and my plans for it. I guess neither of us is going to get what we want."

She shut the door behind her, unable to see through her tears.

Now what?

Josh rose from Ari's guest bed, stretched and sighed in relief as his vertebrae cracked. He might have recently celebrated his twenty-ninth birthday, but his body would swear it was his seventy-ninth.

Sleeping on an uncomfortable bed would do that to you.

But Ari's offer to crash at his place until Josh's grandma was fully settled was a godsend. He could continue to help her unpack and get settled, without having to worry about commuting from the city. Plus, it enabled him to be closer to Emma, which was a huge plus.

Ari had broached the subject of Josh moving in with him if he ever decided to give up his Manhattan life—something Josh never would have considered before but was looking more and more attractive.

Despite how happy his grandma was about her move into Marble Head, Josh still worried. He wanted the staff to know family cared about her and might pop in unexpectedly. While he understood that she lived in the least restrictive part of the Marble House, he needed to make sure that she was taken care of and treated well. And for some reason, knowing she was there, rather than in her own home, made him worry more.

His grandmother would tell him he was crazy. She would tell him her favorite Jewish saying about worrying: *anxiety in the heart of a person causes dejection, but a good word will turn it into joy.*

It never made sense to him. It still didn't, despite him being a rabbi.

And then there was Emma. This early on, he wanted to spend as much time with her as possible. Commuting back and forth would be difficult.

He paused. Honestly, commuting to see her was going to be tough no matter where they were in their relationship. He thought again about Ari's offer. With Josh's job in Manhattan, it didn't make sense to live here. Even a reverse commute would be difficult, because with the train schedules, he'd spend at least three hours a day traveling to and from the city.

He'd have to commute to see Emma, though. And his grandmother.

What if there was a way to move out here? What if Rabbi Moskowitz needed more permanent assistance?

His stomach churned. There was an entire process and timeline to finding a rabbinic job. It wasn't as easy to make a sudden switch as it was outside of the rabbinate.

He was learning so much at his synagogue in Manhattan, but there might be some incredible opportunities in his hometown synagogue. Plus, he'd get to see his grandma more often, have an easier time seeing Emma.

He parked his car at Marble House, and before he got out, left a message for Rabbi Moskowitz. Then he walked to his grandmother's unit.

"Joshy!" Her voice rose with happiness, and she limped over to him.

He frowned. "How's your leg? And where's your cane?"

She patted his hand. "It's sore but getting better. I'm a little stiff right now. Don't worry, I still use it."

"If you say so." Maybe he should mention it to one of the staff. He entered her apartment, noting the boxes lined up at the sides of the room. "Where do you want to start first?"

"I'd like the kitchenette set up. Everything all over the place is making me kvetchy."

He smiled. "You? You're a ray of sunshine, Grandma."

He remembered how easygoing his grandmother was until he'd leave his stuff all over the kitchen when he got home from school. First, her shoulders would stiffen and her lips would thin. She wouldn't say anything, not wanting to nag, but she'd sigh. Loudly. And if he didn't get the hint, which as a thirteen-year-old boy wasn't unusual, she'd clear her throat. Occasionally, if he was able to get his head out of the cloud of Axe body spray he liberally doused himself with, he'd notice his grandmother's distress and ask if she was coming down with a cold. Usually, he was oblivious, forcing her to ask him to clean up his stuff. And when he inevitably forgot, she'd yell.

Now, his grandmother gave him the stink eye. He gulped, following her into the kitchenette.

He pulled over a chair and pointed. "Why don't you sit and direct me? The room is too small for both of us to unpack and arrange."

"You're managing me, but I'll let you do it this time," she said, sitting on the hard chair and wiggling until she was comfortable. "But only if you tell me what's going on in that keppe of yours?"

"What do you mean?" He held up bakeware, and his grandmother pointed to the correct cabinet.

"I know you. You worry about me when you're at a crossroads. What's the problem?"

"There's no problem," he said. Just because a million questions, concerns and catastrophes occupied his mind, not to mention how much he hated change, didn't mean there was a problem.

His grandmother drummed her red-painted nails on her pants leg. "Gee, if I'm as stupid as you think I am, it's a wonder you've grown up into the kind and successful man you are today."

"Grandma, I've never thought you were stupid. You're brilliant."

"Mm-hmm."

He sighed. "Fine, maybe I have a problem." Or twelve.

"And maybe I'm old."

Josh paused. "If you think I'm going anywhere near that, you're crazy. Just not stupid."

"Okay, tell me what's going on." She patted his back, and for a moment, he wished he was fourteen again.

"New York is inconvenient."

"It's also noisy, fast-paced and has great theater," she said.

"Don't forget the restaurants." He held up two pot holders with penguins on them, and she pointed to the drawer next to the stove.

"I live and work in Manhattan, but you live here now, and Emma is here, too."

"I've lived here forever," she said.

"But not *here* here. What if you need something?"

She took his face in his hands and squeezed his cheeks. "Joshy, the whole reason I moved into this place is to lighten your load. If I need anything, there are all kinds of people who can help me. Me being here isn't a problem."

"It's new and different. It isn't home."

She sighed. "Joshy, you've got to get past this change aversion you have."

"And you've got to learn to cook for one or two instead of twelve, yet here we are."

His grandmother laughed. "In all seriousness, there is no reason for you to have to come home for me unless we plan a dinner or a holiday or something. However, Emma, that's a different story."

For once in his life, he was glad his grandma was focused on his love life. Such as it was.

"She's busy with her bookstore. She's not going to have time to visit me in New York, which means I'll have to come out here if we want to see each other."

His grandmother pinned him with one of her stares, the kind she gave him when he was rude or used bad manners. "You're the boyfriend, Joshy. Even if she didn't have a bookstore, it wouldn't be right for you to make her travel to you."

His shoulders slumped as he swallowed his disbelief. "So much for female empowerment."

His grandma pointed to the cabinet where she wanted him to stack her dishes. "Female empowerment and manners are not mutually exclusive. Women can do anything, but that doesn't mean men should be schlubs."

"I'm not a schlub, Grandma. I'm saying all the traveling is going to be difficult."

"What's the alternative?"

He paused, plate in hand. "I called Rabbi Moskowitz. Is it crazy of me to think about taking a job interview out here?"

She patted his knee. "There's nothing crazy about exploring options, Joshy. As long as you're doing it for the right reason."

He hadn't seriously considered it before today. But the idea appealed to him. "Wanting to be closer to you is a pretty good reason, I think," he said.

"If you're doing it for me, don't."

He frowned. "There is nothing wrong with loving you so much that I want to be near you."

"There is if it diminishes what you can do with your future."

"Rabbis move temples all the time. What's wrong with that?"

"Absolutely nothing. But if the only reason is because you want to be close to me, don't pursue it. Because I'll be unhappy with you hovering."

"It's not just you, though, Grandma. Emma's here, too."

"And you like her?"

"I do."

"Does she like you?"

"Yes. We both want to see where this goes."

"That's not enough of a reason to move here, either. Don't change jobs for a woman. Because as much as I like her, if things don't work out, you've ruined your rabbinic career for someone who doesn't matter."

Someone who didn't matter? Emma mattered…a lot. "She matters to me, Grandma."

His grandma stared at him for several seconds. Josh tried not to squirm. "Good. I wanted to hear you say that."

He would have rolled his eyes, but somehow, he thought it would make his grandmother laugh harder than she already was. Her shoulders shook, and a few snorts escaped.

"Glad you're getting pleasure at my expense," he said.

She bit her lip before rising and walking the few steps to where he leaned against the counter. Wrapping him in a hug, she squeezed. "You always give me pleasure just by breathing. But I wanted to know if you liked Emma. And clearly, you do." She pulled away and held up a finger. "I'm still not thrilled with the idea of you changing jobs for a woman, or anyone, really, other than yourself. But as I said earlier, it can't hurt to talk to Rabbi Moskowitz and review your options. As for how you and Emma are going to find time to see each other? That's a conversation the two of you have to have yourselves, without me. Speaking of conversations, you should probably have one with Ms. Match."

"Yeah, you're right."

"Ah, my three favorite words…well, other than 'I love you.'" She looked at the gold watch on her wrist. "I've got to get ready for a social gathering," she said. "Thank you for clearing up the kitchen. Now I can move around in here."

"How about I stay and unpack the rest of the apartment?"

She stared, eyes wide. "No, sir. I'll never find where you put my things."

He reared away from her. "What?"

"You and I organize differently. You know that."

He did. He tended toward sloppy, and when he arranged things, it was by fit, rather than utility. It drove his grandmother crazy. Still, it would be easier for her…

"Are you sure?" he asked.

"Positive. Tomorrow we can work on my bedroom."

Rising, he broke down the boxes and brought them to the trash room. When he returned to the apartment, he looked around. It was starting to shape up.

"I'm glad you've got social activities," he said.

She nodded. "I told you, this is the right place for me. Now go and talk to Emma. I'll tell you all about my activities tomorrow."

Once in his car, he listened to Rabbi Moskowitz's message and returned her call.

"Rabbi Moskowitz? It's Rabbi Axelrod. Josh."

She chuckled. "Hi, Josh. I'm glad you called earlier. I'd love to have you come in and talk about the temple's needs. As you can probably figure out, we're late to the rabbinic search process, so having you show interest is a godsend."

He scratched his cheek as he thought about his current boss. "I'd definitely like to come in and talk to you, but I also have to let my senior rabbi know I'm looking. Especially since this is outside of the typical hiring process."

"I have way more respect for you for saying that," she said.

"How about you come in on Sunday? We'll chat and discuss next steps. That will also give you time to talk to people on your end."

He pulled up his calendar and made a note. "Sounds great."

They hung up, he left a message for Ms. Match and took a deep breath. He had a lot of work to do.

Emma hadn't looked at her phone all day. She'd been too busy talking to the insurance company and the contractor and the bank, trying to work out how she could cover the cost of repairs, keep moving on the bookstore construction and open on time.

When Josh called at the end of the day and commented on how he hadn't heard from her, she snapped.

"Do you have any idea how busy I am?" Her voice rose in frustration before wobbling with unshed tears.

"What can I do to help?" Josh's concern did nothing to calm her. If anything, it made those annoying tears spill over. Especially since he didn't take the bait and yell back.

"Nothing. I can't talk to you now."

"Have you eaten? How about I bring over some food?"

"Not everything can be solved with food," she cried. "You have no idea what's been happening. There's no *here* to bring food over to."

"What do you mean?"

Emma's breath hitched. She didn't meant to blurt that out, especially to Josh. This was his former home, and he was attached to the past. The news was going to hurt him as much as it hurt her. "Forget it," she said. "Don't worry, I'll take care of it." Somehow.

"Emma, tell me what's going on."

"There was a flood," she whispered.

"I'm on my way over."

"No," she cried, but he'd already hung up.

She slid down the wall in the former living room and covered her face with her hands. She didn't have the wherewithal to deal with Josh. Or anyone for that matter. She needed to get The Book Nook situated, and that was all she could think about.

Not only did she not want to deal with his reaction to his former home, but she didn't know how to deal with him as her boyfriend, if that was what he was. Especially right now when all her focus was on getting her business back on track. How was she supposed to devote energy to him when all of it was needed to solve this problem?

By the time the knock sounded on the front door, her heart was racing, and she was in a full-blown panic, curled on the floor. If she opened the door, she'd have to deal with his emotions, too. She couldn't.

"Hey," his voice whispered at her ear. "Take it easy," he said. "Everything is going to be okay."

He was wrong. Nothing was going to be okay, but she didn't have the energy or the focus to answer him.

A moment later, his body pressed against her back as he sat next to her. His hand rubbed her shoulders in a soothing motion—not too hard, not too soft. He didn't speak. The silence cushioned her. She focused on breathing in time to the movement of his hand. And slowly, the panic receded.

Opening her eyes, his long legs stretched next to her, clad in jeans and sneakers. She reached out her hand and rested the back of it against him. The denim was soft, and the contact grounded her.

Still remaining silent, he placed his hand over hers.

Expelling a deep breath, she sat up, and he cradled her against his chest. He was warm, his heartbeat steady. She could get used to this. Except she had too much to do.

Pushing away from him, she rose.

He followed her. *Dammit.*

"Talk to me?" His quiet voice didn't reflect any of the hysteria she'd imagined. She looked at him askance, sizing him up.

He stood there, letting her gaze run over him, from those soft jeans she liked to the three-quarter zip in a slightly lighter shade than his deep blue eyes, to his dark hair, slightly mussed.

"A pipe burst." Those three words were harder to say to him than the famous three words everyone talked about. She braced herself for his reaction.

There was none. At least, none that she could see.

"Where?" he asked.

She led him toward the kitchen, stopping in the entryway. Surveying the scene from his perspective, she took in the gaping holes where the drywall had been, the multiple fans—and the noise associated with them—situated around the room, and the garbage strewn everywhere.

"Wow."

She cringed, waiting for a torrent of words to come. Except, they didn't. She waited another few seconds before turning to him. "That's it?"

He stuffed his hands in his pockets and rocked on his heels. "Nothing else I say is going to be helpful. I want to support you. Tell me what you need—if you know. And if you don't know yet, I'll be silent support." He looked her up and down. "I mean this in the best way possible, but you look like you need it."

She honestly didn't know whether to laugh or cry or smack him. Probably shouldn't smack him, since he was doing everything he could to be supportive. And at some point, she was going to appreciate that, even if right this second she couldn't get past breathing.

"Twenty thousand dollars."

He frowned. "What?"

"I need twenty thousand dollars. The insurance company can't pay out for a few weeks because it's a brand-new policy, and I missed that fine print when I signed, I can't afford my deductible, I can't increase my loan, and the contractor needs money to do the work. Which I understand, but every day that nothing is done to this..." she swung out her arm to encompass the entire room "...is another day of water damage that increases the amount of money needed to fix it. But as of today, the cost is twenty thousand dollars."

He stepped gingerly into the room. "You need everything in here cleaned out so that it can dry."

"I know. I was going to do that tonight."

He looked at her, eyebrow raised, before pulling out his phone and tapping out a text.

She watched him, too tired to ask what he was doing. She wasn't delusional enough to think he was Venmoing the money to her. Wouldn't that be crazy?

Another knock on the door sounded, and he brightened.

"That's dinner."

"Dinner?"

He nodded. "You have to eat. So do I. I ordered Chinese food."

Her stomach growled. Not usually one to miss meals, she'd been too nauseated to eat today, but now she was starving. She took the food from the delivery guy and brought it into the living room. They sat on the floor and silently devoured the beef and broccoli, lo mein, spare ribs and fried rice.

As Emma started collecting the garbage, the doorbell rang.

Josh rose. "That should be reinforcements."

"Reinforcements?" She had to figure out a way to speak like a normal person again, but for the moment, she couldn't do anything other than repeat what Josh said.

He nodded and opened the door. Three guys walked in, carrying crowbars, hammers and a bunch of other things Emma couldn't identify.

"Hold on," she said, scrambling to her feet. "What the heck is going on?"

Josh turned to her. "I don't have twenty thousand dollars to give you. I can't make the insurance company hurry up their payment or the bank give you more money. I also can't force the contractor to be a mensch and help you out for free. What I can do is provide labor so we can remove all the wet things from the room."

"But what if that causes more of a problem?" Emma asked. "What if we remove something we shouldn't?"

Josh pointed at the big blond guy. "This is Matt. He worked construction over the summers to pay for college. He's an engineer. He knows stuff."

She would have commented on Josh's description, but she was too stunned to do anything but nod. And since Matt was also nodding at what Josh said, she and he probably looked like matching marionettes.

She stopped nodding.

"I'll double-check what's what as soon as we go into the room before we wreck anything," Matt said.

Emma looked at Josh. He hadn't freaked out. He hadn't criticized her. He'd come up with an immediate solution to her problem and handled it without adding to her stress.

She rushed into his arms and squeezed him tight.

Wrapping his arms around her, he held her while she whispered, "Thank you," over and over again into his shoulder.

"Shhh," he said, rubbing her back.

She wanted to stay in his arms forever. All her fears of him finding out, all her disappointment over her parents' reaction, all her stress over the flood, lessened. She wasn't alone. And while she was perfectly capable of opening the bookstore on her own, she needed help to deal with this emergency.

Josh, the man who hated change, who cherished his past and never wanted to leave his home in the first place, had stepped up.

Restored, she pulled away, and Josh let her go.

She gazed up at him. "Thank you," she said again, her voice now firm.

"You've said that a couple times." He turned to his friends. "Ready to get started?"

As a group, they attacked the kitchen, with Emma pulling her weight as well. Armed with protective masks and work gloves, they removed the moldy, wet detritus. Tearing out the soggy drywall was oddly satisfying, and Emma focused her frustration on the necessary destruction.

Thwack! *My parents are unfair.*

Crrrrack! *I was an idiot for not reading the fine print.*

Bang! *Starting a business is hard.*

Sweat poured down her back, her breath came in gasps, and her arms ached. And for the first time since she'd started the bookstore, confidence flowed through her.

As she carried another load of debris to the dumpster, she nodded at Josh. "This might be the best cure for anxiety ever."

He tossed his garbage bag over the rim and reached for Emma's, tossing that as well. "You'd recommend flooding your kitchen? Maybe adding it to the business plan?"

He winked, and her heart melted.

"Not in the slightest. But I might consider adding *do demolition yourself.* It's cathartic."

"I like seeing you smile," he said. He leaned over and kissed her.

"Thank you for your help. I thought… Well, I thought you'd have a different reaction to all of this." She gestured vaguely toward the building.

"It's not about me," he said. "This is your business. You suffered an emergency, and I came up with a possible solution to part of it. Reacting any other way wouldn't have been productive."

She leaned up and gave him a deeper, harder kiss. He smelled of sweat and drywall, and she'd never found anything sexier."

When they parted, he held her upper arms and craned his neck. "Did you sniff me?"

Her face heated. If only she could melt into the ground. But he was still holding her—which was nice, actually—and melting would probably result in her needing more repair money that she didn't have. Instead, she closed her eyes. "Maybe."

His low chuckle made her open them again.

"If I wasn't exhausted, I'd suggest ditching the guys, going upstairs, and maybe christening one of your new rooms," he said.

Sympathy mixed with humor, and she brightened. "A, you're a rabbi, so 'christening' might be frowned upon. At least call it something else. B, the rooms are messy, and the floor is hard. After the work we've done, I want soft. And C, I think I owe you and the guys ice cream and cookies. It's probably wrong to ditch them right now. But I'll definitely take a rain check."

"Rain check?" Josh asked. "Maybe you'll come to our seder?"

Emma's stomach dropped. Passover with a rabbi? And his grandmother? Who probably followed the laws more than she or her own family did. Like, they probably ate matzah the entire time and said all the prayers in Hebrew and… Her mind spiraled in a million different directions. She took a breath and decided to ignore the invitation. Instead, she turned toward the others. "What flavors of ice cream do you want? My treat."

Emma noted everyone's requests and placed the order. She sneaked a glance at Josh, who stared at her, a thoughtful look on his face.

Please don't talk to me about Passover, she thought. *I'm not ready for this.*

Josh's phone rang, and he walked away to answer.

She sighed with relief, hoping whatever call he received would distract him enough to forget about the invitation.

When he returned, his face was ashen. "My grandma's at the hospital. I've got to go."

Before Emma had a chance to respond, he raced from the room, the slamming of the door echoing in her ears.

Chapter Ten

"You threw a kegger?" Josh raged. "What did you do? Move into a frat house?"

He stood in the emergency room, behind the sliding curtain that pretended to double as a privacy cover. Only, his voice was raised loud enough, he was sure the entire wing could hear him. He didn't care. Especially because his grandmother's three friends were also in the same emergency room, with their shocked families by their sides.

His grandmother lay on the gurney and hiccuped. An IV bag was attached to her mottled hand. She was propped on her side. And she stank of alcohol.

She tried to glare at him, but her eyes kept rolling. "There was no beer involved," she said around a loud burp. "It was gin. Daphne has been steeping it for days in honor of my arrival."

"Grandma! What the hell?"

"Don't swear, Joshy. And lower your voice. My head is killing me."

"Good!" He wanted to scream at her, make her understand how she'd freaked him out. Make her see how wrong she was. But her squinty-eyed look tugged at his heart. He lowered his voice.

"Grandma, you're lucky they didn't kick you out."

The director of Marble House had met him at the hospital, gone over all the rules his grandmother broke—public intoxication being the biggest one—and gave her a pass since she was new and still adjusting to being there.

She was damn lucky. If it were up to him, Josh wasn't sure he would have been as magnanimous. His grandmother's other friends were similarly excused, not because they were new, but because they'd been trying to make Muriel feel welcome. They were, however, banned from planning any social activities for residents for the next three months.

"Stop being angry, Joshy, we were having a little fun."

"A little fun is one martini. Or a sing-along. They pumped your stomach."

"Yeah, I don't recommend that," she said with a grimace. "I think next time, she should adjust her recipe slightly."

"Next time?" His voice squeaked like a teenager. "Grandma, there can't be a next time."

"I know, Joshy, I was teasing you."

He shook his head. "You're not funny."

A patter of footsteps outside the curtain made him look up. The curtain slid over, and Emma stood there, panting.

"I'm sorry, I came as soon as I could, but I had to leave money for the ice cream and make sure your friends were okay with me leaving and—"

Emma paused mid run-on sentence. She narrowed her gaze at his grandmother. "You're okay, Mrs. Axelrod… Muriel?"

Josh rose and put his arm around Emma. "She's hungover but fine. You're nice to have come, but I'm about done with my sympathy for her."

"Josh, that's not nice," Emma said.

"Listen to Emma, Joshy."

He inhaled before explaining to Emma what happened. She covered her mouth with her hand. By the time Josh finished his explanation, she was spluttering.

"Can I come to your parties, Muriel? They sound like a lot of fun."

"What?" Josh gasped.

"See, Joshy, you should loosen up a little." His grandmother hiccuped again.

Emma put a soothing hand on his arm, leaning into him. "But in all seriousness, I'm glad you're okay. You worried Josh and me." She turned to him and caressed his face. "I've never seen skin quite that shade of gray."

He leaned into her palm, warmth splaying across his cheek from her touch. Finally, his nerves eased, but he hated the concern that bled from her eyes.

"Thank you for coming," he said. "You're exhausted. Go home and relax, and I'll call you later."

"You're as tired as I am. More so, since you did more heavy lifting than I did. I'm staying."

He rested his forehead against hers, feeling the exhaustion creep over his skin. "Thank you." Pulling away, he turned to his grandmother. "Seriously, I need you to be more careful in the future, okay?"

She patted his hand. "I will. I'm sorry." She shut her eyes momentarily, then blinked them open. "Do you remember the youth group party your junior year in high school?"

He pulled up a chair and sat next to his grandmother, motioning Emma over as well. Pulling her onto his lap, he wrapped his arms around her waist, as much for his own comfort as to keep her steady. "I do," he said with a groan.

"Youth group party? This I want to hear," Emma said.

"It was a shul-in," Josh said. "The youth group was getting ready for our Purim carnival on Sunday morning, so Saturday night, we all went to the temple, decorated the social hall and prepared the games and slept over in the youth group lounge."

"I urged him to go, thinking it would be fun for him to get to know all the youth group members," his grandmother said.

Josh nodded. "I knew the ones in my grade but didn't know anyone else, and honestly, wasn't sure I wanted to, but grandma told me to go, so I did. Anyway, a few of the seniors sneaked alcohol in, and a bunch of us got hammered."

"At the temple? Oh my gosh." Emma's mouth dropped. "I can't believe you did that."

Josh shrugged. "To be fair, I didn't know the punch was spiked, and once I tried it, I *really* liked it."

Emma laughed. "I'll bet."

"I drank enough to get violently ill, and everyone got scared and alerted the youth advisor who called the rabbi and my grandma."

"Oh boy," Emma said.

"Yeah. It wasn't pretty. Grandma grounded me, the youth advisor banned me from the next event, and the rabbi made me read Torah at services for the next three weeks."

Emma's eyes widened. He loved her expressions. "Wow. Didn't that turn you off participating in services?"

Josh shrugged. "You'd think so, but by that third week, I was pretty confident in my Torah-reading skills."

"He volunteered to read during the High Holy Day services," his grandma added.

Josh's face warmed at the pride in her voice. And then he remembered the risk she'd taken.

"You'd think she'd have remembered what happened to me," he said, a challenge in his voice as he glared at his grandmother.

She patted his hand.

A groan from the next bed over, followed by the curtain swiping open between the beds, made Josh glance over.

Daphne struggled to sit up, her face pale. "Why is everyone screaming?"

Great, the hungover mixologist friend.

"Daphne, how are you feeling?" his grandma asked. "You look a little peaked."

"Shh, whisper, please."

His grandmother repeated her question in a whisper.

"What? I can't hear you?"

Josh would have laughed if they were anywhere but in a hospital with the woman who gave his grandmother alcohol poisoning.

Emma's shoulders shook, and she turned away from the older women.

He led Emma outside the curtains, where she gave into her giggles.

"I don't know how you can laugh at this."

She bit her lip. "Come on, it's funny."

He stared at her.

"I know you were worried about your grandma, and rightfully so, but now that we know she's okay, you have to admit that hungover old ladies is kinda funny."

His lips twitched.

She raised an eyebrow in challenge. On principle, he didn't want to let her win, but the laughter bubbled in his chest. He shook his head, partially at her and partially at the traitorous laughter, but it was useless. It burst from his lips in a quick chuckle.

The release also let out some of the anxiety swirling in his stomach. The muscles in his neck loosened. He took a deep breath and paced outside his grandmother's cubicle. "Okay, you're right," he said.

"What's that?" she asked.

"I can see how the situation can be funny...now. But when I first arrived?"

She approached him and grasped his arms. "You had every right to be worried. I was worried, too, and she's not my grandma. I kind of wish she was. But now that you know she's okay, you have to be able to see the humor where it exists. It's okay to lighten the load a little."

Emma was right.

She looked at her watch. "I've got to go. I need to make sure the fans are set up correctly and that the work area is clean, plus make a list of everything that needs to be replaced. When the insurance comes through, I know what to do."

Guilt washed through him. "I'm sorry I can't help you." He turned toward his grandma and annoyance flashed. "Her antics didn't just affect her—"

Emma's hand on his arm stopped him. "It's fine, Josh. Go deal with her. And tell her I said bye."

He pulled her in for a quick kiss. The vanilla scent of her hair was way better than the antiseptic of the hospital, and he breathed it in. Letting her go, he watched her leave, aching to be with her. Instead, he returned to his grandmother's cubicle.

Swishing open the curtain, he entered. While he'd been in the hall, a nurse had entered to take her vitals.

His grandma's cheeks had pinked up a bit, and the nurse raised the head of her bed so she could sit up. Although the privacy curtain between his grandmother and Daphne was closed again, he was still able to see that Daphne wasn't as far along the road to recovery as his grandmother. Since Daphne was the one who started the entire fiasco, a frisson of satisfaction trickled through his veins.

Emma's voice popped into his mind, chastising him, and he paused. A little sympathy wouldn't kill him. He sighed. He'd have a lot of apologizing to do at Yom Kippur.

He needed to figure out why he was still having such a strong reaction.

Just then his grandmother noticed him. His self-reflection would have to wait.

As the nurse left, Josh pulled up a chair and sat next to his grandmother. "You're feeling better, I see," he said.

"Yes, the nurse said I can probably go home in an hour or so."

He looked at his watch. "Gonna be a late night."

"Go home, Joshy."

He pulled away. "And leave you here alone?"

She skewered him with her sharp gaze. "You know I'm older than you, right? So you're not my father, may his memory be a blessing."

"I'm aware. And I'm also aware of my desire to keep you company and drive you to Marble House when you're ready."

"And in the meantime, you're going to lecture me?"

He scoffed. "I doubt you'd listen anyway. And a very smart person told me I have to lighten up."

His grandmother puffed out her chest. "I knew Emma was good for you. Now tell me how things are going between you two."

He told her about the flood, and his grandmother groaned. "Oh I feel terrible, Joshy."

"I know, but it's not your fault. Emma doesn't blame you, either. It's a lot of bad luck."

He explained how he, Matt and Steve helped clear out the kitchen of debris, and she glowed with pride. Her pride in Josh had always been important, helping him through hard times, and now was no exception.

"I hope her inventory wasn't damaged," his grandmother said.

Josh's stomach sank. He hadn't thought to ask. He pulled out his phone, but when he saw it was after ten, he decided to wait. No sense causing Emma added stress at this time of night.

"I have an interview with Rabbi Moskowitz," he said instead.

His grandmother's face lit up like the light above the Torah ark. "Joshy, that's wonderful!"

He put his hand on her arm. "There are a lot of moving parts for this to work. Don't get excited yet. And please don't mention this to anyone, including Emma."

His grandmother made a zipping motion over her mouth with her fingers as the nurse returned with the discharge papers.

Daphne called out, and Josh opened the curtain. "You're going?" she asked. Her face was still a bit gray, and Josh suspected she'd be here until tomorrow.

His grandmother nodded.

"Save me a seat at mah-jongg tomorrow," Daphne said. "I don't want to lose my place to Randi. She cheats."

As they left the hospital, his grandmother in much better shape than when he'd seen her earlier, Josh carried her belongings and ushered her to his car. He was silent on the drive, and his grandmother rested her head against the seat. He suspected their mah-jongg game tomorrow was not going to have the usual players, but he kept his mouth shut.

Once at his grandmother's apartment, however, he spoke. "You know I love you, right?"

She nodded, her gaze soft. "Of course I know."

"Please don't scare me like this again, okay?"

She hugged him, her bony arms stronger than they looked. "I won't. I'm sorry."

In the light of the following day and emptied out with multiple industrial fans blowing, the destroyed kitchen looked simultaneously better and worse than it did yesterday. Emma stood in the center of the room, turned in a slow circle and wondered how on earth she was going to get the bookstore ready in time.

Her mentor in business school had stressed the importance of following a sound business plan. And part of that plan included a to-do list and a timeline.

Before she gave in to the despair threatening around the edges of her mind, she pulled out her laptop and reviewed her plan, trying to ignore her parents' comments.

Although she was used to them, they still hurt.

A half hour later, she studied her revised plan which she thought should enable her to open on time. She stretched her back and neck, and for the first time in days, the anxiety that had trailed her wherever she went lifted.

Grabbing her phone, she called the contractor.

"Hey, Jim, we're going to put the kitchen on hold. I'd like your guys to move ahead with the rest of the lower floor, though."

"What about upstairs?"

"That should be fine, as well."

"Great, we'll be there in an hour."

The Book Nook's grand opening probably wouldn't include the café, but she could still pull off the bookstore piece, bring in some revenue and not completely lose sight of her entire plan. It wasn't ideal, but it would do.

Her stomach growled. She grabbed her wallet and walked into town. The chill January air was bracing, and she wrapped her scarf tighter around her throat.

She needed a hot black coffee to function, and the guys would probably appreciate some bagels. She entered Isaacson's Deli and stood in line.

The garlic and yeasty aroma was delicious. Looking around at the tables, most of them filled with people chatting and enjoying themselves as they ate, filled her with nostalgia. Samantha used to meet her here every Sunday during high school, as well as college breaks. Now that she lived in Manhattan, whenever she was home they'd meet here to catch up.

She missed her friend. As angry and hurt as she was, she'd give anything to return to how things used to be. When it was her turn in line, she approached the counter and gave her order.

Claire, someone Emma recognized from all her time spent here, waited on her. Blond hair pulled up in a ponytail, she gave Emma a wide smile as she poured her coffee and filled a bag with bagels. "No Samantha today?" she asked.

Emma shrugged. "No."

"How's the bookstore coming along? Will you have a romantasy section? I love those books."

"It's good," Emma said, flashing a brief smile. "Definitely, and we can order anything you don't see. Make sure to stop in for our grand opening." She dug a postcard out of her pocket and handed it to her. "Mind if I leave a few of these on your counter?"

Claire turned toward the back. "Hey, Aaron, can we leave promo Book Nook postcards out for customers?"

The owner of the deli, Aaron Isaacson, walked over and took the postcard from Claire's hand. "Sure, put a stack over there," he said, pointing to a spot next to the cash register. He nodded to Emma. "This town desperately needs a bookstore. Good luck with it."

"Thank you," she said, pulling out a stack of postcards. "I appreciate the support." A new idea burst, and she stepped to the side. "Can I talk to you a second?" she asked Aaron.

He nodded and led her toward his office.

"So, my plan has been to have a small coffee and pastry shop in the bookstore, but the kitchen flooded, and I'm going to have to put that idea on hold for the moment. How would you feel if I gave out ten-percent-off coupons for the deli with book purchases?"

He nodded. "I love the idea, but what do you get out of it?"

"Reciprocity? I can print out more postcards and you could give them to customers who buy from you?"

Aaron pointed outside. "The thing about this town is its generosity. I've experienced it myself, and I want to pay it forward. You don't need to do anything. How about I take care of your first month's worth of food with challah bites and bagel bites? And I'll throw in coffee. Nothing that requires a kitchen, everything bite-size and easy to leave out for customers to take with them."

"You'd do that for me?" She wrinkled her brow. "You don't know me."

"Like I said, this town thrives on generosity." He leaned out of his office and called to his brother, Isaac. "Can you grab our calendar?"

Isaac came over. "Got it, what do you need?"

Aaron turned to Emma. "When is your grand opening?"

"April first, as long as nothing else goes wrong."

He nodded. "I get that. Isaac, put it on the calendar. We're delivering bagel bites, challah bites and coffee every morning in March."

"Ours or Caffeine Drip's?" Isaac asked.

"Caffeine Drip's." Aaron met Emma's gaze. "We all work together in this town."

"And they won't mind?" Emma asked.

"Trust me."

Emma left the store in a daze. Running footsteps behind her made her turn.

Aaron's brother handed her the bag of bagels and her coffee. "You forgot these."

She cleared her throat in embarrassment. "Thank you."

She wanted to hug Isaac and Aaron for their generosity. She also wanted to call Samantha and tell her the good news. But she couldn't. Josh? He was stressed about his grandma, but she was probably doing better today, right? She hoped so. Needing to know, she pulled out her phone and dialed.

The sound of his voice when he said hello warmed her.

"How's your grandma today?" she asked.

"I just got off the phone with her, and she seems like her old self."

"That's great!" She let out a sigh. The more time she spent with the woman, the more she cared about her.

"Yeah, I'm relieved. Also, a little nervous about the next thing she does, but..."

"No, no, you need to hope to be as energetic and feisty as she is when you're her age. Like seriously, good for her for having a great time."

Josh shrugged. "I guess so. How are you? How's the kitchen?"

"That's what I was calling to tell you about. Well, in addition to asking about your grandma." She summarized her conversation with Aaron and Isaac.

"That's awesome," Josh said. "It sounds like the perfect solution."

"I still can't believe they'd do this for me, someone they don't know." She thought about her parents and their different philosophy.

"Businesses are good for the town. And like Aaron said, this town is generous."

"Mm."

"What are you thinking?" he asked.

She sighed. "Something kind of awful."

"What do you mean?"

Her stomach clenched. "You and your friends pitched in

when my kitchen flooded. Aaron and his brother are donating coffee and food, and they don't know me. Yet my parents, who are supposed to love and support me, refuse to help me." She gripped the phone hard and swallowed. She shouldn't have said that. Not out loud. Not to Josh. "Forget I said that," she whispered. "I've got to go."

"No, Emma, wait," he cried. "Don't hang up."

"I've got to get stuff done," she protested. She picked at her cuticles, hating herself for making excuses.

This wasn't the time to lean on Josh. They'd barely been dating. She wanted that glowing honeymoon phase, where they each were wide-eyed, holding stupid "you're the cutest, no *you're* the cutest" contests and giggling on the phone and over text. Instead, they seemed to be rushing from one crisis to the next. The last thing she wanted was to confess all her deep feelings of inadequacy and push him away.

"Not until you listen to me," he said, his voice surprisingly firm.

Sighing, she looked around. Standing in the middle of Browerville wasn't the ideal location for a heart-to-heart conversation. With silent apologies to all of the drivers looking for street parking, she climbed into her car but didn't turn on the engine.

"Okay." Her voice came out low, as if her vocal chords were reluctant to give in.

"We're not responsible for our parents' actions," he said. "It's not your job to make them behave or feel or speak the way you'd like them to."

"But—"

"No, don't argue. Because there's a good side to that. And it's this. You don't need to feel guilty about not living up to their expectations or disappointing them. Because if they behaved the way they should, nothing you did would ever disappoint them. The onus is on them, not you."

Her chest was tight, and her temples started to pound.

"I mean, unless you murder someone," he added. "Although, according to my grandma, murder is forgivable, not serving enough food is not."

She choked. It was the closest she could get to laughter.

"Emma, it's not your fault that your parents can't support you. On the flip side, it's totally due to you that friends and strangers do step up and help you out."

"Maybe," she said.

He huffed. "I guess that's better than a no."

"I know you're right. At least, the rational part of me does. But I'm not sure I'm ready to believe it."

"Where are you?" he asked.

"Outside of Isaacson's Deli. I have to go to the house and deliver the bagels to my workers."

"I'll meet you there."

"What? Josh, no, you don't have to."

But the line was silent, her protests given after he hung up.

She drove to the house and put the bag of bagels in the center hall. By the time she finished letting everyone know they were there, Josh appeared.

He stood in the hallway, his body taut, hands stuffed in his pocket. He looked uncomfortable, as she would if her childhood home was being completely redone.

Or as she would be if that childhood home had been filled with as much love as his had.

She sucked in a breath. Maybe she was being too harsh.

Before she could decide, Josh's arms were around her, enveloping her in a hug. She leaned into him, despite how badly she wanted to handle everything herself. His sweater was soft against her cheek, and he smelled like citrus and spice. She breathed deeply, his presence alone calming her like nothing else could. Running her hands along his back, she admired his broad shoulders. She hooked her thumbs in his belt loops and leaned back to meet his gaze.

"Hi," she said.

"Hi." He bent and kissed her, his mouth sure and warm. Tingles of desire flitted over her neck. Her tongue plunged into his mouth, and he pressed his body against hers. Heat surrounded her. Her eyelids fluttered closed, and she let his kiss carry her away—away from the thoughts tap-dancing in her brain, away from the hammering and blaring radio from the workmen. Away from everything except this man.

He cradled her face in his hands, fluttering his fingers along her jawbone before running them through her hair. She smiled against his mouth. He loved her hair. Even if he didn't tell her that, he always found a way to touch it.

As he massaged her scalp, fiery trails of heat cascaded across her scalp and along her spine. She sighed, the breath catching in her throat before escaping as a groan.

He growled, pulling her tighter against him.

She wanted this man and plundered his mouth with her tongue as need built inside her.

When Josh pulled away, she gasped. He blinked, as if coming back to reality.

"Upstairs," he said, voice gravelly.

"But…" Upstairs, the rooms were empty of furniture. Not that there was any downstairs, either.

"When I make love to you, it's not going to be in front of an audience."

She swallowed as she wobbled, knees weak. Nodding, she grasped his hand and followed him up two flights of stairs.

He pulled her into the first open room they came to, empty except for a few moving blankets left behind. Josh turned to her, kissed her and then grabbed the blankets, shook them out and spread them on the floor. He pulled a condom from his pocket.

Her eyes widened, momentarily thrown into reality. "You came prepared," she said.

His gaze softened. "I'm always prepared." He held up a hand. "Not because I expect sex, but because I never want to make my partner feel like she has to be the one to take care of everything."

There was absolutely nothing in the world he could have said to make her care for him more. She blinked back the tears. If she was going to melt into a puddle, it would be from ecstasy, not tears.

She shut the door and kicked off her sneakers before going to him and grasping his face to kiss him senseless.

With privacy guaranteed for who knew how long, their hands reached blindly for each other's clothing, pulling, tearing, yanking until they were both naked.

Josh's sharp, inhaled breath made her entire body heat. He stared, gaze glittery and focused as he raked her body from the top of her head to her toes and back up again. He stopped at her breasts, before moving forward and cupping them in his hands.

"You are exquisite," he rumbled.

Her nipples peaked, and heat ran through her core.

His hands on her breasts set her skin on fire. She stepped closer, needing less space and more contact between them.

His chest was covered with a light dusting of dark hair that formed a dark line in the center of his body. His broad chest was muscular but not overly so, and she traced the ridges of his muscles and ribs as his skin trembled.

His nostrils flared, and he reached for her, massaging her rear as his mouth met hers. His kiss, passionate and hot, made her practically forget her name. And when he trailed his lips from the sensitive spot behind her ear along her neck and across her collarbone, she threw her head back and groaned.

Against her body, he hardened, and she pressed herself closer, sending shards of desire flaring through her. A whimper formed in the back of her throat as his every move, every touch ignited her body like the shammash to the other candles in the menorah.

"I want you," she whispered against his neck, his stubble providing enchanting friction against her lips.

"I want you, too," he responded and slid his tongue down her body.

Once again, her legs shook, and she melted to the floor.

He followed her to the blanket, made quick work of the condom despite his shaking fingers and positioned himself underneath her as he continued to kiss her senseless. She slid along him until she reached his hips at the same time as his body tightened, and he hissed beneath her.

"You like that?" she asked.

He squeezed her hips, positioning her perfectly on top of him.

"Yes." He ground out that single word and let his hands fall to the floor.

She was in charge. His eyes were dark with desire, and she stared into them as she rose and fell in time to her own rhythm. He followed along but let her lead the way. As need built within her, she moved faster and faster. His jaw clenched, and his hands made fists in the blanket on either side of her.

"You first." His voice was strangled, volume barely audible.

"Together," she panted as her muscles clenched around him. Sounds and sights around her blurred. The roar of her pulse pounded in her ears, and she reached one last time for the precipice, before satisfaction exploded, and she shrieked his name.

She barely had time to catch her breath when his hips lifted one last time, he wrapped his arms around her waist and took his release, her name a shout on his lips.

Together, they rode wave after wave of aftershocks as they slowly returned to reality. She collapsed on top of him, the smell of sweat and sex mingling together. She buried her face in his neck, he shifted her to the side, and she waited for her heart to slow to normal.

"I love you," he whispered. "And I'm thinking of taking a position at the Browerville Reform Synagogue so we can be together."

She froze. *It doesn't mean what you think it means. It's because we had sex.*

Armed against allowing her feelings to get the best of her, she stretched her arm over his body and burrowed into him deeper. "This was lovely," she said. "But it's not a reason to change your whole life."

He angled toward her. "What?"

"The sex," she said, rising to meet his gaze. "It was lovely. But it was just sex."

"That's not what I was talking about," he said. "I mean, yeah, the sex was great. But I knew it would be after our first time. I'm talking about you. I love you. I want a future with you."

"You can't," she said, practically cutting him off. "We've barely been dating. You're caught up in the sex hormones."

"That's obnoxious," he replied. "You wouldn't like it if I translated your feelings for you."

She swallowed, realizing she'd misstepped but not sure how to backtrack. Love took time. Lust was immediate. But if he wasn't ready or able to recognize that, she didn't know how to make him understand without hurting his feelings.

His brow was creased, his mouth drawn.

Scratch that. She'd already hurt his feelings.

She sighed. "I'm sorry. I didn't mean to hurt you. You're right, I'd be upset if you said that to me."

He settled, but his body remained tense. Lying with him was no longer cuddly, unless you liked to cuddle something hard and unyielding.

He remained silent, and she couldn't figure out if he was trying not to say the wrong thing or thinking of what to say. Either way, her discomfort increased. She needed to explain why he was wrong, but how?

"Love isn't something that just happens," she said. "It takes time."

"Maybe for you, but not for me."

She winced. It was only now, lying on the hard floor, that she realized how little protection the moving blanket provided. She shifted, trying to find a more comfortable position.

Josh continued. "You don't have to say it back or even feel it."

Guilt weighed on her. He was planning to change his entire life for her, and she couldn't manage to say three little words? She shivered, realizing now that she was naked. She reached for her clothes and pulled on her shirt.

Josh placed his hand over his eyes.

"It's not that," she said. "But it's too soon."

"For you."

"For anyone!" Exasperation made her voice rise. "Love takes time to develop. You have to get to know the person, see their flaws, decide if they're worth it before you change your entire life." Her voice broke.

"No, you love someone despite their flaws," he countered. He jumped up and stepped into his jeans.

"That's not real, enduring love," she said. "Because sometimes, there are flaws that can't be overlooked."

"Oh? Tell me yours." His blue eyes flashed with anger this time.

Part of Emma was sad they'd come to this, and another part of her was triumphant. *See, you don't really love me.* Her sadness deepened. "I have lots of them, but you won't know which ones you can get past until you know me better, Josh. Like how we celebrate Passover or any of the Jewish holidays. Whether I'm a planner or not. A morning person or a night owl. You and I are different, Josh. You don't *love* me, you're in love with me. There's a big difference."

"And you're scared," he said. "That's why you're playing semantics. You're afraid to let me in and examine our differences, because you don't want to get hurt."

"Of course I don't want to get hurt, Josh. No one does. But you can't decide you're going to love someone out of the blue. Any more than you can throw an invitation to a Passover seder without talking about it first."

He shoved his feet into his shoes, practically stamping his feet on the ground. "That invitation really threw you? Why? I don't care how different we are or how different our observance is, I want to share everything with you. And I didn't just decide, Emma."

"It's only been a few weeks. We haven't gotten to the deep confessions part of our relationship. You're a rabbi, and I am so far from a rabbi I could practically be of a different religion."

"So what?"

She gaped at him. "You've got to be kidding. So what? So what if I don't want to keep kosher?"

He shrugged. "We can talk about it."

She stared at him. "We can talk about it? That's your answer? Because so far, we haven't talked about much. And yet you claim you love me."

"I do," he said. "And that won't change."

She shook her head. "You want me as I am right now, before you see how I might change. Because you hate change."

He frowned at her. "You're not making any sense."

"Yes, I am. We barely know each other, Josh. What happens if I turn into something that you don't like?"

"Not going to happen."

He wasn't getting it. A knot formed in her stomach. "Everything is moving at lightning speed, Josh. Your grandma moving, you having to leave the home you grew up in, me opening a bookstore and moving out and trying to succeed on my own. We're in the thick of it. Of course things are going to change."

His jaw tightened. "Not the important things."

"You can't know that. Any more than you can know that you love me."

He ran his hand through his hair, spun around and paced the room. "Fine, you don't want me to love you, I won't. Happy now?"

"No, that's not what I want, Josh."

"What do you want?"

"I want time. Time for us to figure out what we truly feel, what we need, who we want to be."

His shoulders slumped. "With everything changing around us, Emma, you're the one thing I'm truly sure of."

"I don't understand how you can say that. We're different. You're a rabbi—"

"Why is this such a sticking point for you? I've never once pushed you to change how you observe or *if* you observe."

"But what happens—"

"It's not your lack of Jewish faith that's a problem, Emma. It's your lack of faith in me. In us."

Before she had a chance to answer, he swung open the door and walked out of the room.

"Josh!" she yelled, but he didn't respond.

The hammering combined with his feet pounding down the stairs made her temples throb.

She turned to the now empty room. The blanket lay rumpled on the floor, its dirt and grime visible now. Her skin itched, and her nose was stuffed from the dust.

And her heart? Her heart was numb.

Why couldn't Josh understand? She cared for him. He made her happy. Their chemistry was perfect. But how was she expected to give him her heart when it was so easy for the people who claimed they loved her to walk away? Her parents, her best friend…and now Josh.

Especially when it came time to work out their differences. He was a rabbi! She barely observed anything. How did two such different people meet in the middle?

It proved he didn't love her. Not the way she wanted to be loved.

She leaned against the doorjamb, her arms folded across her stomach. She'd made it through life with her parents. She was going to someday adjust to life without Samantha. Josh? Josh was a blip on her timeline. He'd be easy to get over.

Doubt crept through her veins like hidden plaque. Her cheeks were wet, and when she ran her hands over them, she realized she was crying.

She never cried. It must be an allergic reaction to the room. Because she couldn't face the other option.

That she'd let the one person who might truly love her, leave.

Josh left Emma's house in a fury. How dare she tell him how to feel? His feelings were valid, even if she didn't understand them. He got into his Mustang and pounded his fists on the steering wheel.

It was one thing for her not to feel the same. He'd be

crushed but could deal with it. But to accuse him of not knowing his own heart?

He pulled away from the curb, tires squealing.

Flashing lights behind him made him swear under his breath, and he pulled over a few houses down.

Ten minutes and one warning later for not using his blinker, Josh looked through both mirrors and behind him, turned on his blinker and carefully pulled away from the curb.

There was nowhere to go. He'd left his childhood home, which more and more felt like a stranger's place. He didn't want to go to Ari's apartment. He was a guest there, despite the roommate offer, and as much as he appreciated his friend's hospitality, it wasn't home.

Home. Maybe he should go back to the city. His grandmother didn't need him. Emma didn't want him. What was he still doing here?

Your grandma didn't abandon you no matter how awful you were. You can't leave her now.

His inner voice was super annoying.

He'd go visit his grandma, see how she was and maybe get her opinion on going home.

Pulling onto the Marble House property, he looked out his dashboard window at all the activity going on, despite the cold. Residents sat outside talking. Others played pickleball on the courts in the distance. Still others walked the paths, arms linked, talking and laughing.

They all had a life here with friends. For an outsider looking at it, it seemed like a good life.

And him? His life was changing so fast, he didn't know how to control it. He was like the superhero in the comic book, given powers he had no idea how to control.

Except he wasn't a superhero. Not even close.

His phone rang, and he swore when he saw the caller. Ms.

Match. Of all the times to return his call. The urge to let it go to voicemail was strong, but he answered anyway.

"Hello?"

"Hi, Josh, I got your message. I'm sorry things didn't work out with Samantha, but I've got a bunch of other potential matches for you."

He couldn't do this. "No, I… I think I'm going to take a break for a while."

Ms. Match's voice lowered. "I understand how frustrating the process can be—"

"It's not that," he interrupted. "I met someone else. At least, I thought I did… I don't know. This isn't the right time. Thank you, but I'm going to take a break from your services."

"All right," she said. "When you're ready to start up again, please let me know."

He hung up the phone and waited for the relief to appear. He'd decided to take a break from relationships. He should be pleased.

But he wasn't.

Knocking on his grandmother's door made him sadder than he already was. He'd never knocked before entering her home. Her home was his home. Yet this place was different, and it might be an invasion of her personal space to enter as usual.

"Joshy, why are you knocking? What am I, a stranger? And why do you look sad?"

A part of his psyche brightened, hearing her protest his knock. "Sorry, Grandma, I wasn't sure of the new protocol."

"Protocol schmotocol. You're my favorite grandson, you can enter anywhere I am without knocking."

He was also her only grandson, but he wasn't about to quibble. "Okay, next time, I won't knock," he said.

She led him into the living room where they sat together on the sofa.

"Why the long face?" she asked, offering him a bowl of mints.

He took one and popped it in his mouth, as much to stall for time as to satisfy his grandma's urge to feed him.

"Emma and I had a fight."

"Oh no!" His grandma looked horror-stricken. "What happened?"

He summarized their argument, leaving out the sex part. She listened quietly until he finished.

"Do you remember Max Schlossberg? Or Tim Offenbacher?"

"Yeah, Max and I were in middle school together, and Tim was the first friend I made in college."

"Right after your parents died, you came home from school telling me all about the new friend you'd made, Max. He was amazing, you'd never known anyone as cool as he was, you were going to be best friends forever."

Josh leaned back. "I wonder what ever happened to him."

His grandma shrugged. "I don't know. What I do know is for the first month after you met him, you wouldn't stop talking about him, and you made me pack extra food for lunch so you could share with him."

"He was my friend."

His grandma shook her head. "You wanted him to be your friend. And Tim? You called me to send care packages you could share with him and told me about all the times you and he went out to bars and parties. You wanted to join the gym at school so you could play basketball together."

Josh shifted in his seat. "We were all trying to find our place."

"I know. But do you know what those two guys had in common?"

He looked around the living room, as if he could find the answer somewhere among his grandmother's belongings. "No."

"They were the first people you met after big changes happened in your life, and you clung to them like lifelines until you found your footing."

"That's not the same thing at all," he protested.

Holding up her hand, she continued, "Helping me move here and essentially ending another chapter of your life is a big change."

"But that's not why I love Emma."

"Maybe not. But maybe Emma is afraid your love isn't the deep kind that will last, and she's trying to protect herself from being hurt, like Matt and Tim."

That was ridiculous. Emma didn't know about those guys. Heck, Josh hadn't thought of them in years. "Grandma, friends and girlfriends are completely different."

She chuckled. "I hope so." She blinked, becoming serious again, and reached for his hand. "I'm not doubting you love her, and I think that's wonderful. I just want you to see a pattern of behavior that might be influencing some of your decisions. I'm sorry she hurt you by not accepting your feelings or returning them. But I also can see things from her perspective, and I'd hate for you to unintentionally hurt her."

His grandma was usually great at advice, but this time, she was completely off base. Trying to change the subject, he said, "You're feeling better now?"

"I am. But the fact you're asking me that makes me think you've never gotten drunk or suffered a hangover before. I'm not sure whether to be pleased or chagrined."

"Grandma, you want me to get drunk? That's a far cry from what you said to me when I was in high school."

"And you're several years older, so I'd hope it is." She

squeezed his hand before releasing it. "Not only am I feeling better, but I'm planning to attend the cane-decorating workshop Emma is leading this weekend."

Emma was leading a workshop? A small sense of betrayal overtook him. "I thought you were grounded."

"We convinced them this was a mitzvah, since we're teaching the other residents how to do something."

He gave her his best side-eye. "I'm not sure I approve."

"Well, it's a good thing you're my grandson and not my father. Relax. It's a no-alcohol event."

"Thank goodness."

Josh stayed a little longer, tackling some of his grandmother's to-do list.

"Anything else bothering you?" she asked as he was about to leave.

"I'm conflicted about moving synagogues," he said, stuffing his hands in his pockets. "On the one hand, I'm eager to be more hands-on. On the other, my current temple is huge. Maybe I should stay to grab every opportunity there."

An understanding glance flashed on his grandmother's face. "I'm not sure I can give you what you're looking for. Ultimately, you have to decide where you'll be happiest."

If only he knew where that was. Adulting was hard.

"When are you talking with Rabbi Moskowitz?" she asked.

"Sunday," he said. "But there's a lot of coordination that has to happen before I'm allowed to interview with her officially."

She pulled him close to kiss his cheek. "Good luck."

"Thanks," he said. "Love you!"

"Love you more."

Chapter Eleven

Emma's list of things she needed to tackle was longer than her arm, but she couldn't concentrate on it. Teaching the women at Marble House how to decorate their canes was fun, but a piece of her continually waited to see if Josh would show up. Searching for book inventory resulted in an extensive list of self-help books and how to know if your guy loves you.

She was surprised her computer hadn't blared, "Josh, Josh, Josh." While ordering bookcases over the phone, she'd daydreamed about the man's voice on the other end of the line, comparing and contrasting it to Josh's and wondering how soon in this man's relationship he'd declared his love. And whether or not he'd meant it. The follow-up email, listing fourteen large bookcases when she needed twenty and twenty-seven small ones when she only needed sixteen, proved she wasn't focusing on anything she should.

After fixing her mistakes, she changed into workout clothes and went to the JCC to use their gym. Maybe sweating for an hour would help fix her.

As she entered the building, several women chatted together nearby, and the ache of missing Samantha increased. Emma had moved past anger for the moment and was firmly in the sadness part of the five stages of grief. Groaning, she signed in and went straight to the locker room to store her keys before hitting the elliptical machine.

"Hey, there!" A voice made her turn.

"Tracy, wow, I haven't seen you in ages," Emma said. "How are you? What's new?"

Her high school friend held up her left hand. "I'm engaged." Her wide grin made her eyes sparkle like the rock on her finger.

"Congratulations! When's the wedding?"

"Next fall. I'm home looking at dresses with my mom."

Pangs of regret filled Emma's stomach. It cramped, whether from the incline she'd set on the machine or her reaction to her friend's words, she wasn't sure. When Emma thought of getting married, the stress of doing things with her mother outweighed all the excitement she was supposed to feel.

Tracy prattled on about all her wedding plans, and when she stopped for breath, Emma asked, "How did you know he was the one?"

Her eyes gleamed. "Oh my gosh, from the moment I saw him, I knew. It sounds crazy, I know, but it was like this light from above shone on him."

Emma tried to hide her skepticism. "Really?"

Tracy nodded. "He didn't fall quite as fast, though."

"Does he know you fell in love at first sight?"

"Mm-hmm."

"What does he think about that?"

Glancing her way, Tracy frowned. "What do you mean?"

Emma adjusted the settings on her elliptical to be more conducive to talking. "You know, does he believe in that kind of thing, does he doubt you?"

Tracy paused and wiped her face with her towel. "Does he doubt my love? Of course not. He'll be the first to tell you that we all feel love differently and at different times. What matters is that we're going to be together and our love is going to morph and grow over time." She leaned toward

Emma. "Although I will say that he teases me mercilessly about the 'love at first sight' thing." She made air quotes with her hands, and her diamond ring winked in the sunlight streaming through the large wall of windows. "But since one of the things I love most about him is his sense of humor, I can't exactly complain."

They both started up their machines again.

"What about you?" Tracy asked. "What are you up to these days? Are you seeing anyone?"

Emma filled her in on all the details of the bookstore.

"I can't wait to browse. I love mysteries. Will you carry them?"

Emma rattled off a few authors' names and Tracy rubbed her hands together in glee.

"Count me in for your grand opening." Tracy paused. "You must be too busy to see anyone."

Emma's shoulders tightened. She'd hoped to distract Tracy with talk of books, but clearly, people planning weddings focused on relationships. "Well, actually, it's complicated. I was seeing a guy, but I don't think it's going to work out." She didn't want to go into too many details. Although she and Tracy knew each other from high school and had socialized in the same circles, they hadn't talked in years.

"That's too bad. But hey, when you're ready, and after you get The Book Nook off the ground, text me. My fiancé has some single friends, Jewish, who you might like."

Oh no, was Emma becoming the single friend that others were always trying to set up? She took a deep breath. No, Tracy was trying to share her happiness and maybe spread some of it around.

Finished with the elliptical, Emma turned it off and wiped the sweat from her neck. "That's sweet of you, Tracy. I'll let you know, okay? As you said, I have a lot going on right now with my bookstore." And despite her being the one to leave him, she missed Josh.

Tracy gave Emma her number and left, while Emma continued onto the weight room. Although the cardio was healthy, it hadn't erased Josh from her mind, thanks to Tracy. Maybe some weights would do the trick.

Twenty minutes later, Emma's arms hurt, and she wasn't convinced she could focus any better on work than she could before she arrived. After a quick shower, she returned to her car.

Driving through town, she noticed the huge snowflakes hanging from the streetlights. Winter scenes decorated most of the storefronts along Main Street. The yearly window-painting contest was in full swing. Even if you didn't own a calendar and paid no attention to weather, the entire town oozed a cozy winter vibe.

Everywhere she looked, something reminded Emma of Josh. As she drove, memories of his warmth and charm during the winter festival flooded her senses. She fumbled for the music app on her phone, hoping to drown him out with one of her favorite artists. But the country songs were all about relationships, the emo songs made her feel things she didn't want to feel, and nothing else appealed to her.

Her phone rang, and relief washed through her as her sister's face appeared on the screen.

"Hey, Alyse, your timing is perfect."

"Oh? Why?"

Emma swallowed, realizing she'd spoken without thinking. She hadn't told her about Josh. And there didn't seem to be a point now. "Just in need of a distraction. What's up?"

"Well, I've got a distraction for you, but probably not one you're going to appreciate."

"That can't be good."

"Heads up that mom and dad are planning to stop by The Book Nook to see what you're doing."

Emma's stomach knotted. At this point, it knotted so often, she didn't think the kinks would ever get loose. "When? Why?"

"I'm not completely sure, but I'd expect them soon. We were talking, and I suggested they take a look at what you were doing."

Emma put her car in Park and sat outside The Book Nook, banging her forehead on the steering wheel. In other words, her parents were complaining about her to her sister. *Lovely.* "Thanks for the warning," she said.

"For the record, the only reason I suggested they visit you was because I don't think they can wrap their brains around what a great job you're doing. They need to see it to believe it. Please don't be mad at me."

"I'm not mad at you," Emma said.

Her sister sighed. "You're mad at them, though."

Did she know about their money conversation? Emma hated keeping things from her sister, but at the same time, she didn't want to put her in the middle any more than she already was. She scoffed. "I'm kinda always mad at them at this point. But it's fine. I'll show them around as soon as I find my flak jacket."

"I'm impressed you own one," Alyse said.

"Not only do I own one, but it's pink and monogrammed," Emma said. She groaned. "Oh, jeez, I think they just pulled up." She cursed to herself. "Here goes nothing."

"You've got this," Alyse said. "Love you."

"Love you, too."

Squaring her shoulders and wishing she owned that make-believe pink monogrammed flak jacket for real, Emma climbed out of her car.

"Hi." She plastered on a bright smile and walked over to her parents. "This is a surprise."

"We realized we haven't seen anything you're doing with the bookstore," her dad said.

Translation, Alyse the wonder child suggested you come over.

Her mom remained silent but kissed her cheek before looking around the neighborhood. "I pictured it more residential than this," she said.

Emma pointed down the street. "While it's not on Main Street, it's one street over, and as you can see, there are a few boutiques and doctors' offices on this street. Plenty of traffic, easy to walk to from Main Street and plenty of on-street parking for those who want to drive."

"And this is zoned for commercial use?" her dad asked.

Emma nodded. "Come on in, I'll show you around. But be careful because the workmen are here. It's noisy and dirty inside."

A part of her hoped her parents would change their minds and drive off, but no, they followed her in silence.

Once inside, she showed them the main floor and how each room would function as part of the bookstore. She described the bookshelves, the reading areas, the checkout section, and pointed to the kitchen. "In the future, the coffee and snack bar will be back there. But right now, it's stripped to the studs."

"You've got the inventory for all of this?" her dad asked.

She nodded. "The Book Nook will specialize in certain genres—romance, mystery, fantasy, sci-fi and a few nonfiction genres, at least to start. I can always expand based on customer requests."

"And you think those are the best books for your readers?" Her mom's question hung in the air, touching on all of Emma's insecurities.

Emma blew out a breath. "I've talked to people at the library and around town, any time I saw people reading books. Plus, I've done research and asked lots of people at town hall meetings when I was there for zoning issues. Those genres seem to be the ones people are most excited about. For now, yes. And as I said, I can always alter orders in the future."

Her mom nodded. "Responding to reader's needs might actually be a benefit."

Was her mom actually praising her? Emma didn't want to spend too much time thinking about that, in case she was wrong, but a tiny corner of her soul thawed.

She led them into the front hallway and pointed to an alcove. "Thanks to the generosity of Isaacson's Deli and the Caffeine Drip, we'll have fresh coffee, bagel bites and challah bites daily, until I can get the kitchen up and running."

Her dad's posture straightened. "I guess that makes good business sense for them."

Emma nodded. "They want to support up and coming businesses in town, and they're excited about The Book Nook. They also let me put postcards in their stores."

She brought them upstairs to the second floor. "I'll be living in the two top floors. The guys are going to convert this floor to a living room, kitchen and bathroom.

Her parents followed her from room to room. The two of them exchanged a lot of looks but didn't say anything.

So much for their visit changing their minds, she thought. Whatever hope she'd gotten from their questions downstairs fizzled.

She brought them to the third floor. "And this will be where the bedrooms are, plus another bathroom." Although she showed them each room, she avoided the bedroom where she and Josh had had sex. She couldn't go in there. Not now.

Finally her mother spoke. "It's a lot of space for one person," she said.

Emma nodded. "I don't plan on moving again, and it's got space if I get married someday. Plus, I can always rent the upstairs if I ever decide I no longer want to live over the bookstore."

"It's good to think ahead like that," her dad said.

Emma's knees wobbled, but she remained upright and smiled at him.

Once downstairs, she led them onto the porch, where it was quieter. "I can show you the architectural plans if you'd like, now that you've seen the actual space." She didn't expect them to want that much detail. They'd shown interest in her progress, and now they'd leave.

But instead, despite the cold, they both lowered themselves to the front steps. "Yes, we would," her dad said.

Even her mom nodded in agreement.

They moved over to make space for her, and Emma put more value in that movement than something as simple as giving her body room to sit. Her parents rarely made emotional space for her, unless they were depositing her into the box they labeled Unmet Expectations.

Emma sat on the wooden front steps carefully, hyperaware of the contact of jackets and arms and legs. Her hands shook as she pulled out her tablet, tapped on an app and scrolled to the architectural plans. She showed them each room, reminding them of what they'd seen and showed them renderings of how it would look when completed.

This time, her parents' silence didn't fill her with dread. The deeper into the plans she delved, the more confident her voice became and the less her fingers shook, until by the end of her demonstration, her chest swelled with pride.

Suddenly, her mother leaped up and raced down the walkway. Her father followed.

All of Emma's hopes fell. She crouched over her legs, making herself into the smallest human ball she could. Her stomach ached, and despite her best efforts, tears poured from her eyes.

Why am I never enough?

She couldn't do this anymore. She needed to leave, except this was her space, her home, her bookstore. Rage filled her at the need to wait until her parents left in order for her to find peace. Just as she was about to demand they leave, their footsteps got closer and she was wrapped in an embrace.

She jerked her head up and found her parents encircling her. Their heads touched hers. A hand, probably her mom's, stroked her back.

"What the hell?" She didn't realize she'd spoken those words out loud until her parents glanced at each other with small looks of approval on their faces.

Their wet faces.

She'd never been one for geometry or physics, but she was pretty sure the angles were completely wrong for her tears to land on their faces. Not in this position.

What the hell?

"I'm proud of you," her mom whispered.

A strong urge to look behind her overwhelmed Emma. Surely her sister must have sneaked up when Emma wasn't looking.

"What?" she asked.

"Me, too," her dad said.

"I don't understand," Emma said.

"You created all of this yourself," her mom said, gesturing to the house. "You had a vision, and you've executed it."

"I know you didn't think business school was for you,

but you accepted the task and created something perfect for you," her dad added.

Emma was stunned, her mind numb, yet at the same time spinning like a dreidel on Hanukkah. She'd dreamed of this her entire life, knew exactly what she would say and do if it ever happened. But now that it was real, everything she'd wanted to say jammed in her throat.

"It's not finished yet," is all she managed to say.

"That's okay," her mom said. "It will be, and it will be beautiful."

Who was this woman, and what had she done with the mother Emma grew up with?

Her shock must have shown on her face, because her mother actually blushed. "You have every right to be surprised, Em, but seeing that you are hurts my heart. Not because of anything you've done, but because it shows me how wrong I was."

"How wrong we both were," her dad added.

Emma's gaze bounced from one parent to the other. This was a dream. It had to be. And man, was she going to be disappointed when she woke up.

"I've set unfair standards and compared you to your sister for your entire life," her mom said. "And I was wrong."

"Did you know I went to art school?" Her dad's question, out of the blue, shocked her.

"No," Emma said. But as much as she wanted to know all about it, she wanted to hear more from her mom. But her mom was nodding at Emma's dad.

"I did," he said. "It's where I met your mom. I had grand plans to be an artist, and your mom wanted to own an art gallery."

She'd never heard this story before. "Why didn't you?" Emma asked.

"I painted an entire show's worth of landscapes, and no one bought a single one. Mom started work for a gallery owner but couldn't manage to sell any of that gallery's paintings. Since her salary was based on commission, we struggled."

"And then I got pregnant with your sister," her mom said. "And we were both terrified. Terrified of being unable to support our family, of being unable to give our children the best possible foundation for a successful future."

"We pivoted," her dad said. "I gave up my art dream and went to work at a bank, getting my business degree at night. And mom worked at a doctor's office. We fought hard for success, and we became blinded to the possibility of following dreams." He paused. "Maybe blinded is the wrong word. Maybe fearful is better."

He glanced at Emma's mom, who nodded.

Her mom continued, "Your sister, well, she followed the more traditional path, and we were confident she'd be successful. But you were *so* like us." Her voice turned wistful. "You took all the dreamy parts of our personality—plus our stubborn parts—and became this person we loved but feared. We didn't want you to suffer the way we did."

"Instead, we forced you to follow our plan and made you suffer, rather than trusting you to develop your own," her dad said.

Emma was stunned. She was like them? She thought about her childhood but couldn't see any similarities between herself and her parents. At all. She stared in them in shock. "I don't understand. Why were you so hard on me then? You succeeded!"

Her mom bit her lip before answering. "But only because we changed what we wanted to do. You never would change what you wanted, and we were afraid you'd fail."

Emma rose and paced the porch. "But so what if I failed? At least I'd be happy."

"And poor," her dad said.

"There are worse things in life than being poor," Emma said. "Like growing up thinking you could never be good enough for your parents."

Both her parents' faces whitened.

A part of Emma wanted to apologize for hurting them. Another part of her needed them to understand the consequences of their actions. But guilt sliced through her just the same.

"Oh, Emma," her mom whispered, rising and walking toward her. She stopped a couple feet away, as if she were afraid of being rebuffed.

"Why did it take until now for you to believe in me? I did everything you asked. I went to business school, I graduated with a plan, and I've carried out that plan. You've seen me do it." Emma hated the raw pain in her voice, hated giving into it, hated that she cared what her parents thought after all these years. But she couldn't help it.

"I don't know," her dad said. "When you came to us for money, all my fears of what might happen blocked me from seeing what could happen."

Alyse was the one who'd convinced them to see her bookstore. "Why is it always Alyse who can get through to you? Why not me?"

Her mother reached for her hand. "I know you think it's because we love her best, but I promise that's not true. It's because she's got that rational, logical part of her brain that can cut through all our emotions. And she pointed out, rightly, that unless we saw what you were doing, all that fear was going to grow."

"And we realized she was right, so we came to see," her dad said.

"I know we were wrong, and we have been for a very long time," her mom said. "I know we've made lots of mistakes."

"And we'll probably keep making some of them," her dad added.

Her mom continued, squeezing her hand, "But I want you to know how sorry we are, how much we regret the way we treated you and how we've made you feel. It's not on you to forgive us, it's on us to prove to you that we deserve to be forgiven."

"You don't have to say anything to us," her dad added. "We don't expect anything from you at all. You've done well for yourself on your own and are clearly more capable than we've given you credit for. But we want you to know that we love you, we see what you're doing, and we're proud of you."

Emma swallowed, her throat thick with tears. The apology was everything she'd always wanted, yet fear sliced through her. "How do I know this is real?" she asked. "How do I know that if I mess up or something happens, you're not going to say I told you so? Or think it?"

Her mom slumped. "It kills me that we've betrayed your trust. I don't have an answer for you, other than to tell you we won't do that."

Emma stood there, looking at her parents. They'd always seemed disapproving. But despite all of their faults, she did love them. And maybe leaning into love was something she was going to have to do, until she was able to trust them.

"Okay," she said.

The relief that washed over her parents, faces made Emma's eyes water. And when they crushed her against them in a hug, she let the tears fall. The three of them stood bawling together. And when she finally pulled away, she was free.

"Thank you," she said, wiping away her tears.

Her dad pulled a piece of paper out of his pocket and handed it to her.

She opened it and gasped. "You're giving me money?"

"We want you to have this," he said.

"I'll pay you back."

He shook his head. "Think of it as an investment. If the entire community can invest in your dream, the least we can do is join them."

Emma wasn't sure what shocked her more. Her parents completely changing their minds, or the fact that all she wanted to do was run and call Josh to tell him the news.

Three months later, Josh sat on the sofa in his grandmother's apartment, surrounded by his grandmother's friends, windows open wide to take advantage of the spring breeze. His grandmother stood in the kitchenette, preparing some of her favorite kosher-for-Passover appetizers. Her friends brought kosher-for-Passover desserts. Josh brought matzah ball soup and brisket that he'd ordered from Isaacson's Deli.

Most of Muriel's friends spent the first night's seder with their families, and now, for second night, they were celebrating together. Sophie and Daphne were critiquing their daughters-in-laws' matzah balls. Lisa was complaining about the length of her son-in-law's seder. She leaned over to cover Josh's ears.

"We probably shouldn't complain in front of a rabbi," she said.

Josh shook his head in amusement. Their complaints were the least of his problems. He was a twenty-eight-year-old man, hanging out with his grandmother and her friends and leading their seder.

Not that he didn't want to be with his grandmother. He did. But looking around, he realized she had a better social life than he did.

He'd spent the last three months trying to figure out his life. He lived in his overpriced New York City apartment during the week and visited his grandmother on the weekends.

Those visits often included social activities with her friends. And since she'd moved to Marble House, the number of her friends increased.

Meanwhile, his friends in the city were starting to pair off, move in with girlfriends and boyfriends and focus on the next stage of their lives.

He'd focused on his rabbinic life.

His senior rabbi supported his desire to move to the Browerville synagogue. And Rabbi Moskowitz was paving the way for a smooth transition. If the temple board voted in his favor, which she assured him they would, he'd be able to sign the contract and start in Browerville in July, focusing on the teen and youth programs that he loved.

And yet, he wasn't satisfied.

"Joshy, help me with the gefilte fish," his grandmother called.

He rose and held his hand out for a platter.

"Come in here," she said.

He entered the kitchen. "What can I do, Grandma?"

"You can tell me why you look morose."

"Morose?"

She put her hands on her hips. "Don't tell me you don't know what the word means. I know how smart you are and I paid enough for your education that you should have a decent vocabulary."

"I wasn't going to say that. I was surprised you noticed. I thought I hid it better."

Her sharp gaze softened. "I always see it. I can read you better than anyone. You want to tell me now what's going on or wait until later?"

He nodded toward her friends in the other room. "I'm not sure I'll be ready for a big conversation after the seder."

"Pfft," his grandmother said. "These women couldn't stay up past nine if there was money on it."

"Not even for Passover?"

"Nope. Just watch."

At seven fifty-eight, after the fourth cup of grape juice was drunk—Josh forbade any of them to drink wine while he was presiding over the ritual—and the desserts were eaten, Daphne stretched, grabbed her cane—which Emma had helped decorate—and heaved herself off the sofa. "This was fun, ladies. Josh, thanks for a great seder. Happy Passover!"

Sophie collected her ten plagues finger puppets and joined her. "Happy Passover!"

One by one, all of his grandma's guests got up, wished each other Happy Passover, thanked Josh and returned to their apartments.

His grandmother pushed a plate of jelly candies toward Josh and commanded, "Tell me."

"The temple vote should be a piece of cake."

She nodded. "Of course it should. You're the one they're voting for. I don't see why that should trouble you, though."

He shrugged. "It doesn't. I'm moving in with Ari and will save a boatload on rent."

"Still don't see the problem," his grandmother said.

"What if I run into Emma?"

His grandmother's expression shifted, but all she did was point to the candies. "Finish these. I don't want it all to go to waste."

Josh snagged another one, popping it into his mouth. "You know," he said, after he swallowed, "if you made less, you wouldn't have to worry about that."

"But I'd worry there wasn't enough."

They cleaned the kitchen in silence. When they finished, she pulled him into a hug. "You've never been afraid of anything, well, other than change. And you seem to have conquered that fear very well." She cupped his cheeks. "Maybe all your change and growth will bring you what you truly want."

He hugged her, picked up his Haggadah and walked toward the front door. He'd swear she was trying to send him a message.

But he had no idea what that message was.

Emma stood in the center hall of the bookshop. The front hallway, housing the checkout area, was set up. The rooms to either side were complete—all that was left was to arrange the books. The kitchen was still in process and wouldn't be ready for the grand opening, but it was progressing nicely. Her upstairs apartment wasn't ready quite yet, but all in all, everything she needed for The Book Nook's grand opening was moving forward.

Everything except the one person she wanted to share it with. It had been months since she and Josh broke up. Missing him became a dull ache in her chest, something she'd learned to live with but something that never quite disappeared. Every time she thought about calling him, her hand froze. How was she supposed to be sure that the one man who hated change above all wouldn't prevent her from changing and growing as her confidence grew? Especially now that her relationship with her family was changing?

And worse would be if he stayed with her only because he hated change. No matter how much she missed him, she needed to learn to live without him.

She looked at the varnished wood floor and counted the boxes of books waiting to be unpacked. Twenty-five, with more to come. It was time to get started while she waited for the high school student who applied for the stock position to arrive. She turned on some Broadway show tunes, her favorite genre to keep her energy high. Hefting the box at the top of the stack, she sliced open the tape and looked at the stack of cozy mysteries.

"Perfect," she said to herself, and she carried them into the mystery section, dancing a bit and singing off-key.

Her dream was close enough to taste. Her parents had turned over a new leaf, and while far from perfect, they were trying. Her dad offered to help out on weekends, an offer she'd accepted.

The phone app she'd hooked up to the doorbell as a security measure rang, and she pulled out her earbuds and looked at the time. Her potential employee was early, always a great sign.

She swung open the door. "Welcome, you're—"

Her mouth dropped. Samantha stood at the door. Her temples pounded as the anger she thought she'd moved past reared once again.

"—here," she finished.

"Hi, Emma." Samantha looked as polished as always, in wide-legged jeans, a black vest and silk scarf. Her cheeks were red. From the cold or because she stood on Emma's porch, Emma didn't know.

Nor did she care.

The only sign Emma could see of Samantha's nerves was the way she bit her bottom lip and the tilt of her head.

Somehow, knowing she was nervous cooled some of Emma's anger. "Hi," she said, blocking the doorway with her body.

"Can I come in? It's chilly out here." Samantha blew on her hands before stuffing them back in her pocket.

No matter how angry she might be, Emma wasn't a monster. She stepped back and let Samantha in, shutting the door firmly behind her.

Samantha looked around. Her eyes wide, she peeked around the boxes.

At one time, Emma would have flushed with pride at her accomplishments, dying to show her best friend everything she'd done. But that was before.

Now? Now was the time to decide how petty she was going to be. And that decision couldn't be made in two seconds. First, she needed to know why Samantha was here. She folded her arms and waited.

"I was hoping we could talk," Samantha said. "About our friendship."

"What friendship? You destroyed it." Emma's words came out harsher than she intended, but Samantha didn't flinch.

"We both did," Samantha said. "And I'd like to see if we can fix it somehow."

Emma's pulse raced in anger, and she opened her mouth to speak. But somehow, through the anger, a little voice in the back of her head said, *Wait*.

She closed her mouth and turned away. The floor was dirty, with streak marks from the deliveries. Using the toe of her sneaker, she tried to rub them away made as she considered her response.

"It wasn't fair of you to declare Josh off-limits after you decided you weren't interested," Emma said.

"I know."

Emma swallowed. She never expected Samantha to be as reasonable as she appeared to be.

"But you threw yourself in the middle of the two of us, and all of a sudden, all our roles blurred," Samantha said. "I didn't know what to do or how to act. And I always felt like I was playing catch-up with the two of you."

"You were using me as a go-between, and even though I *was* the one who suggested I go with you on the first date, keeping me in the middle was weird," Emma added.

Samantha nodded. "I know. I went about the entire thing all wrong. But I saw the two of you, and all of a sudden I was thrown back to when you took my boyfriends, and I panicked."

"You can't keep punishing me for something that happened long ago and for which I apologized."

"I know. And I don't know why I keep doing it." Samantha shrugged. "I just know I have to start figuring out what I want and need in life and what I'm afraid of."

Emma's heart squeezed with sympathy for her friend, and more of her anger drained away. Samantha had always been the confident one, and now? She'd lost a lot of it.

"I wish you'd talked to me about it," Emma said. "I kept trying to call and text you, and you ignored me."

"I know. I didn't have answers, and I didn't know what to say."

Emma sank onto the ground and leaned against the wall. "We've been best friends since elementary school. You don't need the answers, and you don't need to know what to say. You just have to be there."

Samantha's her cheeks turned red. "I know," she whispered.

They remained silent, together, the only sound the construction noises coming from upstairs. After a few minutes, Samantha joined her on the floor.

"I'm sorry," Emma said. "I'm sorry for making you feel like I was taking the man meant for you. If it makes you feel any better, we're not together."

"It doesn't. But I'm sorry for putting unreasonable expectations on what it means to be my friend," Samantha replied.

Emma bit her lip. She'd wanted this conversation to happen for months. She'd needed to clear the air between them and make Samantha understand how much she hurt her. But the jealousy, something Samantha never showed before, sat between them like a third wheel.

"I hate knowing you're jealous of me," Emma said.

Samantha deflated. "I'm sorry. But every time I saw how your family loved you, and then how boys always, always fell for you. It just wasn't something I could control."

Craning her neck to look at her, Emma frowned. "I know my homelife was better than yours, but it wasn't great. You had a front-row seat to how my parents always showed preference for Alyse."

"They knew you existed. Their worry showed they cared."

Arguing with Samantha was useless. Yes, Emma saw her point. Her parents *did* care, despite, at least in her opinion, how they cared about the wrong things. But their love was fraught with unreasonable expectations. Now, after talking things through with her parents and feeling more confident in their love, Emma didn't agree with Samantha's take. In her mind, she and Samantha had bonded over their similar family issues. It hurt to know that bond never existed in Samantha's mind.

"Boys liked you, too. I remember Craig in middle school and practically the entire lacrosse team in high school. Plus you were never without a boyfriend in college."

"I know. And I'm sorry. Somewhere along the way it became a competition with you."

"That's not fair," Emma said. "I never wanted to compete with my best friend. I never wanted boys to get in between us. And I apologized up, down and sideways for all the mistakes I made."

Samantha expelled a sigh. "I know. It's another thing I have to work on." She looked directly at Emma for the first time. "I have a lot to work on, honestly. I need to figure out what the heck is going on with me if I ever am going to be happy."

Wow. Emma stared at Samantha. Her confident best friend was replaced with someone Emma honestly wasn't sure she liked that much. But she did respect her. "I give you a lot of credit for admitting that. Especially to me."

"I'm hoping, once I figure out who I am, maybe we can be best friends again?"

Emma swallowed, reached for Samantha's hand and squeezed. "I'd like that."

With a nod, Samantha stood up and glanced around. "This looks good," she said. "I love the greens and blues you chose for the walls."

Emma rose and followed Samantha around. "Thanks. We're almost ready for the grand opening."

When they'd been best friends, Emma would have asked Samantha to come for the big day. She sighed. When they were best friends, she wouldn't have needed to ask. Now? She kept the question to herself, unsure of many things with Samantha.

Zipping her vest, Samantha turned to Emma. "Can I give you a hug?"

Emma's throat ached. Another thing they'd never asked each other before. She nodded, and as Samantha wrapped her arms around her, Emma hoped that one day, they could find their way back to best friends.

Chapter Twelve

A week after his seders with his grandma, Josh clicked Send on his rabbinic contract as his cell dinged with a text message. He frowned as he saw the sender. Samantha.

hi, was hoping we could talk

He leaned against his chair and glanced at the time. Seven thirty. He was getting ready to go to the gym before coming home and crashing for the evening.

ok, call me

She must have been waiting by her phone, because ten seconds later, his phone rang.

"Hi, Samantha," he said. He refrained from asking why she was calling him, although he was dying to know.

"Hi, I know you're probably wondering why I'm calling you now."

He huffed. "Well, it did cross my mind. How are you?"

She exhaled. "Better than I was, not better enough, though. I wanted to apologize to you."

"For what?" They hadn't parted on bad terms. Maybe odd ones, but not bad.

"For breaking up you and Emma."

Hearing Emma's name made his breath hitch. He rubbed his chest as if there was a physical ache there. "You didn't, Samantha. We broke up for other reasons."

"That may be so, but I certainly didn't help the two of you to stay together. I was totally out of line asking Emma to avoid you when you and I weren't together. It was unlike me, and I'm embarrassed I did it."

The last thing he wanted to do was talk about Emma. He didn't like thinking about her or the pain that still racked him when she did slip into his mind, which was all the time. But Samantha was talking to him, and he needed to answer.

"Don't beat yourself up about it," he said, looking for some grace. Forgiveness was a mitzvah, after all. "It's water under the bridge at this point. But I appreciate your apology. You didn't have to say anything."

"I'm trying to fix things I've broken, including myself." Her voice was quieter than he remembered, like she was speaking from deep inside herself. "And part of that process is admitting I was wrong. You and Emma belong together. I think that's why I was against it."

He contemplated her words while she paused.

"Anyway," she continued, "if anything I did or said contributed to the two of you breaking up, please ignore it and accept my apologies. And, Josh, don't give up on her. She's worth it."

"Thank you," he said. They were the only words he could say, since he couldn't begin to fathom the rest of her message.

They hung up, and he changed into gym clothes, all the while thinking about what Samantha said.

You and Emma belong together.

Well, wasn't that just fan-damn-tastic, since the only one who mattered—Emma—didn't think so. He'd told her he loved her, and she'd told him he was wrong. He didn't know how they could come back from that, especially since his feelings for her hadn't changed, no matter how much he wished they would.

He spent the next hour lifting weights and running on the treadmill. He worked up a sweat, but he couldn't get past Samantha's advice. *Don't give up on her.*

He hadn't given up on Emma. She'd given up on him. On them. All because she didn't believe him.

She wasn't willing to give them a chance. Instead, she'd dismissed him like a child. For the past several months, he'd tried to forget her. He'd gone to a Valentine's singles event in Manhattan, hoping to find someone and move on. But nothing he did worked, and while he'd gotten past the immediate bruising of her rejection, no one appealed to him the way Emma did.

Maybe he and Emma did belong together. By the time he'd returned to his apartment and showered, he was no closer to figuring out his Emma conundrum. Because whether or not they belonged together, if Emma didn't return his feelings, Samantha's words were meaningless.

Unless Samantha knew something he didn't.

He grabbed his phone and texted her.

Do you think Emma and I have a chance?

He stared at his phone, hoping for an immediate response, but nothing came in. He huffed. Samantha was always busy. Clearly, no matter how many changes she was making to her life, answering texts immediately wasn't one of them.

His body was exhausted, but his mind continued to spin until finally he fell into a restless sleep. The next day, he reached for his phone. She'd answered.

Yes. But leave me out of it.

His heart raced. He was tempted to ask for more details, but he didn't want to sound like a twelve-year-old boy. And he still had the same problem as before—Emma didn't believe him. He needed to convince her. His only hope was that she was still interested in him.

He wondered how Samantha knew. The last time he'd been with Emma, she and Samantha hadn't been speaking. What changed?

He'd fallen for Emma, and maybe he'd fallen too fast. But instead of fighting, he'd let her end the relationship, which only proved her point. If he cared for her, he would have fought back, proven to her that she was worth it.

He would have used his strengths, his focus, his deliberate choices, to choose her.

Sinking onto a nearby bench, he looked across the street to Congregation Emanu-El of New York. The light-colored masonry and art deco ornamentation always made him pause whenever he passed it.

To an outsider, he and Emma were completely different. His grandmother raised him, and his Judaism was a central tenet to who he was. He loved the culture and religion, not to mention the food.

Emma, on the other hand, wasn't raised the same way. Still, she'd shown interest whenever he talked about some ceremony or tradition from his childhood.

He was more serious, more deliberate—the thought made him smile—while she was more spontaneous, willing to try new things.

But they were both loyal, both driven, and he thought—he hoped—good together.

Why hadn't he made more of an effort with her?

His face burned with shame. He should have fought for her, for them. Instead, he'd frozen, so caught up in the idea of her leaving him that he hadn't stepped up and confronted both of their fears.

It was time to change that.

He hoped Samantha was right, that Emma still cared about him. Because he'd spent the last several months trying to change, and he was about to show her the results.

Emma sat in The Book Nook, three days before the grand opening, and checked off another item from her still scarily long to-do list. She'd hung the banner outside the store, and she'd asked the contractors to help her put the store sign in the ground. Now, anyone walking or driving by would know about the bookstore.

She needed them to purchase books.

Exhaling a breath, she got ready to work in the kitchen, when a knock on the door made her pause.

She opened it and gave a huge grin. "Muriel!" She hugged the older woman and held out her arm. "Come inside! I'm glad to see you. How are you? Can I show you around?"

Muriel laughed as Emma struggled to take a breath. "Someone's excited, I see."

"Excited, nervous and jittery with caffeine," Emma acknowledged. "Probably not the best combination, but yes."

As Muriel entered, Emma peeked outside. How had she arrived? Had Josh brought her?

"This place looks wonderful, Emma, dear." Muriel's eyes twinkled. "Lisa brought me here. If you're looking for Josh, you won't find him with me."

Emma bit her lip. "I...um..."

Muriel patted her cheek. "Show me what you've done with the place."

Emma examined the woman's face, searching for any sign she missed her home, but Muriel looked happy and at peace.

Emma led the woman from room to room, her chest expanding with pride. Each time Muriel exclaimed over an architectural touch in a reading nook or the quality of a comfy chair's upholstery, another bubble of excitement burbled beneath the surface.

"Three days," Muriel exclaimed when they finished the downstairs tour. "Your grand opening is in three days. I'm proud of you!"

Emma's chest swelled with pride. "Thank you. I hope customers come."

The older woman nodded. "They will. I've already talked it up with my friends, and they can't wait to check this place out. There's talk of hiring a jitney." She leaned closer to Emma and whispered, although they were the only two people there. "Especially when I told them about your spicy romances."

Emma hugged her. "I'm happy to point them in the right direction when they arrive."

"Excellent. That's what I told them. Now, for the real reason I'm here." Muriel looked around. "Where can we sit?"

Scanning the rooms, Emma led her toward one of the new sofas recently delivered. They sat at opposite ends, and Muriel wiggled and bounced for a moment. "Comfortable," she said, her voice oozing approval. She ran her hand over the nubby blue fabric. "And it'll wear well, too. Now, I want to invite you to Friday night services with me."

Emma's stomach dropped, and she focused on the sofa fabric, the blue-and-green patterned rugs, the newly sanded and stained floor, anything to avoid looking at her. She wasn't a temple-goer, not since her bat mitzvah when she was thirteen. When the silence stretched too long, she finally met the older woman's gaze.

"That's not my thing." Emma paused. "Unless you need a ride, in which case I'm happy to drive you."

Muriel shook her head. "I know you're not religious, sweetheart. But this service is going to be a camp Shabbat. It imitates the types of services the Jewish camps have, so it's much more casual and has lots of singing. It's about as relaxed as a service can get. You can wear T-shirts and camp gear if you like."

It sounded more appealing than Emma originally thought. Still... "Why are you inviting me?"

Muriel shrugged. "While you and Josh were dating, you'd expressed interest in some of the Jewish traditions you were less familiar with. I'm not trying to force you to do anything you're uncomfortable with, but I thought you might enjoy this service."

Emma stared at her for a few moments, trying to figure out if there was an ulterior motive. But Muriel hadn't brought Josh with her, so if she had one, Emma couldn't figure out what it was.

"When is the service?"

"Tonight."

Emma blanched. "Tonight? My grand opening—"

"—isn't until Monday." Muriel looked around. "You're in great shape, and by this evening, you're going to need a break. Please?"

It was the *please* that did it. How in the world was Emma supposed to resist begging from this woman? "Okay, I'll go."

Muriel's face brightened, and she actually clapped her hands. "Wonderful. Pick me up at six forty-five."

After making sure Emma knew the exact address, Muriel left, and Emma spent the rest of the day thinking about the night's service.

That evening, dressed in jeans and a sweater since she

didn't own camp clothing and wasn't about to show up in a ratty T-shirt and shorts, Emma walked into the synagogue with Muriel. A trickle of sweat ran along her back, and her heart pounded against her rib cage.

She didn't know why she was nervous. It was a synagogue and a Friday night service. That was all. The woman was probably lonely and wanted company. Emma would do a mitzvah and be done with it. It wasn't as if the rabbi was going to call her up to the bimah in front of everyone to recite Hebrew.

They found seats in the third row, and Emma swallowed.

"Wouldn't you be more comfortable back there?" She pointed toward the back of the sanctuary.

Muriel shook her head. "That's where all the teens sit, so they can chat without disturbing the rabbi. I want to see and hear what's going on."

Oh boy.

They sat in the pews, and Emma flipped through the pamphlet the usher gave her, ignoring the chatter around her. The pamphlet was filled with songs and adapted prayers they'd use instead of the large prayer book. Guitar strumming filled the space, and all chatter stopped.

Emma looked up at the musicians who played and kept time with her hand against her thigh as the congregants around her began to sing. She flipped to the front of the booklet where the lyrics were and tried to join in.

When that song was over, the cantor led a few more. Some of the teens in the back rose and led the congregation in prayer. And then, a man in a kippah and prayer shawl stepped forward.

Emma's mouth dried.

It was Josh.

Her body went hot and cold. She whipped around to look at Muriel.

The older woman wore a beatific smile on her face as she perched on the edge of her seat.

Emma had been played. She had no idea why or how he was here, what he was doing up on the bimah or why he was giving tonight's sermon, but she needed to escape.

She moved to rise, but Muriel's hand on her leg stopped her. She'd strand the woman here if she left. That, and the silence in the sanctuary meant everyone would hear her get up and see her leave.

Josh would see her.

If she stayed in her seat, it was possible that he wouldn't notice her, even if they were in the third row.

Except that after he straightened his papers on the lectern, he glanced over the congregation in general and focused on his grandmother. His gaze shifted and connected with Emma's. Surprise widened his eyes, before a small smile stretched his lips.

Emma couldn't breathe. She opened her mouth to drag air into her lungs.

Josh began his sermon, and Emma couldn't look away.

Despite all of her anger and frustration, he looked good up on the bimah. Confident. Happy. Passionate in his beliefs.

This was where he belonged. If she'd ever possessed any doubts, listening to his sermon erased them all.

"Change is an essential piece of Judaism," he said. "We are obligated to change. Abraham's story in the Torah teaches us the value of change, as our people go from a skeptical, wandering people in the desert to a cohesive, holy community. But right there is the paradox. Because if you look at our people as a whole, I don't think anyone would describe us as cohesive. In fact, we thrive on our differences."

Josh took a breath and looked right at Emma. His dark blue eyes bored into her, daring her to break contact.

And God help her, she couldn't. She stared, drinking him in. His voice, smooth and deep, the passion that flared in his eyes, his hair shining beneath the lights… She couldn't look away.

"Our differences make Judaism unique. We don't all have to worship the same way or believe the same things. Heck, we can be Jewish even if we don't believe in God. Our religion is a striving, living, breathing thing. It constantly changes, constantly adapts and constantly welcomes those who have questions."

Emma's face heated. It was as if he were talking directly to her.

He laughed. "As someone who hates change, you'd think as a rabbi, I'd have a problem with this part of Judaism. But you'd be wrong. Because no matter how different we all are, the very fact that we're allowed to be different, to learn and to change our minds is exactly what drew me to becoming a rabbi in the first place. In my personal life, I struggled with changing circumstances. But through it all, Judaism became my rock, my anchor. Well, my grandma did, too."

The congregation laughed.

Emma's eyes welled.

"But my Judaism has taught me that change can be good. It can be scary and frustrating, too, but it can also be just. It's what obligates us to look at something that isn't fair and to fix it. It's what leads to tikkun olam, repairing the world. And so, I leave you this evening with a challenge. What can you change in your life that will help repair the world?"

The choir sang, and finally, Emma tore her gaze away from Josh and looked at the carpeted floor. Her stomach hurt, her mind was filled with questions, and she couldn't stay in the sanctuary one moment longer. She needed to leave. Even if it meant ditching Josh's grandma.

"I have to go," she whispered to Muriel. "Can you get a ride home?"

The older woman's face creased with worry. She opened her mouth and closed it, finally nodding.

And as the choir's voices rose in song, Emma made her escape.

That night, her phone rang, and Emma groaned. But manners made her answer anyway. "Hi, Muriel."

"Oh good, you answered."

What was she, a mind reader? "I can't ignore you when you call." *Even if I want to.*

"Excellent. It's time to discuss my grandson."

Emma wished she'd ignored manners. "I'd rather not."

"In my next life, I'm going to be a shadchan, a matchmaker, so I need the practice now," Muriel said. "You and he are perfect together."

Emma shook her head. "No, we're not."

"Tell me why."

How in the world was Emma supposed to complain to Muriel about her own grandson? "He doesn't know me," she said.

Muriel frowned. "I'll admit, the two of you were only together for a short time, but knowledge comes with time. And during the time you two were together, you fit. You made him happy." She paused. "Did he not make you happy?"

Emma's throat ached. He'd made her happy. "He did."

"Do you miss him?"

She wrapped her arms around her stomach. "Yes."

"Then what is the problem?"

"It was never going to last," Emma said.

"Nonsense. Have you met my grandson?"

Emma sighed.

"My grandson hates change. He fights against it. If you think he's going to suddenly stop caring for you, you don't understand him at all."

Emma struggled to find the right words. "He may hate change, but there's no way I can possibly live up to his opinion of me. Eventually, he's going to be disappointed in me, and I don't want to be responsible for that. He deserves to be happy."

Muriel's voice softened. "Oh, honey, who taught you to have such little faith in yourself?"

Emma swallowed. She'd never been enough for anyone. Not her parents, not her best friend. Why would Josh be any different?

"My grandson has suffered great loss in his life, and that loss has taught him two things. One, to hate change. I'll admit, he has to get over that. To his credit, he's working on it. And two, to hold onto the ones he cares about as soon as he realizes it for as long as he can."

"That proves he doesn't care about me," Emma said. "He let me go."

"Have you done anything to ask him back?"

Emma's face burned. "No," she whispered.

Muriel continued, "He hasn't stopped caring about you, sweetheart. But he doesn't want to get in your way. And maybe he's waiting for you to show him whether or not you care for him."

Emma remembered their words when Josh said he loved her. She'd denied his feelings. Her cheeks heated. She'd told him he didn't know himself well enough, never mind her. She'd been so focused on doubting him, she hadn't thought about her own feelings for him or given him any hint about them.

She wasn't sure she understood her feelings for him.

Except for the past few months, every time she'd thought about Josh, she missed him.

She returned her focus to Muriel. "And yet, you're the one who's calling me, not him."

"If he knew I was, he'd yell at me."

Emma could picture that easily, and it lessened some of her anxiety.

"I know I'm overstepping," Muriel said, clearing her throat. "It's what Jewish grandmas do. And I know that me saying he still cares for you doesn't mean anything unless he tells you. Or better yet, shows you." She sighed. "I guess I'm hoping the two of you can set aside whatever your differences are and somehow find your way to each other. Because I think the two of you together are unbeatable."

"Even though we're different?"

Muriel sighed. "Bubbelah, difference adds spice to relationships. Haven't you read any of those spicy romances you're going to carry?"

"I've never known anyone like you," Emma said, struggling to retain some decorum. "You're immediately accepting and—" She paused. No matter what conflicts might arise with her parents, she wasn't about to betray them to someone else.

The understanding tone in Muriel's voice brought a lump to Emma's throat. "Your parents love you, bubbelah, don't ever doubt it."

Emma exhaled. "I know they do. And we've made a lot of progress. We used to be different, and I never thought they understood me, but now, well, I know they do. But they still point out how different Josh and I are, when it comes to religion."

"And how wonderful is that?" Muriel asked. "Making space for religious differences and trying to learn from each other is what helps Judaism to thrive. You don't have to observe in the same way, as long as you respect each other's practices. Tell me, did Josh try to make you do anything that made you uncomfortable?"

Emma whispered, "No."

"Did you try to make him less observant than he is?"

Again, Emma said no.

"Maybe some of the problem is your own fears."

Josh pulled up in front of The Book Nook, turned off the engine and wiped his sweaty palms on his thighs. This was it. Opening day for Emma's bookstore, and hopefully, the first day of their relationship.

He looked out the passenger window. A wooden sign with The Book Nook in fancy lettering swung from the rafters of the wide front porch. A nylon flag that read Open fluttered from the large oak tree in the front yard. And a chalkboard sign with *Come in and escape* in colorful chalk letters was set up on the sidewalk.

Even better was the steady stream of people who walked up to the store.

Satisfaction filled him. From the looks of things, Emma's store was a success.

He never doubted it would be. Every time she talked about it, she'd been excited, and she'd transformed that excitement into a solid business plan.

What was surprising, however, was his lack of nostalgia. As he sat outside The Book Nook, he didn't feel any remorse that his home no longer existed. All he felt was pride in Emma's accomplishments.

Maybe he had figured himself out. Finally.

It was that pride that made him turn the engine on and pull away from the bookstore without entering. He needed to talk to her, to apologize, maybe grovel. Whatever it took to win her back. But he wasn't about to rain on her opening day.

The chalkboard sign specified the time The Book Nook closed today. Eight this evening. He'd return, after she'd had time to handle her sales and close up. In the meantime, he had things to do.

He drove into town and entered the synagogue parking lot. The Assistant Rabbi parking spot was empty, and he pulled into it, turned off the car and sat for a moment, as if he was testing out the feel of the spot.

He scoffed. A parking spot was just that, a place to park. It didn't mean anything.

Except it did.

Grabbing his satchel, he locked his car and rang the bell. The buzzer rang, and he entered the foyer, where the administrator, Ruth Meyers, met him.

"Nice to see you again, Rabbi Axelrod," she said.

"It's nice to be here." He handed her a box of black-and-white cookies. "For you."

Ruth smiled. "You definitely know the way to my heart."

He shrugged as he followed her into the office.

"Rabbi Axelrod, come on in," Rabbi Moskowitz said. "We're glad to have you here. Your sermon this week was fantastic."

"Thank you," he said. "It's great to be here. I'm looking forward to working together."

"The kids are going to love you," she said.

For the next hour, the two of them discussed the specifics of his role, which wouldn't officially start until July, but he'd help out as much as he could beforehand. After their meeting, Ruth showed him his office, where he sat behind his desk with his hands laced behind his head, absorbing it all. He filled out paperwork, and by then, it was time to visit his grandma.

"Hi, Grandma," he said, kissing her cheek as he entered her apartment.

"Joshy! I was on my way to mah-jongg."

He frowned. "Oh, I didn't realize you were busy. I'll come back later."

"No, let me let them know I'll be late." She pulled out her phone and texted, using her index finger. The large print on the screen was big enough for him to see her message without any effort on his part.

"There we go," she said. "Now come in and sit with me."

"I'm all official."

She patted his leg, squeezing it a little with satisfaction. "I can't wait to attend your first Shabbat service."

"You were at Camp Shabbat, Grandma."

His grandma demurred. "That doesn't count. You weren't official yet."

Josh wanted to ask about Emma, but his throat thickened. He swallowed, avoiding the one topic he wanted most to address. He'd find out all he needed tonight. "Well, unless you're going to sneak in with the teenagers, that might not be for a few months."

"Pfft, Rabbi Moskowitz has to take a vacation at some point or lead a funeral, and when she does, you'll fill in."

"True." Josh relayed his conversation with the rabbi to his grandmother and described his new office. "You'll have to visit me there."

She nodded. "Absolutely. The next time I go to The Book Nook, I'll visit you, too."

"The next time? Did you stop by the opening today?"

"No, I was there a few days ago."

He twisted his body to face her. "You were? But it wasn't open."

"I needed to talk to Emma, of course."

He got a sinking feeling in his stomach, like he'd eaten one too many matzah balls. "About...?"

"You."

He dropped his head into his hands. "Grandma, tell me you didn't."

"Only if you want me to lie to you."

"Grandma, why are you butting into something that doesn't concern you?"

"Everything having to do with you concerns me, Joshy."

"What did you say to her?"

"I wanted to find out if she still cares for you."

He groaned. "Grandma, this town already has a matchmaker. It doesn't need you, too." Raising his gaze, he noted her smile. "Why are you smiling?"

"Because I told Emma you'd hate that I was talking to her about you. I was right."

"Yet you did it anyway."

She shrugged. "Sometimes, important things overrule feelings. Don't worry, she wasn't upset."

"Maybe not, but I am." He turned to her. "I was planning to talk to her tonight, after her grand opening. But now, thanks to you, she's going to assume the only reason I came was because you made me. Which makes me look like a child."

His grandma pursed her lips. "Hmm, I can see why you'd think that, but I don't think Emma will."

"Grandma, enough! I love you, I promise, but I need you to stay out of things with me and Emma. If the two of us are going to get together—and now I have more doubts than I did before—it's got to be because of her and me. Not you."

She didn't answer, and he went for the one thing he thought would make her understand.

"What did you love most about Grandpa?" he asked.

Her gaze grew dreamy. "Everything."

"No, come on, what was one of the things you loved the most? You used to tell me all the time when I was growing up."

"His confidence."

"Right. And if you interfere, you're taking away mine."

Her cheeks grew blotchy. "Oh no, Joshy. I'm sorry. I didn't mean to do that. I wanted to give you two a push in the right direction. Because you're perfect together. I didn't mean to make it harder for you."

He leaned over and kissed her cheek. "I know, Grandma. And I'm not mad." He let out a sigh. "Promise me, you'll let me handle things from now on, okay?"

"Okay."

"I'll let you get back to mah-jongg now, Grandma."

"And you'll let me know what happens with Emma?"

"I promise."

He left, going over his planned conversation with Emma in his mind. Now that he knew his grandmother had interfered, he didn't think his original plan was going to work. But he wasn't sure he had any better ideas.

In rabbinic school, his mentor gave him a great piece of advice. Josh had been preparing his first sermon for a congregation, and he was nervous. He wanted to make sure he set the right tone, gave the right examples, left the congregation with the right message.

His mentor saw his struggles and pulled him aside. "Speak from your heart and the rest will follow."

Josh had taken the advice, desperate for any help he could get. And it worked. As first sermons went, it definitely needed some work. But the congregation loved it.

Emma wasn't a congregant, and his words for her weren't a sermon. But he was still taking the advice.

Once again, he pulled up to the bookstore. It was quieter

now. The sky was dark, the stars not yet shining, and everything possessed that monochromatic look things got in the evening. But the lights shining from the front windows held an extra glow.

He jogged up the porch steps and knocked on the door.

Emma answered. Her hair was as curly as ever. The sight of her made him ache. He'd missed her.

"Josh." Her voice was quiet, her gaze shuttered.

"Emma."

"We're closed."

"I know."

"You missed the opening."

He exhaled. "I didn't want to take away from your special day. But I drove past earlier, and it looked successful."

She gave a slight smile. "It was."

"May I come in?"

"Why?"

Her question gutted him. *I want to see you, touch you, be with you.* "Because I want to talk to you."

"Did your grandma send you?"

Part of him hated the question. Actually, most of him did. He swallowed the bile that rose in his throat. But a small part of him was glad she asked it now, rather than later. "No."

Emma remained where she stood for a moment, and he wondered if she'd refuse. But she backed up and let him inside.

His chest eased. To buy himself time, he scanned the part of the store he could see with interest. "This looks fantastic," he said.

"Thank you."

God, he hated how little she engaged with him. Talking with her was never this difficult. It would never get easier until he fixed…everything. "I never should have told you I loved you."

Her face fell, and he reached for her.

"Not because I don't, because I do. Still. But because telling someone you love them means something. It's important. It carries weight. And although my feelings are true, I should have waited until I had more time to show you how much I loved you, so that the words didn't sound empty."

Emma wrapped her arms around her waist. "It's not that they sounded empty, it's just… When you said them, I didn't have much experience with people loving me regardless of what I did. But I shouldn't have thrown your words and feelings away or told you that what you felt wasn't real."

"I think I understand why you did," he said. "It kills me that I do understand, now, that you were basing love on your past experiences. I wish I hadn't gotten angry."

"I wish I told you how I felt," she whispered. "We're different. I was afraid that at some point, you'd get tired of those differences or would want more from me than I could give. Especially because our relationship was new."

His chest ached for her. "I know. Look, I can't promise that we're going to work out forever, as much as I'd like us to. But I can tell you that I've dated other women and never felt for them what I feel for you. And that I'm stubborn and I don't give up easily. I'm not the kind of guy who walks away when things get hard."

Her expression lightened, and a spark of hope ignited inside him. "That whole 'hating change' thing," she said.

He nodded. "Yeah, although I'm working on it."

She turned away and paced the small front entryway. The only sound was her rubber soles pattering on the floor. Finally, when he thought he'd go crazy in the agonizing silence, she spoke. "I'm sorry for doubting you and for assuming you were the same as other people in my life."

"It's hard not to make those assumptions when they're the only thing you know," he said.

"My parents and I had a long talk. I think things are getting better between us."

His breath hitched with excitement. "That's great. Right?"

"Yeah, it is. They're making an effort to change, and I'm trying to find the space to let them be less than perfect. And… if they can recognize the mistakes in their behavior, I have to learn to accept that not everyone is going to treat me like they do. Including you."

"I'm not like them," he said, his voice forceful. "I'm not perfect, and I don't expect others to be. I might disagree with something you do or want or say, but my feelings for you don't depend on those things. I hope you'll give me a chance to prove it to you."

"I'd like that," she said. She bit her lip. "I haven't been able to stop missing you no matter how busy I was or how hard I tried."

He couldn't help the smile that spread across his face. "Is it wrong of me to like that?"

She nodded. "Very." She took a step toward him, her gaze intense. "I've never felt like this about anyone, either. This time apart, it's made me realize how much I care about you. Every time something good happened, every time I suffered from a bad day, you were the only one I wanted to share it with. I'm pretty sure that means I love you." She wrinkled her nose as she gave him a lopsided grin.

He'd been afraid to move toward her, not wanting to crowd her for fear of chasing her away. After all, the intensity of his feelings drove her away once before. But now? He was ready to take a chance.

He stepped toward her, not removing his gaze from her. In a heartbeat, they were toe to toe.

"I know I love you, Emma. Still. I know I'm not what you expected. I come with a lot of unknowns. But you are everything I've ever wanted, and I'd like to see if we can make this work."

She reached for him, her hands cool against his cheek.

He closed his eyes for a moment and took a deep breath. When he opened them, she was still there.

But this time, she was smiling. "I do love you. I do. Despite all my insecurities, your love is the one thing I'm confident about. I'm not sure I'm the right partner for a rabbi, but I'm willing to try."

"I don't think I could ask for a better one," he whispered as he pulled her toward him and kissed her lips.

She sank into him, and for the first time in months, everything around him settled.

When they pulled apart, her pupils were wide, her lips parted, her breath coming fast. "I hope you'll never want to," she said.

Epilogue

Ms. Match exhaled as she consulted her notes one last time. Josh Axelrod had found his match, despite—or maybe because of—his grandmother's interference. As she closed out his file and stored it away, she vowed it would be the last time she accepted a client she hadn't personally vetted. No more well-meaning relatives starting the process. Nope, Anya promised herself, no exceptions. The single person had to speak to her, sign the agreement and be personally involved from the first moment.

Her purple bejeweled nails sparkled in the late summer sun that slanted through her window. Luckily, Josh had found a match, even if she couldn't take credit for it. But Samantha?

Anya pulled up her file and frowned. Samantha *was* her client or had been until she'd received the email this morning terminating their arrangement. That was probably for the best. The young woman had broken the rules and hadn't seemed interested in anyone else Ms. Match had suggested. Nor had she provided helpful feedback for Anya to refine her selections.

Even still, a niggling of concern prevented her from deleting Samantha's files. She was a pretty good judge of character, and something about Samantha made her heart hurt. That woman needed to find *herself* before she found a suitable

Epilogue

Ms. Match exhaled as she consulted her notes one last time. Josh Axelrod had found his match, despite—or maybe because of—his grandmother's interference. As she closed out his file and stored it away, she vowed it would be the last time she accepted a client she hadn't personally vetted. No more well-meaning relatives starting the process. Nope, Anya promised herself, no exceptions. The single person had to speak to her, sign the agreement and be personally involved from the first moment.

Her purple bejeweled nails sparkled in the late summer sun that slanted through her window. Luckily, Josh had found a match, even if he couldn't take credit for it. But Samantha?

Anya pulled up her file and frowned. Samantha *was* her client or had been until she'd received the email this morning terminating their arrangement. That was probably for the best. The young woman had broken the rules and hadn't seemed interested in anyone else Ms. Match had suggested. Nor had she provided helpful feedback for Anya to refine her selections.

Even still, a niggling of concern prevented her from deleting Samantha's files. She was a pretty good judge of character, and something about Samantha made her heart hurt. That woman needed to find *herself* before she found a suitable

He stepped toward her, not removing his gaze from her. In a heartbeat, they were toe to toe.

"I know I love you, Emma. Still. I know I'm not what you expected. I come with a lot of unknowns. But you are everything I've ever wanted, and I'd like to see if we can make this work."

She reached for him, her hands cool against his cheek.

He closed his eyes for a moment and took a deep breath. When he opened them, she was still there.

But this time, she was smiling. "I do love you. I do. Despite all my insecurities, your love is the one thing I'm confident about. I'm not sure I'm the right partner for a rabbi, but I'm willing to try."

"I don't think I could ask for a better one," he whispered as he pulled her toward him and kissed her lips.

She sank into him, and for the first time in months, everything around him settled.

When they pulled apart, her pupils were wide, her lips parted, her breath coming fast. "I hope you'll never want to," she said.

partner. Anya only hoped Samantha would do some significant soul-searching. Her match was out there. Somewhere. Anya would stake her reputation on it.

* * * * *

Find out how Ms. Match helps Samantha find her true match—without any third-wheel best friends— in the next Harlequin Special Edition romance in the Matchmaker, Matchmaker... series, coming to you in the fall of 2026